STRIVERS ROW

During the 1920s and 1930s, around the time of the Harlem Renaissance, more than a quarter of a million African Americans settled in Harlem, creating what was described at the time as "a cosmopolitan Negro capital which exert[ed] an influence over Negroes everywhere."

Nowhere was this more evident than on West 138th and 139th Streets between what are now Adam Clayton Powell, Jr., and Frederick Douglass Boulevards, two blocks that came to be known as Strivers Row. These blocks attracted many of Harlem's African American doctors, lawyers, and entertainers, among them Eubie Blake, Noble Sissle, and W. C. Handy, who were themselves striving to achieve America's middle-class dream.

With its mission of publishing quality African American literature, Strivers Row emulates those "strivers," capturing that same spirit of hope, creativity, and promise.

G-SPOT

Ballantine Books

New York

G-SPOT

An Urban Erotic Tale

NOIRE

G-Spot is a work of fiction. Names, characters, places, and incidents are the products of the author's imagination or are used fictitiously. Any resemblance to actual events, locales, or persons, living or dead, is entirely coincidental.

Copyright © 2005 by Noire

All rights reserved.

Published in the United States by Strivers Row, an imprint of The Random House Publishing Group, a division of Random House, Inc.

Strivers Row and colophon are registered trademarks of Random House, Inc.

Library of Congress Cataloging-in-Publication Data

ISBN 0-7394-5028-X

Printed in the United States of America

This book is

dedicated to urban scribes far and wide.

Keep doin' the damn thing.

Acknowledgments

All props go to the Father above for
blessing me with the ink that flows from
my pen. Thanks to Jay, Missy, Tyrone,
and Man for having my back 24/7.

Stay black.

NOIRE

G-SPOT

In the beginning . . .

Have you ever rolled over in the middle of the night and realized you were doing shit you swore you'd never do? Sexing brothers you vowed you'd never touch? Bending backward and stooping lower than you ever thought you'd stoop? Well, if you can feel me even a little bit, then let me hit you with a story that might just blow your mind. And I swear, as crazy as it sounds, every word of it is true. Let me take you to the G-Spot. A gentlemen's club in the heart of Harlem. A place where playa-hating and disrespect can cost you your life, and betrayal guarantees you a fate worse than death. My name is Juicy Monique Stanfield. I lost my soul in the G-Spot and this is my story. . . .

Chapter One

It was right around midnight and bodies were heating up at the G-Spot. I should have been at home studying for a chemistry test but instead I was sitting with my girl Brittany in a private booth at the most expensive gentlemen's club in Harlem.

"This place is the shit, Juicy." The music was loud and Brittany was dancing in her seat. "Your man is large," Brittany said. "Old as dirt, but large. If Cecil owned a fly joint like this instead of a detail shop, I'd be hanging lovely every night. I can't believe they charge a grand just to get in the door, but with all these rich-ass basketball players and rap artists up in here I guess cheddar ain't nothing but cheese."

Saturday night was Ladies' Night at the G-Spot Social Club. Although the lap dances and private parties catered to the men, one night a week sisters came out to drool over some of the sexiest brothers on the New York street scene.

Brittany was steady running her mouth. She was in my finance class at Fordham University, and I had invited her down to the Spot because I liked having company.

"Juice," she said, "this place is not only classy, but it's also hot! Thanks for getting me in for free, but damn, girl, when are the brothers coming out?"

"Hold on," I told her. "The male strippers are coming up next." *And that's when my trouble will really begin,* I thought, crossing my legs.

"Don't get me wrong," Brittany said. Dressed in a short white skirt and a silk halter, she was drinking double shots of Alize and had three lines of coke laid out on the table in front of her. "I mean, the girls are working it, but where are the men with the fine bodies? I want to see some hard asses and Mandingo backs. Maybe even get me some dill-zick, if they slinging any!"

As soon as she said that I looked around for G and saw him walking up the stairs like he did every night at this time. G was a man of habit. I could put my money on it that every night at exactly midnight, he would disappear upstairs to check on his drug operation and make sure each nanogram of his powder was accounted for.

The house rule was to get the men to spend every dime in their pockets, and every girl had to do her part. It was about getting them to buy drinks all night, pay for lap dances; and if they wanted to fuck, they paid for the sex and the room, too.

And Brittany was right. Money wasn't a big thing for the drug dealers and playas, but I could see how it would turn her on. The dollars had my nose open at first too, but not anymore. These days chasing the thing that I wanted most could get me killed. It was like being addicted to candy and working in a chocolate factory where the product was off limits. Night after night I sat in the G-Spot, the biggest sex den in New York City, and watched others get what I needed.

Let me just put it out there.

I was a nineteen-year-old Harlem girl with a healthy appetite. But it wasn't sweets that I craved. And it wasn't drugs. It wasn't jewelry, and it wasn't Prada skirts or fur coats neither. All that stuff was at my fingertips, mine for the taking. I was miserable in spite of all the bling. Because even though I rolled with the richest man in Harlem, I couldn't get my g-spot hit. I was Granite McKay's woman, and I craved dick.

I guess you could say G inherited me from my grandmother, who had been good friends with him and his mother. Even though he was twenty-seven years older than me, I had known him all my life. When I was a kid we lived on 136th Street in Harlem, and I used to run numbers for my grandmother. I could remember what everybody on the block played, and I never forgot a bet. Grandmother was sanctified but she played her some numbers every day. I would run up to the number house and put the numbers in, then keep track of who hit without ever writing any of it down. Every afternoon when whoever hit got paid, my grandmother got her cut and me and my younger brother Jimmy got a Nehi grape soda, a pack of watermelon Now & Laters, and some rainbow jawbreakers.

G owned the number spot and a lot of other businesses in Harlem, too. He had been married to a Puerto Rican woman at one time, but people said she disappeared one day and nobody ever went looking for her. G had a son named Gino, but nobody had seen him in years. He went to college in another state because G wanted him to live a different type of life.

By the time I was fifteen I was looking at Granite McKay with grown-woman eyes because he had a body that was out of this world. I had heard all kinds of rumors about older men like him. Old men give you worms. Old cum turns into buttermilk. Old balls sag and have gray hairs on them. I didn't listen to none of that shit because I didn't think it applied to the way G was laying it down. Young or old, he was the finest man I'd ever seen in my life. G was tall and had dark skin and hair that was real black and wavy. Every six months he was driving a spanking new car. People on the street worshipped him and treated him like the king of Harlem.

But one day me and Jimmy and Grandmother watched from our window as G beat a man down on a street corner. The man was bleeding and begging for his life, and G held him down and bent his fingers back one at a time. All ten of them. I could feel his bones crack. A cop car drove up and when the patrolmen inside saw that it was G administering the ass-whipping they pulled away and kept right on going. When I asked Grandmother what the man could have done that was so bad, she told me he was G's cousin, and that he'd cheated G out of twenty dollars on a bet. I couldn't understand it because G was so rich. He owned all the drug dealers in Harlem. He owned the number spots and restaurants and clubs. Twenty dollars was nothing to a man like him.

But Grandmother said it was the betrayal and not the money that almost got the man killed. She said G had killed other people for less than that and the only reason G didn't kill this man because they were family and had grown up together and G loved him. I saw the man not too long after that on Malcolm X Boulevard and both of his hands were in a cast. One of his eyeballs was gone out the socket and he had no front teeth. Grandmother said G let his cousin live as a lesson to everybody walking the streets of Harlem: Nobody betrayed G and got away with it.

"Girl, you sure the dranky dranks are free?" Brittany picked up her glass and guzzled her drink down. She sniffed a line from the table and then offered me some. I shook my head. My mother had been a junkie ho so I never used drugs.

The crowd started clapping and Brittany pointed up at

the stage. Her mouth fell open as the spotlight shone on a
sister who was squatting with her back to the crowd. The
girl was named Honey Dew, and dollars was being thrown
up on the stage like mad. Honey Dew bent over and spread
her butt cheeks and picked up a full bottle of Coke using
just the muscles in her pussy.

"Oooh! Did you see that!" Brittany and everybody else
was going crazy. "I gotta learn that move!"

"I don't know if she's giving lessons, but drink all you
want." I turned away from the scene on the stage. "Go on,
Britt. Order another round. Whatever you want is yours
tonight."

I wished I could say the same thing about myself. I
couldn't get what I wanted if I tried. None of the men in
Harlem were crazy enough to touch me. G would never
cheat on me, and he played me so close I couldn't cheat on
him either. He allowed me go to college three days a week,
but that was only to keep me from getting bored.

"A busy mind will keep the devil out of you," he said. So
I went to Fordham University in the Bronx and studied
dance. My dance instructor said that although I had never
taken classes before I was one of the best students she had
ever seen. She said I moved my body like it was for sale, and
in a way it was. G paid all the bills for me and Jimmy, even
for Jimmy's special doctors, and I gave up my life in return.
Since he was letting me go to college I had wanted to enroll
for a minor in political science. But G said that would only

make me sound like one of those smart-mouth bitches who needed their tongues cut out. And whatever G said was exactly what went.

Even though I was in school, G liked to take me out with him to the club every night, just to show me off. He'd pick out my clothes and tell me how much makeup to put on, then march me around in front of his friends. "You a fine chick, Juicy. Pretty hair, caramel skin. You got the finest body I've ever seen. Don't make me kill none of these motherfuckers over you."

So you might ask, if I had a rich sugar daddy who looked good, adored me, let me get my education, and kept me and my brother in the finest condition, why was I so unhappy? Well, I can tell you! G was a lot older than me and the truth was he just couldn't keep up. Even though he had the right package, the goods just didn't function like I needed them to. Besides, G didn't trust women so he was sexually limited. He didn't eat pussy and he didn't tongue kiss, which were two things I was dying for. G said pussy was nasty and he only put his dick in it because he had to.

I remember the night G made me his. It was two years ago and even though I was only seventeen, I was more than ready. I had always been a sexual person. I started masturbating as soon as I discovered what my clitoris was, but fear of my grandmother had kept me from messing with boys. One time I got a sex flick from my girlfriend Rashida and snuck it home and watched it while Grandmother took Jimmy to the doctor. Seeing all of those hard dicks made me so hot I tried to push a cold fat cucumber up inside me, but it hurt too bad and I had to stop.

G had been looking at me for a long time and I knew it. I was a senior in high school and I worked part time at a beauty shop on Amsterdam Ave run by Dominicans. G used to park his freshly waxed car outside the shop and just watch me through the window. All those old women in there swore he was looking at them and they would be posing all up in the window and shit, trying to get his attention. They just couldn't believe a big-time playa like him wanted my young dumb ass.

A month later I graduated from high school and the next day my grandmother laid down for a quick nap and died in her sleep. G came by the apartment with a sympathy card and enough cash for us to put her away nicely. Like most people I was scared of the dead, but I was even more afraid of cemeteries and dark holes. When I was little some hysterical saint from the First Baptist Church had almost pushed me into my mother's open grave, and that was the last time I'd stepped foot inside a cemetery.

I told G I didn't want to go to Grandmother's burial, and he said he understood. He arranged for Grandmother to have a private burial and even paid for her headstone and let me pick out the type of letters and what I wanted it to say. The next night he picked me up from the apartment and took me over to the Spot. He made security lock all the doors and turn on the bright lights. He told them to turn off the music, get the hoes out the back rooms, and then he called out all his staff, even the cleaning people.

"All right. I'm gonna ask y'all once and I expect the motherfuckin truth." He held me by my arm and walked me up on the stage. "This is Juicy from 136th Street. Who in here done had some of this? Anybody in here done sucked her or fucked her? I wanna know if you so much as *smelled* this pussy. If your fingers been in it. If your tongue been in it. If your dick been in it. If you've rubbed your clit on it."

All I heard was a bunch of "no G, no"s.

"Good, then. Juicy is *mine,* and that's all I'm gonna say."

Everybody knew what that meant. I was smiling inside because like I said, I had never been touched. Plus, I was hyped about G's money and thought I had just hit the number big time. I just knew I was going to lay up in that phat apartment he kept on Central Park West and have neck-cracking sex with an experienced man in a round waterbed.

Instead I was so disappointed I could have died. G's entire bedroom was done up in mirrors, the walls, the ceilings, and even the floors. There wasn't a streak of dust on them either. The bed wasn't round and it wasn't a waterbed, but it was huge and it felt like the mattress was made of pillows. He had taken me shopping during the day and to a classy, expensive restaurant afterward. He'd been so nice to me, holding doors open and buying me roses. I just knew my whole life was set. Back at the apartment that night I took a long bath and put all kinds of lotion all over my body. It was the first time I had ever been in a bathtub so deep or felt water so hot. I was so excited about what was about to happen that just the sensation of rubbing my own flesh turned me on. I waited until G got in the shower, then stuck my towel between my legs and thought about what he was going to do to me. I was ready for the real thing by the time he turned off the water.

When G walked into the room wearing only a pair of white silk boxers I almost fainted. He was old, but he didn't smell like old people and he didn't look like old people neither. G was in his middle forties but he ate right and lifted weights. He had a ripped stomach and a built chest, and when I saw all that long black dick pressed up against his stomach I felt blessed. But as soon as he got in the bed it all changed.

"Oooh, baby." I was rubbing my hands all over his body. I felt his arms and his chest and before I could stop myself, I grabbed his big dick with both hands. He pulled away.

"Girl, what the fuck is wrong with you?" He sat up in the bed looking at me like I was crazy.

"Nothing, baby. I just want to make you feel good." I took off my thong and bra and held my breasts in my hands. I rubbed and squeezed them like I did when I was alone. I was ready to finally get them sucked. I wanted to push my nipples in G's mouth, but instead I leaned over and tried to put my tongue between his lips.

He slapped me so hard I almost flew off the bed.

When I sat up the room was spinning.

"Juicy, I know you young and don't know shit. But I'm gonna tell you something you bet'not never forget. Don't you ever put your mouth on my lips, or on nothing I have to drink or eat. And don't worry about me putting mine on you neither. And let this be the last time you rush me, too. I'm the man up in here, so I'll come for the pussy. Don't you be chasing my dick like you no ho, else I'll put your ass to work in the G-Spot."

I cried inside. All the moisture that had been soaking my panties suddenly dried up and I laid back on the silk sheets, not knowing what else to do.

"That's right," G said. He pressed a button near the headboard and the lights went dark. "Just lay back and let Daddy get a little bit of this and everything will be everything."

And all he got was a little bit, too. He squeezed my right breast twice and then pinched my nipple so hard I wanted to scream. Then he climbed on top of me and pushed my legs apart. "This is gonna hurt some, Juicy. But I promise to go slow, okay?"

I tried to stop the tears that were coming out my eyes. This was not how I had imagined my first time going. Yes, he had gotten the dinner and the roses right, but why did he hit me? What about the foreplay? And what did he mean don't worry about him putting his mouth on me? I wanted my pussy licked! I had waited a long time to do the things

I'd read about in magazines and seen in movies, and now he wouldn't do them to me?

G went easy on me like he said. He pushed into me real slow, whispering in my ear until I almost forgot the stinging on my cheek and the mean words he'd said. I put my hands on his ass and pulled him into me. It hurt real bad when he broke my cherry, but a moment later the head was in and then nine more thick inches slid in behind it.

"Oh yeah." He moved on top of me. "You just as juicy as your name. This some good pussy, baby." Ten seconds later he shook a little bit and it was all over. I was still moving my hips as he breathed above me. His dick was getting soft and I worked my ass faster, feeling the beginnings of my very first sex-induced orgasm.

My eyes were closed and I was almost there when he rose up on his arms and hollered real loud, "Girl, what the hell you think you doing?"

I opened my eyes and again he was staring at me like I was some freak. "You fucking with me or something, Juicy?" he said. He pulled his soft dick out. "What? You can't tell when the shit is over, or I just don't keep it going long enough for you? You need more than what I'm giving you or something? What you doing, girl?"

The good feeling between my legs disappeared. I was laying in a cold wet puddle and it really confused me. G had been really good to me and I thought I loved him. But I now understood my situation like it was written out on the wall.

This was what sex would always be like with Granite McKay. There was no escaping it neither because he had declared me to be his, and so I was. Leaving him was out of the question because it would put his rep on the line. Plus, me and my baby brother needed what G was putting out, so I had to do what I had to do. I was in deep with no way out.

G was still staring at me. "I said, what you think you doing, Juicy?"

"Nothing, G," I answered him, and took my hands off his ass. I put them at my sides. "I'm not doing anything."

The DJ changed the music and the naked girls cleared the stage. They almost had to drag this skank named Monique off, she was so busy shaking her big ass and playing with those three nipples she had. A sexy beat picked up and the lights went down low. "Here they come!" Brittany started clapping her hands along with the other women in the house.

This was the best part of my week. I prepared for my normal routine by leaning back into the booth and crossing my legs, squeezing them together as the first man appeared on stage. He was a black god. His skin was dark and every muscle on his body was bulging. And so was his dick inside those skimpy red bottoms he wore. I swung my crossed leg to the beat of the music as I watched him. Already I was turned on.

Each time I pumped my leg a jolt of pleasure screamed in my clit. Brittany was still running her mouth and going on about how fine he was. I wished she would shut up and let me concentrate. A minute later he was joined on the stage by three other men, all of them with beautiful bodies that they knew how to move. I kept my eyes on the first guy. He moved the best and seemed to be looking right at me although I knew he couldn't see me in the darkness.

"Ahh . . . shit! I like the way you work it!" Brittany was digging his rhythm as much as I was. "Be right back," she said. She went searching in her purse, then she ran up to the stage and grabbed dancer number one. She was on her knees as he grinded in her face, and she screamed and stuck some money down in his shorts.

I leaned back all the way in the booth and let my fingers tickle my nipples. I had on pants but I opened my legs and slid my zipper down and quickly stuck two fingers inside my panties. I kept my eye on Brittany as she danced with the guy onstage and let him rub all over her body. I imagined it was me up there, sweating under the lights and getting stroked by those strong hands, hard dick being pushed all up in my face. I could feel his hardness on my lips and smell him, too. A moment later I closed my eyes and my hand moved faster as I hit the rocks and waves washed over me. I caught my breath and zipped my pants as the heat seeped out my body.

And then the shame hit me. I was tired of masturbating

on the sneak tip, but it was all I could do. Living with G I had to learn to get my orgasms quick and quiet. I did it mostly in the shower or laying next to him while he slept, but there were times when I couldn't help myself. I found out that I also liked to get off in public. There was something about the risk of getting caught that really turned me on. I liked to cross my legs on the subway and fantasize about the men as the train rocked me back and forth.

One time I was standing up on a crowded train from 125th Street downtown to 34th Street. The lights were flickering on and off and I realized the guy behind me was riding my ass. I didn't even turn around to see who it was. I had on a short denim skirt and I just gave that ass up to him. I pushed back and worked my hips and let him rub his dick up and down my crack. He put his hands under my skirt and stuck his fingers past my thong. He held on to my hip with one hand and fingered me with the other until I came right there in the middle of the crowd. Part of me wanted him to take his dick out and stick it under my skirt, too.

When I realized what that meant I jumped off the train at the next stop, even though I still had three more stops to go. I was scared the guy was following me but I didn't want to look back and see his face. I felt guilty and dirty for weeks after that, and I vowed not to even think about another man touching me. For a long time I didn't even touch myself. I thought about my mother and wondered if I was turning into her, but I told myself I wasn't a ho. I was just frustrated because I needed to be satisfied and G wouldn't do it.

I picked up my purse and Brittany's, too, and went into the ladies room to wash my hands. When I looked into the mirror I saw a little girl they called Juicy-Mo staring back at me and she looked sad as hell.

Chapter Two

I was born and raised in the heart of Harlem, but the way G dressed me and kept me looking people thought I was big money from the suburbs some-where. G hired a professional stylist to do my hair once a week and another girl to do my nails. I got a massage twice a week at the G-Spot from Ursula, a blond girl G had turned out when he was vacationing in Sweden.

Ursula was really nice, but I got the impression she wanted to do a lot more than just massage my muscles. As soft music played over the speakers, I would lay on my stomach with my eyes closed as she worked her hands down my back to my lower spine. But she wouldn't stop there. She loved to massage my ass, kneading my buns like dough as she stroked my cheeks with both hands. I hate to admit it but I loved the way it felt. So erotic and sexy. G never touched me like that.

"You have beautiful body, Juicy," Ursula would tell me in her Swedish accent. "You smell delicious, you have pretty color and soft skin. Your ass is magnificent. Many people would love to be G."

Sometimes I would feel my pussy get soaking wet as she rubbed my butt into a rhythm, and I'd feel so confused! I would jump up and take my towel and run out the room. Ursula would be laughing as I left because she knew I'd be coming back for more.

I was so frustrated I didn't know what to do. I obeyed G because, like everybody else, I was scared of him. Plus, being raised by old folks had made me obedient. G had enough years on me that I just naturally did anything he said. Grandmother said we were lucky she'd taken me and Jimmy in after our mother got killed for dipping in Big Sonny's pot. Mama's jive little trick game coulda got us all shot, so it was only natural that Grandmother accepted us with a reluctant heart. She was scared I'd turn out to be a no-good street ho just like her daughter, so she whipped my ass on the regular and made damn sure I minded her.

Everything I did as a child, I had to sneak and do it. I didn't do nothing more than hide candy under my pillow or listen to 98.7 KISS FM when she left the house, but at least once a week Grandmother would anoint my whole body with holy water and pray over me until she got hoarse. But maybe I was my mother's child, because by the time I was twelve my female urgings had come on strong. I kept a notebook called the Juicy Journal that was filled with my sexual fantasies, and I couldn't even see a man without my panties getting wet—and he didn't necessarily have to be fine neither. Grandmother could pray all she wanted to, I'd vow as I hid under the covers and explored the softness of my insides. I was gonna get me some dick if I had to buy me some.

But I never did. Grandmother was real strict on me and she had to be, because the streets of Harlem were nobody's joke. So I fantasized and masturbated my ass off, careful not to make enough noise to disturb Jimmy, who slept on the love seat across from my sofa bed.

But while Grandmother was busy watching me, she tried not to press Jimmy too hard. Our father, James Joseph, was a mental case and had been locked up on the crazy ward at Bellevue ever since Jimmy was a baby, but his genes must have been real strong because Jimmy was something else. A real live piece of work. Grandmother feared he might get sent to the crazy house just like our daddy, and just the thought of losing Jimmy sent chills through me because as much mess as he got into, I was Jimmy's heart and my baby brother was my soul. I'd lay down and die for him without a second thought.

Don't get the idea that Jimmy was a bad boy or nothing, because he really wasn't. He couldn't help the things we'd been through no more than I could. Life had really shit on us, so of course Jimmy bore scars from it. When he was little he had to be watched all the time. Grandmother would send him to the Spanish store on the corner and that boy would be out there throwing rocks through car windows. On check day Grandmother would tell him to go downstairs and wait for the mailman, and we would find him on the roof hours later. Striking matches and watching them burn out.

Grandmother used to throw rent parties every month, and one day we left Jimmy at the house while we went to get some fatback to go in the collard greens. That crazy boy took and threw my kitten Fee-Fee out the bathroom window. "Where's Fee-Fee?" I ran around the house crying when she didn't meet me at the door like she usually did. I saw Jimmy's eyes slide toward the bathroom. I ran in there and the window was pushed open and my cat was bleeding on the ground in the alley downstairs.

"I thought she had nine lives," Jimmy cried like a damn fool when I jumped on him. I kicked him in the balls then punched him on the arm so hard he got a frog in his muscle.

I cried for weeks over that cat. Grandmother prayed for a while, then said that was the last straw, and she put Jimmy in a special day school so the doctors could find out why he did so many crazy things. Like she didn't know! It took all the money we had to pay for Jimmy's new school and his doctors, but we did it. Jimmy was a lot better now, but every now and then it seemed like he had a flashback that made him do something straight to the left. I tried to keep him as close to me as I could, praying like hell that that crazy bug wasn't still living in his head because except for G, me and Jimmy were all alone in the world with only each other to hold on to.

So even though I felt cheated, I thanked God for sending G our way. He took good care of me and Jimmy, and without him we probably would have ended up in a shelter someplace. G was the father we never had, and he gave us everything we missed having when we were kids. The only difference between G and what I imagined having a father was like, was that I slept in the bed with him and he climbed on top of me twice a month. But even that part was over with so fast I sometimes thought I had dreamt it.

The apartment we lived in had four bedrooms. I shared the largest one with G, and Jimmy had a nice one that was down the hall on the other side of the kitchen. G gave us the best of everything. Jimmy had a wide screen television in his room, Xbox, and all the latest games that came with it. He was only seventeen, but he was as almost as tall and fine as G. Everybody in Harlem knew what had happened to my mother, so G understood the problems Jimmy had and didn't mind paying for his special school or the medication my brother took to keep his brain straight. In fact, G didn't mind paying for anything we wanted, and when I stepped out in the street people didn't know what to do with me. I was just that fly.

G was like that with his people, too. Everybody who worked for him, from the cleaning ladies on up to Greco, who was in charge of the staff, and Moonie, who was the chief of security, got paid out the ass. G was conniving and cutthroat, but he believed in sharing the sugar, and his philosophy was that when everybody got fed, everybody stayed happy. I guess he was right because he'd been running things in Harlem for years and, while one or two had tried, none of the young bucks out there were bad enough to take him down. The wall of soldiers surrounding him was just that solid.

The only thing G asked his people for was exactly what he expected from me. Honesty. Honesty and loyalty. He was hip deep in hustlers and hoes every day, and in a woman he wanted somebody who had been touched only by his hands. And for what he was putting out, that should have been a simple request. But in the back of my mind I knew it was only a matter of time until I failed him. G was forty-six and I was only nineteen. He liked it cold and I liked it hot. There was just too much wrong with that picture. It wasn't even a matter of if I would mess up, but when, where, and with who.

Chapter Three

There were twenty-six students in my dance class, including me. I didn't socialize with most of them because I didn't want them asking questions about my life. I could tell we were different. They lived in the dorms and went to campus parties at night. I had a Samoan driver named Pacho who dropped me off at school and picked me up after my last class. Then I hung out with strippers and hoes until the sun came up.

I liked school and would have been a better student if G would let me stay home and study sometimes. I was failing my science class. I could not get the hang of chemistry with all those symbols because I did not study. When I told G he said not to worry about getting an F in the class. Just take it again next semester.

There was a guy in my dance class named Vincent. We got paired up together a lot because we were both

so good with our bodies. G said men who danced in tights
were all gay, but I thought he was wrong. Vincent had a
strong body and nice eyes. He smiled a lot and I liked the
way his hands felt when he held my waist or lifted me up in
the air. Sometimes it seemed like we moved so good together
it was almost like we were only one body.

For our dance midterm we were giving an evening perfor-
mance on the school stage. I wanted G to come because I
wanted him to be proud of what I had learned. But I should
have known better. G had a front row seat, and waiting in the
wings I could see him sitting there twirling his onyx ring.

The lights were shining on me and Vincent as we danced
to Latino beats, then brought the tempo down easy with a
few jazz routines. For the finale Vincent lifted me in the air
and slid my body down against his until I reached the floor.
We had been practicing this move for weeks and each time I
slid down his front I felt his erection. At the end of the dance
I put my leg up on his shoulder and bent my back until my
head almost touched my ass. We stayed like this with our
crotches touching as the audience clapped and the music
faded. When I turned around to take my bow, G's seat was
empty.

I didn't bother changing my clothes after the show. I just
grabbed my bag and ran outside but there was no car waiting for me. No G, no Pacho, no ride home. I wanted to cry
as I walked slowly back inside. I didn't have any money to
call a cab so I would have to change clothes and jump the
turnstile to catch the downtown train to the G-Spot. This

was the first time G had ever let me go home alone, and I knew it meant something bad.

Vincent walked out of the men's locker room as I was going in the door.

"Good job, Juicy," he told me. "You felt good out there."

I corrected him. "You mean I looked good out there."

"No, Juicy. I meant just what I said. You *felt* good. Your body always feels good to me."

I didn't know what to say. But I knew what the look on Vincent's face meant. I had been seeing it in men's eyes from the time I was twelve. Back then it used to make me feel nasty. Grandmother told me I didn't have no control over how I was shaped. She didn't know where I got all my titties, but said hips and ass ran on her side of the family. At twelve a stare like that from a man could make me run and hide in shame. At nineteen it made me feel hot.

"Are you going home?" Vincent wanted to know.

"Yeah, I have to take the train because my ride left."

"Oh!" He looked at me with those eyes of his. "That was your father sitting out there, right? I saw him watching you. He looks like one of those back-in-the-day brothers. Sharp dresser for an old head. He didn't wait for you?"

I was so embarrassed. "Yeah, that was him. He had to leave. He had to check on his business."

"Then can I walk you to the train?"

"Okay, let me change my clothes first."

I walked with Vincent to the station. I told him I had lost my wallet and he gave me his MetroCard. Although we had danced together I still felt shy with him. It also felt nice to be with a man my own age who was interested in the same things as me. We got to the train station far too quickly, and when Vincent said good-bye he kissed me on my cheek with soft lips.

I didn't know how to act. I ran down the stairs and jumped on the first train that came. Good thing it was the local instead of the express because that gave me enough time to cross my legs and have three silent orgasms before I reached my stop. All I had to do was think about how Vincent's hands felt on my body and the touch of his lips on my cheek.

When I walked into the G-Spot Pacho was sitting at the bar. He gave me a funny look as if to say, Beats the hell out of me what just went down. Moonie was behind the bar drying glasses. To those who didn't know, Moonie looked like the average bartender. He was a short narrow-faced brother with eyes that saw everything that moved, and a lot of stuff that didn't move, too. But I knew the scoop. Moonie was G's right-hand man. His position behind the bar was just a front. He took care of security for G's entire operation, and even in the middle of a big crowd, Moonie knew exactly who was in the Spot and what they were doing at any given moment.

"Hey Moonie. You know where G is?" Of course he knew. He was real soft-spoken and looked downright harmless. But Moonie kept his shit understated on purpose. That's why so many niggers slept on him. They usually didn't even see his Glock until it was pressed against their foreheads.

He grinned at me with all them big-ass teeth. "What's up, Juicy. I think he went back to his office a minute ago."

I walked to the back of the club to where G's office was located. I passed by the Jacuzzi, the sauna, and the cinema room where they showed skin flicks all night long. On the far side of G's office was a stairwell that led down to the Dungeon, two words I'd been warned never to even whisper. I don't know what all went on down in that basement, but I'd heard it was soundproof.

Right next to G's office was a large storage room where the cleaning people kept their supplies. Two maids were standing inside gathering paper towels and toilet tissue, and I nodded hi to both of them before knocking on G's door.

"Come in," he said in a deep voice.

G was sitting at his desk with his hands behind his head. A lit cigar was in his ashtray and Barry White was playing on his stereo. There was a baby picture of his son Gino on the wall. Another picture was facedown on G's desk. One time I had picked it up and looked and saw that it was his ex-wife. She was pretty as hell. I wondered why he kept it facedown like that.

"Hi. I looked for you after the show. I didn't see the car so I took the train home."

"Sit down."

I sat down and my hands and knees were shaking. I didn't know what the look on G's face meant but I knew it wasn't good.

"Dig, girl. You looked trifling out there tonight. If that's what you're doing all day I might as well keep my money instead of throwing it away on you and that school."

"I was just dancing, G. I thought you said you wanted me to study dance."

"That wasn't no motherfucking dancing! If you wanna dance like that you can get your ass in one of the back rooms and stand over some nigger's lap and make me some goddamn money!"

I didn't say anything because I was nervous and didn't know what to say. Whenever I did something wrong G said things like that, things about turning me out, and it terrified me.

"Pacho is gonna take you home. Make sure you clean all three bathrooms before I get there."

I was scared half to death. We had two maids for the apartment. One for the weekdays and one for weekends. One time G had caught me sweeping the floor and he snatched the broom from me and broke it over his leg screaming, "My woman don't have to push no broom! That's what I pay these damn maids for. You just concentrate on looking good and keeping your man happy."

And now he wanted me to scrub the toilets? I knew he was punishing me and I guess I deserved it. G was slick and smart. Game recognized game. He had sensed the throb be-

tween me and Vincent, and he was sending me a serious
message.

When Pacho dropped me off at the apartment, Thomas,
one of the five doormen, let me in. Jimmy was in his room
listening to his music loud and playing another damn video
game. I opened his door and waved at him and he nodded
and kept on playing.

Jimmy was happy here and it made me feel good to know
that I was taking care of him. I thought my grandmother
and my mother would be proud of me for looking out for
my baby brother and for hooking up with G so that we
could live like this. I really believed Grandmother would understand about me being G's woman, but she would frown
at all the sexual thoughts I had and the way I was dying to
get satisfied. She would tell me the devil was in me and I
needed to pray harder.

I was in the bathroom cleaning the toilet and missing my
grandmother when Jimmy came in. "Why you doing that?
Ain't that what Constantina is supposed to do?"

"*Isn't* that what Constantina is supposed to do," I corrected him. I wanted to distract him from what I was doing.
I didn't want him to think anything was wrong between me
and G. He was doing so good in school and taking his medicine without me telling him to. I couldn't risk him back-
sliding and falling back into his old ways.

"I'm just helping Constantina out," I lied. "You know I

can clean a bathroom just as good as anyone else. Grandmother made sure of that."

Jimmy looked like he believed me.

"I'm getting me a job, Juice," he said. "G said since I'm almost eighteen I can come work down at the Spot."

I stood up so fast I dropped the rag in the toilet. Hell no.
I didn't want my baby brother down there. I didn't care what
G said. Jimmy was supposed to go to college and be smart.
Not hang around playas and drugs and naked women every
night.

"Jimmy, you should just concentrate on school. There is
nothing at the G-Spot for you. Plus you don't need to be all
up in that environment. That's why G keeps his own son out
of there."

"That's how much you know. Gino is about to graduate
from college and G said he's coming back to Harlem and I'm
gonna be working for him."

I turned away because I didn't want my brother to see the
worry in my eyes. I didn't know what G was planning, but
Jimmy didn't need to be involved in any of it. I didn't say
anything else though because Jimmy had a big mouth and
could blab it off, too. Sometimes he took G's side against me
but I knew that was because he had never had a father until
G came along.

"We'll see," I told him. "College is gonna be here before
you know it."

"I ain't going to no college, Juicy. I ain't trying to be educated like you are. I can make more than enough money by just doing whatever G tells me to do. Hanging with G, I can be set for life."

I got the rag out the toilet and finished cleaning the bathroom. I didn't like the way Jimmy was talking and I wondered what else G had been pumping into my little brother's head. I made sure every bathroom in the house was spotless. I even cleaned the kitchen. Then I went in our bedroom and got on my knees and rubbed glass cleaner on all the mirrors on the floor. I changed the sheets and took a bath.

I was sleeping when G came home and got in the bed.

"What's that faggot's name?"

He was right in my ear and I woke up in a hurry.

"Huh?"

"You heard me. What was that faggot's name who had his hands on you."

"Vincent."

G grunted then rolled me over on my stomach and got on top of me. This was something he had never done before. I had always wanted to try it doggy style but after my first night with G I knew he only liked it if I was on my back and he was on top.

I wanted to make up for earlier. I moved my ass real slow so he didn't think I was taking over, but enough to try and turn him on. I felt his big dick pressing behind me. G yanked at my panties and ripped one side of them off. A strange feeling went through me. I wanted him to do the same thing to my bra. His hands were rough on me and I liked it. He pushed one of my knees up and yanked me back until my ass was in the air. I was getting excited and felt myself throbbing and wet.

G hauled off and slapped me on my ass and my pussy quivered. *Yes, yes, yes,* it was saying. He slapped my ass again. Harder. Then he slapped the other side. My ass was burning but my pussy was begging him to keep the fire going. I bit into the pillow and whimpered as I pushed my ass out for more.

"You like this shit, huh?"

I nodded as he whipped me. I felt his dick on me. He pushed it against my wet pussy but didn't go all the way inside. He dipped it in just a little bit until the head was wet, and then without warning he rammed it straight up my ass.

I screamed holy hell. I tried to throw him off of me but he was all muscle weight. He held me down and ass-fucked me until I thought I would die. All the while he was dicking me he was whispering that I better not never let another man put his hands on me, faggot or not. I felt his balls slapping against my pussy but it was completely dry. I cried into the pillow and begged him to stop. For the first time G didn't come in thirty seconds. He went at it until I couldn't scream anymore. I thought I was dying. My voice went hoarse and I was exhausted from fighting against him. When he finally did come I was crying loud like a baby.

"Sssh. You all right, girl," he said. He put his arms around me and smoothed my hair. I felt G's hands stroking my back and even though my asshole was on fire I was grateful for his touch. "Don't make me do you like this, Juicy. You mine, girl. Don't make me hurt you this way."

He even got up and got a warm towel and cleaned me up. I fell asleep crying but loving the feel of his hands caring for me. The next morning my ass was still bleeding. I went to my guidance counselor at school and got my major changed from dance to business.

Chapter Four

The scuffling sounds coming from the window awakened her. She pulled her thumb from her mouth and stuck her hand into the panties she'd peed in for the third night in a row, scratching between her legs. Shivering and half-awake, the little girl scooted closer to her brother on the wet mattress they shared. Surrounded by old shoes and bags of dirty clothes, the mattress lay on the floor of the alcove that was part closet and part bedroom.

A thud resounded near the window and she opened her eyes wide. It was just Uncle Cliff, she told herself. Outside guarding the window with his gun. Moans drifted through the apartment and a headboard banged rhythmically against the wall. She closed her eyes in the darkness and tried to go back to sleep, but the wetness soaking her panties sent her climbing over her younger brother, her feet noiseless on the cold tile as she sidestepped the bags

of rotting garbage and headed toward the moaning sounds com-
ing from her mother's bedroom.

The little girl opened the bedroom door and squinted into
the semi-darkness. Cara, her mother, was naked, her stunning,
milky body moving like a storm as she bucked up and down on
top of the strange man stretched out beneath her. In the filtered
light streaming in from the window the girl saw her aunt Ree,
as beautiful as her mother but darker, straddling the man's
face, rolling her privates all over his lips and chin. Her mother
reached out and grabbed both of her own full breasts and
squeezed her cherry nipples, her hair falling down her back in
silky curls, a wicked smile on her face.

The child hated her mother's bed, but somehow she felt safe
there, too, so she crept into the room and slipped beneath the
sheets at the foot of the bed, pulling the covers over her head.
Lulled by the familiar rhythm, scents, and fuck-sounds, she
stuck her finger in her mouth and drifted back to sleep.

The tinkling of shattered glass broke into her dreams and
scared her so badly she almost sat up. She lifted the edge of the
blanket and saw that the window had been kicked straight in;
splinters of sharp glass were like a moustache around an open
mouth as the wind swept into the room. Peeking from under the
sheets the girl saw a tall muscular man coming in through the
window. He was dressed in black and his head was smooth.
Forcing herself to remain still, she squeezed her thighs together
and bit into her thumb as a stream of hot urine slipped from her
and pooled into the bed. She'd get her ass whipped good now.

That was for sure. Mama would call her a stinking little piss-
pot and then tear her ass up.

"What the fuck you doin?" Her mother cursed and jumped
off the man in mid-stroke. "Niggah, you must be outta your
fuckin mind!"

"Where's my money, you trick-ass bitch?"

"Cliff!" Aunt Ree screamed toward the window. "Get your
black ass in here! This motherfucker got a gun!"

"Yo, niggah!" The man in the bed sat up against the head-
board and fumbled around for his pants. "What's up wit this
shit? I put out my money for this pussy and I wanna finish get-
ting mine—"

Fire flashed from the slice of metal in the tall man's hand
and the room exploded in thunder. The man on the bed
slumped over slowly, leaving a puddle of blood, hair, and shat-
tered bone sliding down the headboard. The girl's mother stared
at the corpse she'd just finished riding. The odor of shit and
brains filled the room as his lifeless penis curved and shrank.

"How long you bitches thought you could run this fuckin
game? Who's got the tool this time? Me or that simple nigger who
was standing outside your window with his dick in his hand?"
The man laughed. "I just put that nigger dead to sleep." He
looked at Aunt Ree, then aimed the gun again. "But since you
want him so bad, no problem, bitch. I'll send you out to meet
him halfway."

The gun boomed and the little girl's right ear went deaf.
Aunt Ree fell back, her head cracking into the girl's shin. The

child yelped in pain and fought back the covers to sit upright. The cold air chilled her and she shivered in her tattered Wonder Woman T-shirt.

Looking right through her, the little girl's mother scampered on her knees and clamped her hands over the hole in her sister-in-law's chest. "Ree! Lord no, Ree!" Dark blood bubbled up breaking through the slits in her fingers, then gradually lessened to a steady trickle as Ree shuddered and took her final breath.

The man moved again. "I said"—he aimed the gun between Cara's eyes—"I want my fuckin money. That was Big Sonny's dope you lifted, you skank ass ho, and I want it back."

Cara babbled incoherently, her creamy skin turning gray with fear, her eyes darting around the room as she clutched the sheets in fear.

"I'll get it! I swear to God, I'll get it." She nodded and licked her lips as she begged for her life. "I didn't know how important you was! Didn't know you was working for Sonny! Just gimme a few days, Mistah. Please! Just a few days."

The man swung wildly and the pistol slammed into her mouth, whipping her head back and breaking her jaw. Cara screamed as blood flew from her nose and her lower jaw swung back and forth, completely sprung.

"Mistah, noooo." She moaned and spit out blood. She jumped from the bed and yanked open a nightstand drawer. Bags of weed, vials, pipes, and a tube of Vagisil fell to the floor. She reached deeply inside and came out with a fistful of bills. "Dis

all I got tonight." She pointed to the man's corpse. "This square ain't had no more'n dis is his pockets. Just gimme a few days and I swear on my mother I'll get you the rest. I swear!!"

"Bitch." The man slapped the bills to the floor. "You ain't got a few days. You ain't got a few minutes unless you can come up with my dope or my fucking money." He aimed again and the little girl cringed. "Big Sonny might kill me, but I can guarantee your ass is gonna get to hell first—"

"Wait!" Cara screamed in desperation. "I got jewelry! Expensive shit! And a fur. I can turn that shit over in a few hours. I can sell pussy. Suck dick. Cut crack. Please . . . just gimme a little time," she cried, blood streaming from her nose and mouth.

The next time the man spoke his voice was so cold the little girl almost peed again. "You got ten seconds to come up with something that I can take to Sonny right now."

Cara whimpered, her eyes scanning the room crazily, skimming over the bodies of Ree and the naked man before coming to rest on her seven-year-old child.

"Ten, nine, eight . . ."

Cara looked down at her daughter with a inconsolable expression on her face.

". . . seven, six, five . . ."

Cara's whole body shook as she glanced at the blood seeping all over her bed.

". . . four, three . . ."

Cara's fear smothered her. She reached out and snatched her daughter from the tangle of sheets and thrust her toward the gunman. *"Here!"* She stared into the man's eyes and made one last attempt to save her own life. *"Please . . ."* she whispered. *"Take Juicy."*

The gun belched, and Cara flew backward, landing atop the dead man, her arm circling his neck. The strange man stared down at the little girl, then muttered something under his breath and stroked the side of her face with the hot muzzle of the gun. *"You look just like that ho-bitch,"* he said thickly as he circled her jaw with the barrel and began unbuttoning his pants. The child held still as he ran his rough hand over her plump arms and already shapely legs before pulling the crotch of her wet panties aside.

He pressed his fingers to his nose and laughed. *"You smell like that ho-bitch, too."* He pushed her back on the bed and put the tip of the gun to her mouth. The child closed her eyes as he yanked off her panties and straddled her small body. The gun was pressed against her lips as he fumbled with his penis, and suddenly that dreadful noise rang out again as the boom of a pistol exploded in the air.

The breath was knocked from her lungs as the man fell upon her, his forehead bursting apart like a Chinese apple. She sputtered through the spray of blood that covered her face and slid into her mouth, and then wriggling from beneath the dead weight and gasping for air, Juicy looked toward the door and into the eyes of her savior.

"I love you, Juicy-Mo," her baby brother said, the pistol in his hand dangling at his side. *"Jimmy-Jo loves his Juicy."*

• • •

I woke up fighting the sheets. It was still dark outside and G was asleep with his back to me. The powder blue nightgown I had on was soaked with sweat, and so was the mattress on my side of the bed. I struggled to catch my breath, gulping air through my mouth and hoping G didn't hear me. I rolled over onto my stomach and pressed my face into the pillow. A scream was trying to come out of me and I squeezed my eyes shut and bit down on my lip. But the fear still gripped me, had a tight hold on me, and I crawled from the bed and tried to stand, my knees weak, my entire body shaking.

"Girl, what's wrong with you?"

My legs nearly gave out at the sound of his voice. There were a million reflections of me in the mirrors as I did my best to calm my breathing. "Nothing, G." I pulled the wet nightgown over my head and let it drop to the floor. I stood there naked. Shivering. "I had a nightmare, that's all. Hag musta rode me."

G snorted, then turned over and squinted at me. "I done told you about all that mojo and superstitious bullshit. Your grandmomma done fucked your head up with all that mess. Next thing I know you'll be sprinkling salt across that god-damn threshold to keep the evil spirits counting until the sun comes up." He snorted again, then dug himself deeper into the softness of the bed.

I kept quiet. G mighta been right if it had a' been a hag

riding my back. But the spirit world didn't have nothing to do with what I had just experienced. This was pure-dee prophecy. *Warning before destruction* was something Grandmother swore by, and sure enough bells were ringing dead in my ear. Our nightmare wasn't over. Somebody was gonna catch a bad one, and that somebody was either Jimmy or me.

Chapter Five

By the end of my first semester in college I'd figured out that I didn't really want just a business degree. Grandmother had taught me how to sew, and I was the type of chick who could make a dress out of a sock, so I wanted to see where my creativity could take me. With G's approval I took a satellite class at the Fashion Institute of Technology, and twice a week instead of taking an elective at Fordham, I sat in on an apparel design class at FIT.

When I was younger Grandmother used to have this old Singer sewing machine that was so ancient it had a knee pedal instead of one for the foot. I would get the scraps they threw away in the fabric stores and make fly-ass dresses for all of my dolls.

When I started taking classes at Fashion, G bought me an expensive sewing machine and I shopped at fabric stores up and down 125th Street and on the Grand

Concourse in the Bronx. G liked to shop for me and bring me nice things, so I still stepped out in designer shit left and right, but every now and then I would sew for two days straight then show up at the Spot wearing a "JuicyOriginal" and shame every other sister in the place to death.

That's how I spent most of my time. Designing my private line of clothes, chilling at the Spot looking luscious, and going to school three days a week, grateful to get a break from the fast life and to be around people my age who were actually about something.

Marguerita Gonzales was a Puerto Rican girl who sat next to me in my English class. Blacks and Hispanics were cool with each other in Harlem because basically we were all poor and all had the same issues. Rita was one of those real dark Puerto Ricans. She had the prettiest brown skin and a head full of long curly hair just like mine. She was neat about herself, too. Always dressed real nice and made sure to fold her blazers and leather jackets on the crease before hanging them over the back of her chair.

I liked Rita, but I was slow about letting anybody get in my business. I had a lot of respect for her too, because Rita seemed like the kind of chick who could hold her own in any situation. She told me her father had fucked her for ten years, and then on the night of her fifteenth birthday she had held open her sheets, then stuck a knife in his heart and watched him bleed to death naked in her bed. She didn't serve a single day in jail for doing that skag, and now at twenty, Rita was the top computer programming student at Fordham and she'd just gotten a side job writing programs to help support the two younger sisters she'd won in a custody battle with her mother.

I was scribbling in the Juicy Journal when Rita leaned over and whispered, "This shit is so boring." I tuned in to catch the professor running her mouth about predicating a bunch of verbs. Rita hated English class and anything that had to do with writing, but math? Please. Now, I knew I was sharp with numbers. I could memorize number sequences and detailed equations like it was nothing. But Rita? Rita was math-momma. Her brain worked numbers and logic equations ten times faster than mine did, which is why she was such a good programmer. Damn right she was bored up in this class. Wasn't no numbers being thrown around for her to chew on.

I nodded at her and smiled, then tried to get back into my journal. I was deep into a story where this sister was getting her toes sucked like they were seedless grapes. Her niggah was paying attention to her whole foot, too. Starting at the arch and working his way around. I wiggled my toes. There was no way in hell I'd ever know what that felt like. Not unless I was ready to twist my body up like a pretzel and suck 'em my damn self.

"Wanna go to a party?" Rita almost yelled.

"Sssh!" Just like a Puerto Rican! Girl was loud!

"What?" I whispered, frowning.

"A party. Can you come to a party next Saturday night? In Brooklyn?"

I shook my head. Hell no. Weekends were for getting fly and striking poses at the G-Spot. I had to sit up there and look damn delicious, as G would say, because everybody needed to know that I represented him.

"Okay." Rita shrugged. "But it's a Naughty Girls party so don't blame me if you miss out."

Naughty Girls? I waited until the teacher turned around to write on the board. "What's that?"

Rita grinned. "You don't know? Don't worry. I'll break it down to you after class."

I could barely wait until the period was over. I had a finance exam next, and Rita had a two-hour break until her logic class. "C'mon," she said, swinging her hips in a pair of brown Guess jeans. Rita was really skinny up top with little titties, but she had wide hips and cute legs. "I'm heading to the math building to hook up with a few programmers."

"I thought this was a free period for you?"

"It is. Got a meeting. Through the Back Door. You know, we hack shit up!"

"Girl, it's hard to believe you're one of those crazy nerds who go around letting loose viruses that shut down banks and shit. You don't even look like no damn computer geek."

Rita laughed. "That's the whole idea. Why do you think we call it Through the Back Door? Besides. We don't shut down banks and don't think we tap into the school's mainframe and change people's grades neither. It's not about that. It's about revealing programming weakness to keep the folks at Microsoft on their game."

I waved my hand. We were almost at the math building. "Whatever. Tell me about this Naughty Girl Party thing."

"Gurlfriend." Rita's eyes got all big and this sly look was on her pretty brown face. "They got an arsenal of shit up in there. Rabbits, butterflies, you name it, they got it. Last time I bought me a hammerhead and I rocked my own pussy so good I didn't even need no man!"

Didn't need no man? Rita was laughing her ass off and I tried to join her, but my mind was racing. I wanted to know more! Like, what the hell was a rabbit? And a hammerhead! Have mercy! What kind of stuff did they sell where you could beat your pussy up by yourself all night long?

"You sure you can't get away for one night?"

I frowned. Rita didn't know much about my life in the G-Spot, but she was from around my way so I knew she'd heard of G. Everybody had. "I don't know," I said. We were right outside of my finance class and I stood there frowning with my hand on the doorknob. Rita looked hopeful. Like there wasn't an ounce of stress on her plate. It must be nice, I thought. To be in control of your own damn life. Free to come and go when you wanted to, and free to make your own decisions about where you spent your Saturday nights. The way G had me clocked was almost just as bad as living under Grandmother's roof, and suddenly I was pissed off. Mad at G for making me old before my time, and for all the fun stuff I had to miss out on in the name of being his woman. Shit. Fuck him. G wasn't my goddamn daddy. I smiled at Rita. "I'ma try, girl. I'll see what I can do."

The Spot was jumping, especially for a Monday night. Greco had hired some new meat to work the poles, and all of that fake-fucking up on the stage had created an aura of sex so thick you could lick it from the walls. The stage was on fire and Honey Dew was up there leading the charge. With her butter-smooth skin and bodacious titties, she had those new girls grinding those golden poles like they were flesh and blood dicks. And it was working, too. The hoes were burning up the back rooms; running men in and out the doors so fast the housekeeping crew had run out of clean sheets. Nothing made G happier than taking in bank, and I could tell by the way he was walking around nodding and shaking hands with the rappers and high-rollers that he was pleased.

But his attitude had been a whole lot different earlier in the day. The ice machine was acting up and he'd sent me in his office to get the number to the repair shop off an invoice. I looked in the filing cabinet where all the warranties and stuff were kept, but I couldn't find it. I had just given up and was stepping out the office when I damn near got hit by a guy Pluto, one of G's bodyguards, was slamming against the stairwell door.

I screamed and jumped back, looking down at the bloody

brother who was balled up on the ground moaning and crying. His head had rammed the door so hard the metal was
still shaking as G fumbled for his keys. I stared into the
man's face and he looked back at me with pleading eyes, begging for help.

"Stupid motherfucker!" Pluto kicked the guy in the stomach so hard he spit out blood. I stood there with my hand
over my mouth as G unlocked the Dungeon's door. All I had
a chance to see was blackness with the hint of a light coming
from the bottom of the stairs, and then Pluto kicked ole boy
straight into the darkness and G, his eyes glowing mad, gave
me a look, then stepped through the doorway and locked it
behind him. It took me a minute to get my shit together
after witnessing that. I kept thinking about how bad the
man looked, the scared look on his face, that darkness down
in the Dungeon.

Pluto came back upstairs after that, sweating like he had
just run a race. I figured he had kicked old boy's ass real
good, maybe even killed him, so I walked real close to the
wall when I passed him and acted like I didn't see him grab
his dick and shake it at me.

A few hours later I was sitting at the bar drinking a ginger
ale when I felt somebody plop down beside me.

"Juicy!"

I turned around and smiled. Dyneatha Jones was a live
one. She was about thirty-five, and had a big yellow pie
face that was covered with freckles and a head of kinky red

hair that wouldn't lay down no matter how many times she permed it. Dicey had a loud voice and a loud personality. She was one of the few people Grandmother had trusted around me and Jimmy when we was little, even though she took a fall when she was in her twenties and had just gotten back on her feet a few years ago. As a kid I'd looked up to Dicey a lot because she did things for me that nobody else did. She took me shopping on Delancey Street and down in Chinatown, rode me and Jimmy around City Island and bought us ice cream, and a couple of times we spent the day at South Street Seaport, just chilling like tourists. Dicey was the first person to tell me about sex, hustling, and even my period, giving me the whole low-down on Kotex, tampons, and whatnot the year I turned eight.

But G couldn't stand Dicey. He said her mouth was too big for her own good. Dicey had only been working at the Spot for a couple of weeks. She'd been living with her sister in Queens for a while and had just come back to Harlem recently. Even though he didn't like her, G had hired her anyway. He gave her a job working upstairs in the cut room because he used to be good friends with her father, and some even claimed G was Dicey's godfather.

"Hey, Dice!" I said, and reached out to hug her. I looked at my watch as she climbed up on a stool beside me. "What you doing down here so early?"

Dicey shrugged and touched her stomach. She'd put on regular clothes to come downstairs, but up in the cut room

Dicey had to wear what everybody else wore: a paper-thin smock and not a damn thing else. G didn't take no chances in his distribution center. He was paranoid like a mother that somebody might try to steal some dope from him. Females who worked upstairs weren't even allowed to wear panties to work, and they were barred completely from the cut room when their Aunt Mary was visiting.

"I got my period, girl. Shit came on without me even knowing it, so you know what your man said. 'Care your bloody ass on home!' "

We laughed because as street as G was, he could sound real country when he was mad. "But at least he still pays us full-time while we're on the pad," Dicey said, and signaled Moonie for a drink. "And that's more than I ever expected from a coldhearted playa like G."

"G ain't all that bad," I said. Moonie sent his stuttering sidekick Cooter down to us, and Dicey ordered a double shot of gin and I asked for another ginger ale.

Dicey turned to me. "Is that right?" She laughed and threw that gin down her throat like a natural man. "I forgot, Juicy. You a young thing so you probably can't remember some of the stuff the rest of us here remember. You been fuckin G for what, two, three years?"

"We been together two years."

Dicey chuckled, then sat back and rubbed her fat stomach again. "Like I said, you don't know jack shit."

Cooter brought her another drink and Dicey tossed it

back so fast I almost missed it. She nodded toward the door. "Here comes that mining-ass I'll-suck-your-brains-out-through-your-dick country-apple bitch from Alabama."

I looked toward the door and saw that Money-Making Monique had just walked in, rolling her firm body and turning heads left and right. Everything about her was perfect, from her weave down to her shoes, and men laid out top dollars just to watch the way she stepped out of her panties.

Dicey laughed again. "You need to check that ho around your man, with her three-titty self."

"I ain't worried about G. Monique ain't his type cause titties ain't his thing and he don't roll like that."

"Oh, that's right," Dicey nodded. "That nigger's particular." Then she leaned in toward me and said, "You a cool girl, Juicy, and I love you. Your grandmother was my ace, and I used to see your mother and Ree up on Lenox Avenue back when I had just come out and was still selling pussy. You know, before I got myself cleaned up."

I groaned. Everybody knew how stupid my mother had been, and how much it had cost me and Jimmy. I hated hearing about her, even if it wasn't on the regular, because people like Dicey seemed to give my mother life from the grave.

"Your mother was a little older than me, Juicy, and I looked up to her and even tried to swing my ass the way she used to be swinging hers. But don't you get fucked up by the game the way she did, baby girl. The worst thing Cara coulda done was dip on Big Sonny. Maybe she ain't know whose dope she was stealing when her and Ree tricked Ice Man up, but who else's fuckin dope could it have been? Sonny was a blackhearted motherfucker who owned every nigger in Harlem back then, including G. But look at who's long gone, and who's here still here now, standing on top. As mean as Sonny was, he didn't have shit on G, cause when G stepped up strong he treated Sonny like he was somebody's bitch. Took everything Sonny had, except his woman. I bet you ain't heard nobody talk about laying eyes on Big Sonny since right after Cara got shot, have you?"

"G is a businessman," I said, wishing Dicey would stop scaring me and take her cramping ass on home. "He's all about making money, and you know yourself that when people try you, you gotta put them in check. And that don't make G no monster, Dicey. He feeds his people lovely and he's really a good-hearted person when you get to know him."

"Tell that shit to the Haitian sister used to be around here a few years back. Real cute chick. Built just like you, but shorter hair and not as pretty. Ain't nobody seen her well-fed ass lately neither. Or"—she pointed toward Cooter and Moonie at the top of the bar—"how bout you run that 'good-hearted' shit past Cooter Jackson. His baby sister used to lay up with G, too. But I bet you can't even get Cooter to stutter her damn name up in here, and that girl wasn't much older than you when she turned up dead."

I swallowed hard. If it was one thing I had learned from my grandmother it was to heed the wisdom of warnings. "What you trying to say, Dicey?"

She lit a cigarette and took a drag that was so long it steamed the tip. "I ain't sayin shit, Juicy. I know better than to fuck with G. Especially up in his Spot. But let me ask you this: He ever tell you about his wife? The fine Puerto Rican girl from over on Saint Nick he had his son by? The boy who goes to college out in Cali?"

"No, but I saw her picture on his desk."

Dicey nodded and took another drag, then signaled Moonie again. "Uh, huh. I bet G ain't tell you she been missing for over ten years, did he? I heard they got to scrappin' one night and she disappeared just like that. Cops never even bothered to look for her neither. Some say she went to Puerto Rico, and one time I heard she was living downtown in Brooklyn, but don't nobody know what really happened to her except G. And he ain't telling."

I liked Dicey, but she was messing with my head. I knew G was dangerous, but damn. She was really scaring me. My doubts must have shown on my face.

"Okay, okay, lemme ask you something."

I sighed and rested my elbows on the bar. "What?"

"You got any money?"

"What?"

She sucked her teeth. "Money! Duckets! Dollars! Ends! Do G give you any goddamn cheddar?"

"What do I need money for, Dicey? G takes damn good care of me, and trust me, I got everything I need."

"He ever put any cash in your hand, or do he just go out and buy what you ask for?"

I thought for a minute. Whatever me and Jimmy said we wanted, G made sure it showed up at the crib. He shopped for all of my clothes and even ordered in the groceries.

"Juicy," Dicey pressured me, "how do you get your god-damn tampons every month? Do you go to the store and pull the money out your bra to pay for them yourself?"

Hell no. Like I said, G ordered in the groceries, and that included my tampons and pads, too. "You tripping." I gave her the hand. "I get my cotton sticks the same way you get yours. I march my little ass into the store and pick them up."

"Uh-huh. I thought so. Your black ass is broke. So what if G decides to cut you loose? What if he tell you to let the doorknob hit you where the good Lord split you. Then what? You and Jimmy are just ass-out with nowhere to go, right?"

I didn't answer. What could I say?

Dicey stood up and mashed her cigarette out in an ash-tray on the bar. Her eyes got soft, almost sad, and she spoke quietly before turning to walk away. "Go home and listen to you a Millie Jackson CD, Juicy. That old girl know what the fuck she be singing about. Get you your own money, little sister. Don't count on G to see you through, cause when a motherfucker like him decides he don't want you no more you better start digging toward China or have enough cab fare to jet your ass to the other side of the world. Be smart, honey. Go get you some shit in your own name. Collect your pennies and save your spare change so you can open you up a secret bank account. Get you your own money, Juicy-Mo. Even if you gotta steal it."

Chapter Six

Dicey's warnings wouldn't get out of my head. Her words were steady ringing in my ears, worrying me almost as bad as my nightmare had. She was right though. I needed my own cash. G could act the fool at any moment and I needed to be prepared to take care of me and Jimmy. Plus, I wanted to know more about the other women who had been in G's life. I wanted to know what had happened to them, especially his wife. Dicey made it sound like G had a closet full of skeleton bones and part of me believed her, but I was also scared to find out if she was right.

I cut school on Thursday, ditching Pacho when he dropped me off outside of the Rowland Building where I took my finance class. I waited in the foyer and watched him drive off, then I stood outside of the classroom and waited for Brittany to show up.

"Hey Juicy girl." She was chewing gum and wearing

a pair of jeans that fit her like skin. "You do your homework? I didn't get problem four. Couldn't understand it no matter how I looked at it. Did you get the answer?"

I shook my head and grabbed her arm. "I need a favor," I told her, pulling her to the side. I set my backpack on the floor at my feet. "Something came up and I gotta go see about a sick friend. I left my purse in the back of the limo and Pacho must have turned off his cell phone because his ass ain't answering. Can you let me hold five dollars so I can jump on the train? I promise I'll pay you back."

"Uhm, yeah." Brittany shrugged and dug into her front pocket. Her jeans were so tight she could barely get her fingers in. "You good for five dollars, Juicy. With the setup your man got, you probably good for five thousand. You ain't gotta pay me back. Just hook me up at the G-Spot again and I'll be happy."

I smiled and took the ten-dollar bill she was offering me. "Thanks, Brit. I won't forget this."

I was off campus in five minutes, and heading back to Harlem by train. I was so anxious to get with Dicey that I didn't even pay the men on the train no mind. For the first time in a long time I was riding the subway and there was no fantasizing and no looking at men. My mind was racing, but my coochie was silent.

Dicey lived in a tenement off of 125th Street. I knew because I used to run numbers for her mother when I was little, and Dicey had taken over the apartment when Ms. Jones passed away a few months back. I figured she'd be at home because it was too early for her to be at the Spot, and besides, she was on her period and couldn't work there until it went off anyway. I rang the downstairs bell and waited. A minute passed and I jabbed the bell again, this time leaning on it.

"Who the fuck is it?" Dicey had her face pressed to the window and her red hair was spiked up all over her head.

"It's me, Dice. Juicy. Can I come up?"

She buzzed me in and I walked up the two pissy flights to her apartment holding my breath all the way. Dicey was wearing a white nightgown and walking in her bare feet. She didn't have on a stitch of underwear and her nipples were sticking straight up under her gown. The inside of Dicey's apartment had changed since her mother died, and it was nothing like the rest of the run-down building. Since Dicey had quit doing drugs a few years ago, her new addiction must have been shopping because her joint was laid out with butter-soft leather furniture, a phat stereo, and wall-to-wall carpeting.

"It's nice up in here, girl."

She waved her hand. "Homeboy shopping network. You know how much shit can fall off the back of a truck. What you doin slumming over here this time of morning? G put you out already?"

I dropped my book bag and sank down into the cushions on the chocolate brown sofa. "Nah. I'm playing hooky. Just didn't feel like going to school today." I wanted to tell her that I was craving more of what she had to say, but instead I stared at the collection of ceramic elephants she had on a shelf. Dicey was real quiet, and when I looked up she was staring at me with a funny look on her face.

"Look, Juicy. Don't let that shit I was talking the other day get you down. You fine as hell so G probably planning on keeping you around till he old and gray."

I gave her a look.

"You eat yet?"

I shook my head. "No."

"Come on in the kitchen."

I followed her into the tiny kitchen that was decorated in purple and black from the curtains to the rug. I sat at the table while she fried turkey sausage and scrambled us some eggs.

"You like fried onions in your eggs?"

Hell yeah. Grandmother used to make them that way. "Yep. Cheese too."

Dicey fixed our plates while I made us some toast, then she gave me a fork and a napkin and we carried our food into the living room and ate sitting side by side on the floor. I loved her place. It was peaceful and happy and had the same kind of vibe that Dicey had.

"Check this out," she said. "I know you don't hear no good shit like this up in G's Spot." Dicey took a CD from the rack and popped it into the stereo. "This Miss Millie

Jackson, honey. You need to sit back and suck up what she be saying."

I closed my eyes and listened as Millie Jackson talked about taking your life back and getting all you could out of a man, sexually and otherwise. I didn't listen to much music growing up cause Grandmother forbid it, but the stuff Millie was talking about made a whole lot of sense and before I knew it we had listened to the whole CD and over an hour had gone by, with Dicey singing out loud the whole time.

"I might go to a party next weekend," I blurted out when Dicey got up to turn off the boom box. I didn't even know I was gonna tell her about the Naughty Girls party, but Millie's energy had me on a roll and I opened my mouth and started telling Dicey everything Rita had said.

Dicey was stoked. "You're gonna love it, Juicy. I been to one myself, up in the Bronx, but it was a long time ago. Them women had shit like the D.P.—"

"The D.P.?"

"You don't know? That's the double penetrater. A dick for your pussy and one for your asshole too. At the same time."

"Oh, lordy."

Dicey stood up and lit a cigarette. "Of course you probably don't need nothing like that, right? G look like he can bang your head all night long."

"Shit," I sucked my teeth. "Bang hell."

Dicey was on it. "Oh, so Mister Big ain't all that in the sheets? I always wondered why he chased after young girls,

and everybody knows he will only fuck a virgin. He probably couldn't handle no professional fucker."

"He can't even handle me," I confided. "That's why I
wanna go to this party. I'm tired of wanting what I can't get.
My friend Rita said they sell shit that'll make you not need
no man."

"Please!" Dicey laughed and turned toward the kitchen
with our paper plates in her hand. "They ain't invented
nothin that can take the place of a hard hot dick drilling up
in you, but you should be able to find something that'll
come in second place. But why settle for all them tools when
you got a real live nigger in your bed every night? Either take
charge and make G fuck you right, or go find you some dick
you can live with."

She paused in the doorway. "On second thought, scratch
that. G can be a maniac over his pussy—just ask them niggers down at the Spot. You better go to that party on Saturday and stock up, baby girl. Matter fact, if I don't have to
work I might just roll out with you."

G ruled his empire with an iron fist, and if he came off
as ruthless it was because the streets were hard. But sometimes he was stank and nasty for no good reason at all, and
the way he did poor Nae-Nae that time just didn't make no
sense.

Nae-Nae was one of the younger girls who stripped at the

Spot. Back in the day I used to see her walking with her sisters to the public school we went to a few blocks from my house. When I was in the third grade the school was closed down because of some hazardous stuff in the insulation, and while me and Jimmy got transferred to another school right up the street, Nae-Nae and her sisters got sent to a school way across town.

Nae-Nae was a year older than me, and when she showed up at the Spot a few months earlier she tried to front like she didn't know me. I didn't press her though. From what I remembered she came from a quiet, churchified family, and I figured she was ashamed for me to see her humping poles and giving lap dances all night long.

I had no idea what had happened to her sisters or the rest of her family, but Harlem had gotten to Nae-Nae, and she looked just like a lot of turned-out sistahs who didn't have anything except their asses to fall back on.

One night Nae-Nae came to work carrying a baby on her hip. I was in my usual spot, chilling at the bar shooting the shit with Moonie while Cooter smiled and stuttered all over the customers and poured their liquor. Nae-Nae walked past so fast I barely even noticed her, but a minute later there was such a commotion coming from the dressing room that Moonie told me to go back there and find out what the girls were doing.

"Look at him." Punanee was grinning at what Nae-Nae was holding in her arms. "All that curly hair and just as cute as he wanna be!"

I stepped through the crowd to see what they were all freaking out over and saw the cutest, fattest baby I'd ever seen in my life. He was past handsome. This baby had dimples everywhere and the biggest prettiest eyes in his little butterscotch face that you ever did see.

"Whose baby?" I asked, and daggone if that little fat butterball didn't try to jump out of Nae-Nae's arms and into mine. He stretched his little chubby arms out for me to take him, opening and closing his hands and grinning at me the whole time.

"Mine," Nae-Nae said, passing him to me. "This is Maleek. My little man."

I took that handful of fat and dimples into my arms and almost melted, he felt so good pressed against me. His curly hair smelled just like baby lotion and he was clean and fresh like he had just came out of the bath.

"Oh, Nae-Nae," I said jealously, hefting him in my arms and squeezing one of his ham hock thighs. "He is too fine. How old is he?"

"Seven months," she said smiling at him. His chin was wet with baby slobber and I wanted to kiss it off. Fifty million hands were reaching for the baby, hoes and strippers totally sprung over his fat cheeks and dimpled grin. I passed Maleek off to the next sister and stood back watching as almost every chick in the dressing room elbowed in to get a turn at touching and sniffing that sweet baby flesh.

"Girl," Money-Making Monique said cooing at the little boy. "Why you bring that cute little fella up in here?"

Nae-Nae frowned. "My babysitter got sick and my mama ain't home. I tried to call in but Pluto said if I didn't show up I was fired. I was gonna ask one of y'all to watch him while I'm onstage, and right after my numbers are up I'll run back in here to take care of him."

Every sister in the room started volunteering to watch him. That poor baby was gonna have arm fever by the time they got finished holding and rocking and spoiling him. Nae-Nae stood back watching the women loving her baby up with a smile on her face. She wasn't funny over him at all like some new mothers were. Making you put a blanket over your shoulder just to hold 'em, and standing guard to make sure you didn't kiss their baby in the face.

I watched Nae-Nae, wondering how it felt to have something depending on you like that. A real live baby of your own, one you produced from your own body and could shape and mold any way you wanted to. I'd probably never have the chance to feel what she must be feeling. G was proud of the fact that he'd had his nuts cut, and was quick to boast about his baby-making days being over.

But mine weren't. I hadn't even gotten started in life yet. But the sad fact was, as long as I belonged to Granite McKay, my ass was shit out of luck if I wanted to have a baby. There was no leaving G for some young virile hard-backed niggah. And if G ever got it in his head that he needed to leave me . . . well, his pride wouldn't let me just step. I thought about the Dungeon and that woman in the picture on his desk and shivered. Pushing my way back into the crowd, I snatched for another turn to hold baby Maleek, and as I rocked him and cooed and fought off the hoes, I satisfied myself by pretending for two precious minutes that the fat little baby boy was all mine.

And two minutes was all the time I got with him, too, because one second I was surrounded by strippers a mile thick, and the next second hoes were scuttling back to their rooms and dancers were jumping into their costumes.

G was on the scene.

He hardly ever came into the dressing area, but I guess since all the hoes were talking baby talk instead of flatbacking in the rooms and turning him a profit, he wanted to see what was going on.

"What the hell is that, Juicy?"

G pointed at the baby like it was a snake. Little Maleek grinned up at him and reached out those chubby arms, trying to jump from me to G.

"Look at him, G," I cooed. "Ain't he cute?"

"Cute my ass. Spiders are cute. Who the fuck brought a damn baby up in here?"

The only sound in the room was little Maleek happily squealing like a little pig.

G looked around, twirled his ring a few times, then stared dead at me. I couldn't tell if he was mad because the baby was there, or because I looked so happy holding it.

"I said, whose fuckin baby is this?"

"Aw, don't be like that," I said, glancing at Nae-Nae and pushing the baby into his hands. You shoulda seen G's face. You woulda thought he was holding a bomb. Maleek squealed and laughed and grabbed a handful of G's nose and tried to pull it off.

Everybody started laughing. Even a hard-ass like G had to have a soft spot when it came to such a cute little baby.

But he didn't.

"Goddamn it, Juicy!"

And that's when I knew Dicey had been right. G had a cold black heart. That niggah was so mean he actually bent his ass over and plopped that fat little baby down on the cold, dirty floor.

"Get it out of here," he said, standing back up and grilling all of us with his stare. "And whoever the bitch is who shit out that little puppy, you get your black ass out of here, too."

And then he stepped his ass over that baby and slammed out the door.

We were all stunned. There wasn't a thing we could say though. G had spoken, and poor Nae-Nae was on her own. She picked up her laughing baby and wrapped his blanket around him tightly and headed back out the door.

Chapter Seven

spent the rest of the week busting my brain trying to come up with an excuse that would get me to that Naughty Girls party with Rita. I had the money because I lied and told G I'd lost two textbooks and needed to repurchase them. I half expected him to give me a lecture about being organized and responsible or send Pacho to the school bookstore to pick them up, but he didn't even blink when he pulled a C-note from his gold money clip and handed it to me. I pushed that money into my pocket so fast I chipped my fingernail, but I still had a problem. I'd never stepped out on G before and since he did such a good job of keeping me away from the few friends I had, I couldn't think of a single person I could count on for an alibi.

I had a standing eleven A.M. hair appointment at the Spot each Saturday, and Jewel, the sister G hired to do my hair, had just called the bar phone to say she was running late. I was so nervous over the lie I was trying to cook up for G that my stomach was churning and my muscles were in knots. I was planning to get in the Jacuzzi and let myself de-stress, but changed my mind when I saw the door to Ursula's massage room standing open.

"Good morning!" Ursula said as soon as I poked my head through the doorway. The massage room was serene and relaxing, done up in all white with overhead heated lights. There was soft music playing in the background and Ursula had poured scented water over a big pot of hot stones to cook up her special aromatherapy.

"What's up, Ursula. Why are you in here so early today?"

She shook her head and her blond hair fell around her shoulders. "I could not sleep, Juicy. I think I need vacation. Why are you here?"

"Today is my hair day," I told her. "Jewel's running late so I'm just killing time until she gets here."

"You want quick massage?"

I shrugged. Why not? I went behind one of the partitions and got butt naked, draping my clothes neatly over the hangers that were on a long hook. I took one of the freshly pressed silk robes from a cabinet and slipped into it and walked back out to see Ursula spreading a large soft towel over the padded table in the middle of the room. When she was done I lay down and closed my eyes. The warmth of the overhead lights and the aroma of the scented water evaporating over the stones was calming and relaxing. I lay there think-

ing about the Naughty Girls party tonight and my whole
body was tingling in anticipation. I sighed deeply as Ursula
chopped my calves, massaged my ankles, and rubbed my
feet until they went limp.

She moved up to the top of the table and slid my robe
down until it covered my feet. I got lost in the soft music
and my own sensual thoughts as she rubbed hot oils into my
shoulders and down my arms and the small of my back, and
the moans slipping from my lips truly caught me by sur-
prise. Ursula was working my ass, and as usual that spot between my thighs was slippery and throbbing. But this time,
instead of jumping up all embarrassed and ready to hit the
door, I stayed right there. Bit by bit I found myself rotating
my hips as she squeezed and palmed my cheeks, and my
pussy was so stoked I wondered if she had poured some of
that hot oil down my crack.

"So pretty, Juicy," Ursula was whispering over and over,
and I just couldn't help it. I squeezed my thighs together and
grinded my stuff into that table, shivering and moaning out
loud and fighting back shame at the same time. I felt her
nudge my legs open slightly, and when she slid two fingers
into my wet pussy from behind, there wasn't a damn thing I
could do to stop her. I almost screamed out loud as Ursula
pressed down on my lower spine with one hand as she
rubbed my swollen clit and played in my pussy with the
other. I was amazed when I felt her hot breath on me back
there. Her lips were wet on my ass and I yelped as she spread

me open and stuck her tongue into my hole. I was turned on beyond belief, whimpering like a baby and just about to come when I heard footsteps lumbering down the hall. I froze as Ursula pulled her hand from my pussy and flung the robe over my naked body.

Cooter Jackson, Moonie's flunky, was standing in the doorway smiling and holding the cordless phone. "D-d-dicey on the phone, Juicy. Sh-sh-she say she sick and can't come in t-t-today. You wanna tell G, or you w-w-w-want me to tell him?"

I reached back and made sure the robe was covering my shoulders. "You can let him know when he gets here, Cooter. I was just about to go in the back and wait for Jewel to fix my hair."

I waited until Cooter walked away, then without speaking to Ursula or even looking at her, I wrapped myself in the silk robe and went behind the partition to get dressed. I tried to calm myself down. To bring my ass back to my senses. I didn't want to get fucked by no woman. Wasn't even attracted to females that way, and I sure wasn't gonna let no dyke bitch from Sweden take advantage of my situation and turn me out. When I stepped out from behind the partition I was fully dressed.

"Ursula." I spoke quietly even though my body was on fire and I could still feel her hands on me. "This G pussy you fucking with, and if he ever finds out you stuck your fingers in it, that vacation you claim you need might just be a permanent one."

I didn't wait for her to answer. I ran down the hallway, barely controlling myself long enough to get into the bathroom. I rushed in and locked myself in a stall, then quickly unzipped my pants. I leaned against the door and stuck my fingers into my panties, then bit down on my lip and finished what Ursula had started. I didn't even feel bad when I was done and my nipples were getting soft again. Wasn't no need in feeling shame now because I was happy as hell. Dicey had just called and given me my alibi, and I was gonna go to that party tonight and find out exactly how naughty I could get.

It was good to know that I wasn't the only sister out there who craved orgasms and needed to get sexed on a regular basis. There were a bunch of women in Brooklyn who weren't hardly shy about their bedroom needs, and it felt good to be around regular horny sisters like me instead of lap-dancing hoes who just did it for the money.

Getting out of the Spot had been real easy. Cooter had given G the message about Dicey being sick, and I made up a lie about her bleeding through her pads and passing huge nasty clots that made G's black ass turn gray. As soon as I mentioned her period he spazzed out and waved me away. Told me to tell Dicey to stay her ass out of the cut room until she got that shit taken care of. Of course I missed my Saturday night event; watching the men do their thing on-stage for Ladies' Night, but it wasn't no big thing because I

planned to come home with some toys that would put my
fingers and my fantasies to shame.

G told Pacho to drive me over to Dicey's, so of course
that's where he expected him to pick me up from. And there
wasn't a thing wrong with her either. We watched from the
window together until Pacho drove off, then Dicey waited
ten minutes before calling a Black Pearl cab to come take us
all the way downtown to Brooklyn.

"You got some funds, right?" Dicey asked as we sped
down FDR Drive. I nodded. The hundred dollars I'd gotten
from G was safe inside my purse. Dicey was wearing this
leopard-print top and a matching skirt and she really looked
nice. She'd dyed her red hair platinum blond, and had stuck
about thirty earrings in each ear. At first I wondered if I was
dressed right for a Naughty Girls party and worried that I
would look out of place because I had on a pair of Donna
Karan jeans and a white silk shirt that had cost over a yard,
but looked really simple. But when we got there it was all I
could do not to laugh. These sisters were hooked up just like
the hoes back at the Spot. They were parading around the
apartment wearing g-strings and push-up bras, lace teddies
and satin thongs.

The apartment belonged to the aunt of one of Rita's
friends named Vickie. Vickie was another programmer who
went to Fordham with us, and since her uncle was a truck
driver who was out of town on a long run, her auntie let her
host in her apartment for the night. There was fried chicken,

empanadas, yellow rice, macaroni salad, and a bunch of other stuff spread out on card tables, and even though we were getting our grub on, food damn sure wasn't our focus. The whole mood was up, up, up. Wasn't a buster in the crowd. Just a bunch of hot women, young and old, who were feeding their sexual fantasies and weren't shy about it neither.

Brooklyn naughties sure knew how to throw a party. There were gift bags stuffed with sexy favors, card games where the winners got to choose from a table full of whips, handcuffs, and nipple clamps. And one sister even got up and read from a book of erotica she had written and was try-ing to get published. I dug down into my gift bag, and when I saw what was in there I felt faint. Anal beads and two butt plugs. Not even. They could have kept that mess. G had cured me of any asshole desires I may have had, and I traded those shits with Dicey for some vanilla-flavored clit cream and a penis ring.

I chilled with some really cool women, naughty girls for days, and just sitting around talking shit and watching them guzzle fruit punch spiked with Bacardi made me feel good. Made me feel young and freaky. This was the type of stuff I should have been doing every weekend. Chilling with girls my age, partying, eating home-cooked food, getting my hair braided and playing cards. The whole scene was live. It re-minded me of one of Grandmother's rent parties, and just seeing how free everybody else was made me realize how tight G was choking me. His habits were stifling my groove. Squeezing all the juice out of Juicy.

By the end of the night I had spent every dime G had given me and had even borrowed twenty dollars from Dicey. We called another taxi, and as Dicey gave the driver her address I sat back clutching my packages. I couldn't wait to get home and try out my Ben Wa balls. I'd wanted to slip into the bathroom and put them in and enjoy myself all the way back to Harlem, but I made myself chill. There would be plenty of time for that later.

Instead, I sat quietly as Dicey chatted all the way home. When she wasn't scaring the shit out of me about G's missing or dead ex-women, I liked listening to Dicey talk. Getting with G meant I had to drop the few friends I used to have, and aside from Brittany and Rita, Dicey was the only woman in my life. She was street-down and she had a knack for saying stuff that lifted me up and made me wanna be my own person. I felt she was dropping knowledge bombs on me and I did my best to get right up under them so I could get hit.

Of course, tonight the conversation was all about sex. Dicey was telling me that it was natural for me to want more than G was giving me in bed.

"Look, Juicy," she said. "You too young to be so frustrated. If you had some balls them shits would be blue and backed all the hell up. Don't let nobody deprive you of what God gave you to enjoy. You just gotta be real careful 'cause you fuckin with a maniac, and that's the goddamn truth. Dig," she said, "I probably fucked over two thousand men when I was out there hoeing. They tell you a ho ain't supposed to get off when she getting fucked by no trick, right?"

I nodded. I'd always heard that hoes got run up in so often that they couldn't even feel a dick when it was inside them. It had something to do with the high mileage.

"Well, don't you believe that shit. I made sure I got my nuts one for one."

"One for one?"

"Damn straight. Every time a trick busted him one, I busted me one too!"

We laughed until tears were coming out of our eyes, and by the time we pulled up outside of Dicey's apartment it was after two A.M.

"You gonna stay the night?" she asked.

I shook my head. I had never stayed out all night on G before, and he was sure to get suspicious if I tried to start tonight. Besides, my night wasn't over yet. I had a whole lot of activities planned. I called Pacho on his cell phone and told him I was ready to go home, then I sat outside on the stoop shooting the shit with Dicey until my limo rolled up.

I had Pacho bypass the Spot and take me straight back to the apartment. When I got inside I was mad because Jimmy wasn't home yet and I couldn't think of anything happening in the streets that he needed to be involved in at this time of night. I promised myself that I would slap him upside his head as soon as he showed up, but I didn't want to let my anger spoil the vibes I was still feeling and ruin the plans I had for the rest of the night.

I was so excited I had to make myself slow down. G wouldn't be home until the sun came up, so I brushed my teeth then took a hot bath in some creamy oils made from milk and honey. I'd brought the Naughty Girls' bag into the mirrored bathroom with me, and the whole time I was in the tub I kept glancing at it and licking my lips like there were a tribe of fine black men waiting to jump out those boxes and jump my bones.

With my skin still damp, I rubbed myself down with the same brand of milk-and-honey-scented lotion I'd bathed in until my body was glistening and every one of my nerves was tingling. I had to force my fingers to stay away from my nipples because they were stiff and aching to be rubbed and squeezed.

I wrapped one of those fifty-dollar towels that G had bought around me, then carried the bag into the bedroom and sat it next to the bed. I was like a kid at Christmas. I couldn't wait no longer. I took out the smallest box, the one with the Ben Wa balls, and opened it. I held the two shiny silver balls in the palm of my hand for a hot second, then I quickly opened my legs and slipped them into my coochie.

I didn't have an instant orgasm like I was expecting, but

the more I moved around, the more they moved inside of me. I got up and walked around the room butt naked, watching myself in the mirrors and enjoying the feel of the metal as the balls clicked against each other and made my pussy wet.

Next out the bag was the vibrating eggs with the remote-controlled power pack. They were even better than the Ben Wa balls, but as good as they made me feel, I was worried about what kind of radiation and whatnot that battery pack might be shooting up inside of me so I took them out and put them away.

I decided to try the Fukuoku, which were three lady fingers made out of a soft blue material. Laying back on the round bed, I looked up into the mirrors and watched my fingers move as the tips of the Fukuoku vibrated. I pushed two fingers inside me and ran my thumb back and forth over my clitoris, moaning out loud the whole time. It was a much better experience than using my fingers alone. My pussy got so hot!

I experimented with everything. There was Millie the inflatable mouse; Dong, a ten-inch dildo with a clit stimulator; and an eight-inch thruster with a suction cup. Instead of riding the thruster, I pushed it into me and held it steady with both hands as the head vibrated and the hinges moved it in and out. By the time I'd gone through my whole bag of tricks I had come so many times that I was whipped. Exhausted and too tired to get up and wash my ass, I rolled over onto my stomach, pulled the comforter over my legs, and fell asleep.

When I opened my eyes again the sun was peeking into the room and I heard somebody moving around in the kitchen down the hall. Not sure if it was G or Jimmy, I jumped up and grabbed the shopping bag and searched for someplace to hide it. The footsteps were coming closer now and I knew I didn't have much time. I ran across the room and pulled the leather chaise lounge away from the wall and stuck the bag behind it. Then I ran back to the other side of the room, snatched my robe from the closet, and managed to get one arm in the sleeve and pull back the covers, then dive into the bed before the door was flung open.

I lay there playing possum like a mother. Doing my best to control my breathing so G would think I was asleep. I heard him lock the door to our suite, and then I felt him standing over me, just staring. All kinds of shit was running through my mind. G forbid me to sleep naked, especially without no drawers, and I would have to come up with an excuse as to why my ass was hanging out all over his bed. He was probably wondering what time I'd come home, and then I remembered. He'd told me that when I left Dicey's I was to either come on back to the Spot, or call him on his cell phone when I got back to the apartment.

In trying to get my freak on I had forgotten all about it, and I knew that even a small thing like this was enough to make G suspicious and jealous. I knew he was mad, and

I thanked God that Pacho could vouch for me. He could verify that he picked me up from Dicey's and brought me straight back to the crib.

G was still standing over me. I dared not open my eyes, or even let them shits flutter, but neither did I have to. I could feel him twirling his ring. Probing at me, taking everything in and examining it like a spy, and when I heard him turn and walk away, I wanted to jump up and praise the Lord.

Instead, I cracked one eye open just a peep, and watched as G headed out of the room, but then he turned around and I thought sure he was looking straight into my face.

But he wasn't. He was looking at something on the nightstand, and I almost shit on myself when I saw it. The box from the Ben Wa balls. It was sitting right there in the open. I closed my eyes again as G came back over to the bed. *Oh shit, oh shit, oh shit* was flying through my mind as I heard him pick up the box, and I knew he was trying to figure out what had been in it.

My heart was thudding and my body broke out in a cold sweat. G walked away again, but not toward the door. Peeping through slits, I watched as he opened dresser drawers, searched through the highboy, and even looked under the bed. He'd gone through the closet and had started searching my purse when he decided to check out the Ben Wa box one more time. I had no idea what he was thinking, but when he walked over to the chaise lounge I felt all the blood rush to my head and I was so scared I felt like I was gonna pass out.

I was fully expecting G to find my sex stash and then strangle me with a vibrator cord, but what he did next made me frown and put my brain on alert. G reached up and took a whole mirrored panel down from the wall. Just like that, he lifted it away and sat it down on the dresser. Built into the wall was a metal box with a turning dial. G looked at me just once over his shoulder, and satisfied that I was asleep, he turned his back and spun the dial. I opened my right eye real wide. 32-6-14-41. Hot damn. We were in there.

Chapter Eight

I couldn't tell whether G had put something in the safe or taken something out, but I'd been watching him and hadn't seen him holding anything in his hands. I lay there faking sleep like a pro. I even threw a snore and a fart up in there for good effect, and so far it was working.

32-6-14-41, I repeated the numbers over and over in my head, but there was really no need. Like flies on shit, them numbers weren't going anywhere. There was no doubt in my mind that one day I was gonna get in that safe and see what G had hidden there. I knew he had all kinds of bank, but where he kept it, I sure didn't know. I figured he had it stashed in a bank somewhere, all that money just sitting there drawing interest and making more money.

G had just closed the safe and replaced the mirrored tile when I exhaled. He was probably checking the room looking for some business papers or something he'd misplaced, I told myself. That's all. I was damn grateful that it hadn't been me who had gotten his radar up. But then he moved over to me again and I felt him staring down at me with I don't know what in his eyes.

"Juicy," he growled.

I didn't answer. I was playing possum, remember?

"Wake your ass up, girl."

I rolled over and stretched, then pretended to snuggle into the pillows and go back to sleep. G pulled the comforter clean off of me and I could feel the whole left side of my body exposed to him.

"Get up, Juicy."

Something in his voice prompted me to move. I opened my eyes and tried to play innocent. "Huh? What's wrong, G? What's going on?"

"What did I tell you to do last night?"

I gave him a confused look. "You told me to go tell Dicey not to come back to work until she stopped bleeding."

"What was you supposed to do when you left there?"

I snapped my fingers and sat up. I pushed my hair away from my face and yawned. "Damn, baby. I'm sorry. I know I was supposed to call you when I got in, but Dicey was so sick that I ended up cleaning her house and cooking for her, too. I was so tired when I got back that I took off my clothes and fell straight to sleep."

"Is that right?" His eyes said he doubted me.

"Yes. I'm sorry, G. Next time I'll remember."

"Where your drawers at, Juicy?"

I stared at him. "In the bathroom. In the dirty clothes. Why?"

He didn't answer. "Open your legs," he commanded.

I was scared, but I didn't know what for.

"W-w-why you want me to—"

His hand was around my throat before I even saw him move.

"You questioning me, Juicy?"

It was all I could do to squeak out the word no. When he let me go I spread my legs and brought my heels up.

G kneeled on the bed between my thighs. Then he did something that really fucked me up. He lowered his face down between my legs just like he was gonna lick my pussy, but instead, he spread my lips apart and I heard him sniff deeply as he took a good long whiff of my stuff.

I just knew I smelled like sex. I'd stroked and poked myself to multiple orgasms and had fallen asleep without washing. But, I reasoned, I could only smell like me. I mean it's not like I had no real dick inside of me. Nothing to mix with my stuff and make me smell like a night's worth of real fucking.

G got up and I couldn't read his face. "Go get them panties you had on last night."

I jumped from the bed and scurried into the bathroom and came back holding my champagne lace thong in my hand. G took the thong and looked all in it, then did the same thing he'd done to my crotch. He sniffed those panties like he was a bloodhound, and I prayed that he didn't smell anything that even almost made him think I'd been with a man.

I was standing there with one arm in my robe and one arm still hanging out. G handed me back my panties and started loosening his belt and unbuttoning his shirt like he was ready to hit the bed. I had just turned to walk into the bathroom to put the panties back in the hamper when he hit me from behind.

Heat cut into my upper back, snaking across my right shoulder and burning up my naked titty. A whishing noise broke the air and I whirled around to see G's thick leather belt coming at me like a mad black snake. *Crack!* I was so shocked pee came straight out of me.

"Wh-h-ha—" I pressed my legs together but before I could get my words out G pulled his arm way back to Alabama and let his belt fly again. This blow licked across my hip and curled around my upper thigh. Another one cut into my stomach and ended up sizzling between my breasts. It felt like somebody had thrown lye on me, and thick purple welts started popping up everywhere I'd been struck.

"G!" I screamed, running toward the bathroom. He had this crazy look in his eyes, like he wasn't really there, and for the first time he looked outright ugly to me. His lip was all curled down and spit was actually hanging from it.

"Why your pussy so stink, Juicy? Huh?"

I didn't see the next blow coming, but I damn sure felt it. He caught me square on the ass and I yelped and grabbed myself back there with both hands hopping just like a little kid. I hit the bathroom door still holding my ass and moving fast. But if I was going a hundred, G was going two. He grabbed me by the back of my neck and forced me to my knees, all the while swinging his belt like I'd stolen something.

"Bitch," he called me. "Sneaky little bitch!"

I wanted to ball up in a knot and make myself as little as possible, but he had his foot on my back and my whole body felt like it was on fire. So I screamed. Screamed like somebody was killing me, which is just what I thought he was doing. My face was pressed to the floor, right next to the toilet, and when I opened my eyes the mirrors reflected G standing above me, fucking me up. Bringing his belt down on my ass until I almost passed out.

I couldn't even cry no more. What I was feeling was beyond pain. It took me a minute to realize that somebody was bamming at our bedroom door, and when the heavy knocking got through to my brain all I could think was: *Lord, no. Please don't let it be Jimmy.* I didn't want my baby brother to see me getting my ass whipped like this. I didn't want him to see G so out of control.

"What, motherfucker?" G stopped swinging long enough to bark toward the door.

"Uhm." It was Jimmy. "Ya'll okay in there?"

I bit into my lip, whimpering like a dog.

"Yeah," G said calmly. "We handling shit. Gone to bed. You can talk to your sister when I'm through."

I lay there trembling as Jimmy walked away. I could hear how slow his footsteps were, like he didn't really want to leave. *Go, Jimmy!* I prayed silently. *Just go!*

And now G had me by the neck again, but at least he wasn't swinging his belt. He was taking off his pants. I was too scared to even open my eyes and look in the mirrors to see what he was doing, but then again I didn't have to. I felt him on me. His dick long and hard and pressing into me. This time there were no juices to even halfway ease his entry. He grabbed my hips and rammed his dick straight up my ass, and when he lowered his body down on mine I screamed out loud, my torn skin bleeding and burning in pain.

He fucked me the same way he beat me. Stroke for stroke, his dick was just like a belt, cutting into my flesh. I was so battered and scared I couldn't tell what hurt worse: my asshole, my body, or the top of my shoulder where G was now grinding his teeth, biting into my flesh.

"Aaahh!" I screamed and squirmed as he bit me over and over, sinking his teeth just deep enough to break the skin and cause real pain. As heavy as he was I tried to crawl from under him, but he grabbed me by the hips again and thrust harder and faster, biting me and fucking me with fury until

I felt him bust a walnut inside my ass that was so big his cum filled me up and then ran right back out of me.

Moments later he was on his feet again, pulling up his pants. As hurt and terrified as I was, the tone of his voice cut clear through my pain.

"Stay the fuck away from Dicey, you hear?"

I rolled over on my back, forgetting my fear.

"W-w-why, G?"

Dicey was the only real friend I had. Hell, she was friend, sister, mother, and grandmother all rolled into one. Who else was gonna help me through this life I was living? Who but Dicey would look after Jimmy when G killed my black ass? I stretched my hands out toward him, pleading from the floor. "Dicey's good people, baby. You know that. She's real nice to me and even you said she's one of the best workers in the cut room. She's your goddaughter, too, right, G? You and her father was aces way back, remember?"

G moved toward me and all the muscles in his chest and arms seemed to flex. The rising sunlight was hitting the mirrors and throwing back at least fifty of his reflections. He had a half-smile on his face, but his eyes was so cold I knew there wasn't a bit of joy in him.

"Let me catch you with that bitch again, you hear, Juicy? Just let me catch you."

It wasn't until the next day that I realized how much of a pro G really was. As badly as he had brutalized me, there wasn't a mark on me that could be seen by the public. Every single welt and bruise on my body had been carefully placed so it would be hidden under my clothes. Yeah, my ass was ripped raw and I had a hard time sitting down for over a week, and yeah, G had brought home some cocoa butter and even helped rub it across my back and over my titties where the worst of the welts and the bite marks were, but even Jimmy couldn't tell what all I'd gone through on that bathroom floor.

The next morning when my baby brother looked at me over breakfast and asked what was going on and why I'd been screaming loud enough to wake the dead, I gave him some bullshit story about good sex and rough love play. I told him when he got good enough where he could make a woman scream in bed the way G did, he would know he had arrived.

Chapter Nine

It was the middle of June when the roof really fell in. Ever since the Naughty Girls party G had been playing me extra close. He didn't care that I had been falling asleep in my classes in school and barely keeping up with the work. Every night at six Pacho picked us up in G's fly whip and drove us uptown to the Spot like we was royalty or something. G would send me in the back to get my makeup and hair done, and my clothes would be pressed and ready by eight o'clock when folks were beginning to roll in.

G made me sit up at the bar all night long, and even though I knew Moonie had been ordered to watch me and dip on every conversation I had, I didn't really care. I figured I'd already taken one ass-whipping, so hell, I could take two. I would tell Moonie I was going to the bathroom, then sneak off and go run my mouth with the women who cleaned the rooms in the back, even helping them wipe down the bathrooms and change the sheets in between hoes.

But Moonie was not to be fucked with. He was totally loyal to G, and if you wanted somebody killed he was definitely down for the job. He was slick as hell, too. I couldn't figure out if he had a woman or any kids, or how he kept his eyes on all things at all times, but he had it down pat. Only the best soldiers made it on Moonie's front line squad, and from the highest lieutenant to the lowest lookout standing on the corner or sitting on a project bench, nobody crossed Moonie and nobody got next to G.

The spring semester of school was just about over and even though I had managed to pass all my classes I was feeling low-down. Jimmy kept hollering about working at the Spot instead of going to college, G told me I couldn't enroll in a single summer course unless I had the money to pay for it myself, and to top it all off I was barred from chilling with or even speaking to Dicey. That shit made me feel rebellious like a mother, so once or twice I'd sent messages to her through Cooter, but G had already gotten to her and Cooter came stuttering back and told me Dicey said she wasn't allowed to talk to me no more.

I was so stressed and bored that for weeks all I did was masturbate. In the shower, in the backseat of Pacho's whip, and once or twice I put my life on the line and did it laying in bed right next to G. I went through all my sex toys until they didn't excite me no more. I walked around all day with the Ben Wa balls up in me and practiced clenching my pussy muscles until it was too tight for a tampon.

I couldn't take the sameness of it all. Day in and day out, the same old thing. New York was hot as hell in the summertime but I didn't get to enjoy any of it. I wanted to be in Central Park, or hanging out with Rita in Brooklyn, or just walking the streets of Harlem like I used to when I was a kid. Instead I was either cooped up in the apartment during the day or cooped up at the Spot all night. It didn't take a genius to figure out that a hottie like me was heading straight for trouble, and when I crashed into it headfirst, the only person G had to blame was himself.

I'd been humping those stools for so long that I'd learned how the whole bar operation was run. Liquor was an expensive commodity in the Spot, coming in right behind the drugs and the hoes. By watching Moonie and Cooter I figured out the names of all the mixed drinks and how they was supposed to be shaken or stirred. I dipped on how the finances went down, too. G didn't run no nickel-and-dime game. Playas put their cash on the line as soon as they walked through the door. A grand to step on the carpet, and another grand that went toward your drinks, lap dances, drugs, and any trim you might just want to buy with the room chips you could purchase at any time. If your balance dipped too low Moonie sent some huge thug like Ace or that fat greasy niggah Pluto over to escort you to the cashier in the back room where they'd lighten you up by another grand.

I couldn't stand Pluto's fat ass. Out of all the dealers who worked for G, from the young heads on the streets to the bouncers and security workers who Moonie kept in deep check, Pluto was the only one who stayed up in my shit all the time. Every time I turned around he was either licking his nasty tongue out at me or saying something under his breath. Pluto wanted to fuck me, plain and simple, and if he thought he could do it and get away with it, he'd snatch my ass in a back room and do me all night long.

I didn't say anything to G about Pluto. I was gonna wait until just the right time to tell on his fat funky ass. The only person who knew about Pluto coming on to me was Cooter, and that's because he busted Pluto getting drunk and talking loud shit to me at the bar one night.

"H-h-hey, my man," Cooter had stuttered. "J-j-juicy is a l-l-l-lady. Be cool w-w-with that sh-sh-shit."

Cooter made sure Pluto saw him glance up the bar at Moonie, and then stood there until fatso took the hint and moseyed his wide ass on. We both knew Cooter hadn't scared Pluto off. It was that look he'd shot toward Moonie, and the threat of him getting involved that had done it for Pluto.

When he left, Cooter had winked at me and I smiled. I liked Cooter because he was so nice. Simple, but nice. He was real skinny and had some fucked-up skin, and sometimes he stuttered so bad it was hard to understand him, but he was totally down with Moonie, who trusted him to the max, so instead of trying him and playing him like a duck, most niggahs ordered their drinks and left him alone.

Tonight, the staff had been preparing for Ladies Night just like they did every Saturday when Moonie came out of G's office and told everybody there was gonna be a change in the plan. G was more of a fanatic than Spike Lee when it came to the New York Knicks, and tonight, Moonie said he was closing down the Spot to host a private party for one of the players' birthdays.

All the strippers and hoes were hyped. Basketball players and other professional athletes always seemed to drop the biggest bank. Maybe it was a manhood thing. Harlem wasn't the place for no sherms, and since most athletes usually weren't truly street hard or deep in the game, they spread their cheddar real thick like they had something to prove.

So Knicks, schmicks cause I wasn't starstruck no more. By now I was used to seeing big names roll up in the Spot. All the rappers and recording artists who profiled in the hottest videos, the big-name actors who starred in the black movies, the pimps and playas who held down Brooklyn and the Bronx, they all rolled heavy in the Spot. I could see why the hoes were happy, but this was non-news for me. Didn't make me no difference who came through the doors. I was still gonna be bored and uptight because nobody was coming to see me.

Needless to say, I was looking luscious that evening as I

always did. Sometimes I thought it was such a big waste of energy for me to be getting all primped and perfumed and dressed in all those fine clothes just to sit up on a bar stool or walk laps around a warehouse-sized club all night. I was getting tired of the routine big time. All that cigarette smoke stinking up my hair, my dogs howling in those high-heeled shoes, and I won't even go there about all the fucking I saw going on but couldn't partake in. The sauna, the Jacuzzi, the steam room . . . sperm was flowing by the gallon in the Spot, but not a drop of it in my direction.

I was sitting at the bar when my trouble walked in. I'd seen him a billion times on television, but never before in person. He played on a team that rivaled the Knicks, but he was cool like that so they made him down in New York. Something about him jumped out at me, but I couldn't figure out what it was. It wasn't just that he was fine. I could tell that from the TV, and besides, plenty of fine men swung by the G-Spot. And he wasn't all that tall for a basketball player neither; definitely under six feet, and even though he was damn near the best in the league everybody knew his ass had a problem with showing up for team practices. Maybe it was those cornrows he was rocking, or the way he walked up in the joint like his name was G and he owned it. I don't know. All I could say was the brother put his almond-shaped eyes on mine and smiled, and I got so wet I was ready to jump down and mop up the bar stool.

He was wearing a white sweatshirt and on the front it

read PHILLY. The back read FUCK NEW YORK. Moonie scoped it before old boy got up to the stage, and just by tilting his chin sent a message to three thick-necked bouncers to check him where he stood. He was laughing as he pulled the shirt over his head, and underneath it he had on a white wife-beater with muscles bulging everywhere.

Of course I knew better than to stare. Moonie's eyes never blinked, and I wasn't trying to give him no dog bone to go running back to G with. So I played it chill and glanced at the brother once, then kept my eyes moving right along. But I could feel him looking at me, and when I peeped his way again I knew right then and there that he didn't know shit about Harlem. Hell, he couldn't have known nothing about any borough in the entire city of New York the way he was eyeballing Granite McKay's pussy.

I watched him on the sly as he grilled me all night long: winking, grinning, and licking his lips. He was violating G like a mother, and I was waiting for Moonie or one of the bouncers to check him up and put a gun to his head. He was having himself a good old time. Punanee, one of G's prime strippers, gave him a half-fuck lap dance, and later I peeped him kissing all over Monique's three titties like he needed to be nursed. I knew Greco was tallying his bill up to the penny, and I also knew his pockets were deep enough where he could afford almost anything he wanted in the Spot.

Almost anything.

I watched him hit the Jacuzzi, then stroll into Ursula's to

get a massage. Later, I saw him go into the card room, then come back out and head for the cinema room. Every time he passed my way he gave me a deep, hard look, like he was fucking me with his eyes. He could have been killed for looking at me twice, and even if this was something he should have known, he damn sure didn't seem to care. My body was boiling and I couldn't take it no more.

"I'm hungry," I told Moonie. "I need to get me some grub."

He nodded. "Why don't you send Cooter next door to get you a fish sandwich."

I wrinkled up my nose even though I usually tore those hot whiting sandwiches up. Ronald Be Bad owned the fish joint next door, but there was also a full kitchen right here in the Spot. We sold fried chicken, hot wings, potato salad, and ribs, and the only reason G let Be Bad stay in business over there was because he didn't want us frying fish in the Spot and having it "smelling like no stank ass pussies."

"I got a taste for something spicy," I told Moonie, sliding down from my stool. "I'ma go get some hot wings. You want any?"

He shook his head like I knew he would. I'd never seen Moonie eat, drink, or even take a piss break while he was working.

The kitchen was on the far left side of the Spot, across from the card room and a small room we used in the winter to check leathers and furs. I'd seen the brother with the braids heading that way, and I wanted to get another peek at him. At the counter I asked Raybelle for an order of wings with extra sauce, and the whole time she was fixing my plate I kept peeping out in the hall, my eyeballs crawling all over the place. I was walking past the card room eating a wing and carrying my plate when he stepped out of the men's bathroom and stopped right in front of me.

"Damn," I said, playing it off like I hadn't been clocking for him in the first place. "Why you jump out like that? What you doing in there anyway?" I spoke with major attitude but he grinned all sexy like he didn't even notice.

"It says," he pointed to the sign on the door, "men's room. I was using the bathroom."

He sucked me up with those chinky eyes and had the nerve to stick his hands in my plate and grab one of my wings.

I sucked my teeth. "Don't be putting your nasty hands in my plate! I don't know where they been!"

He just laughed. "They clean, baby. I didn't even use the bathroom. I saw you walking back and forth and I was waiting for you to come back past."

I shrugged and pretended like I was gonna walk around him. "I still don't know where your hands been."

He blocked me. "I know where they wanna be."

I gave him a look. "You must not know who I am. The hoes work out of the back rooms. You can get fucked up talking to me like that up in here."

"Girl, you been peeping me all night long. I know you ain't no ho. C'mere."

He pulled me toward the coatroom snatching my plate so fast the wing I was chewing on slipped from my fingers and hit the floor, sauce everywhere.

"Man, what you doing?" I twisted out of his grasp. The spot where his hand had touched me was hot and tingling.

He put his finger to his lips. "Ssshh . . . c'mon, girl. You know what time it is."

I let him pull me into the coatroom. I melted. "We gonna get caught. . . ." I felt like a kid sneaking a hump in the closet. On some level I knew that I was playing with my life, but the thrill of it all had me on fire. I wanted this guy to do me. I wanted to feel him on me, in me, all over me.

He pulled up my dress in the dimness of the room, and pressed his lips to mine. His breath smelled sweet like choco-late. I felt his hands on my ass and I rubbed my titties against his chest. "Damn, you taste good," he said, his tongue thick and hot and leaving wet streaks on my lips, chin, and collarbone. I was panting, unable to speak. Scared as hell we would get caught but too turned on to even think about stopping.

His fingers were between my legs, urging them wide open. He hiked up my two-thousand-dollar eggshell Ar-mani dress and got on his knees and bit down on my crotch right through my panties. "Oh, damn," I whispered as his teeth raked across my clit and sent chills shooting through my pussy. "That feels so good."

He pulled my panties down with his teeth and lifted my thigh over his shoulders. "Yum," he said, looking between my legs and smacking his lips. "Cute little monkey."

And then it was on. The moment I had been waiting for and hoping for and praying for. His tongue was everywhere, up, down, probing, licking. I felt his lips on my clit and on my asshole, too. He made his tongue stiff and pushed it in and out of me, using it like a mini dick. I cupped his face, pulling him closer as I worked my hips faster. My fingers were wet and sticky with my juices that were covering his cheeks and dripping from his chin. I shivered and shuddered and almost snatched his cornrows out as I held on to his head and came harder than I ever had in my life. My orgasm had to have lasted only seconds, but it was so sweet it felt like forever. The intensity of it scared me. I felt the whole building rock. It was totally unlike anything I had ever felt before and I never wanted it to end. But as soon as it was over I got hit with a blast of reality. I was up in G's spot, wearing his clothes, eating his food, and fucking with one of his customers. How stupid could I get?

"Stop," I said, pushing him away from me. He stood up and pulled his long dick out his pants. I wanted that shit real bad, but I knew better.

"What?"

"I can't do this." I jumped into my panties and pulled down my dress. "Sorry, I just can't. I'm G's woman and this is his Spot."

"Motherfuck G," he said, but at least he didn't try to stop

me. I opened the door and peeked out to make sure nobody was in the hall, then I ran out and pulled it closed behind me.

Back at the bar I sat on my stool and tried to look normal. My pussy was thumping in a delicious afterglow and I kept replaying the act over and over in my mind, feeling his tongue swirling around inside me, rolling over my clit, stabbing up into me. Moonie was standing down at the other end of the bar, so I asked Cooter to go get me a bottle of cold water. Moonie saw me sitting there and came up to the top of the bar. I could feel his eyes studying me, trying to read me like a book.

"Did you get your wings?"

I shook my head and took a swig of water. "Nah. They were frying up a fresh batch and I didn't feel like waiting." I don't know why I lied, but I did. Moonie just looked at me for a minute, then he nodded. "Be right back," I told him, grabbing my purse. "I'ma hit the bathroom right quick." I could feel his eyes on my back as I walked away. At the entrance to the hall that lead to G's office and the ladies room, I turned and looked back. Moonie had left the bar, and was heading toward the kitchen, moving fast.

I went in the bathroom and washed my face. I wet a paper towel in the sink then took it into a stall and did my best to wash myself down there. Then I stood in the mirror and combed my hair and put on some fresh lipstick. G hated to see women who had eaten off all of their lip color. He said it made them look busted.

When I went back out to the bar, there was something on my stool. It was my hot wing. Half-eaten with the crown bit off. I frowned and looked up and saw Moonie standing behind the bar and staring dead in my face. I didn't miss a beat.

"Damn," I said and poked out my lip. "Greco needs to check his cleaning crew." I took a napkin from the bar and picked up the wing, holding it out like it was a used tampon. "Some people are so damn trifling." I switched my ass around to the end of the bar and flung the wing in the trash, then got another napkin and wiped the sauce off the seat real daintylike before sitting down one stool over.

Moonie was still grilling me with his eyes, but so what? Fuck him. He hadn't been in that coatroom holding no light so he couldn't tell shit he didn't know. Besides, I was just getting started. I had finally gotten my pussy licked, and G or no G, I wanted it licked some more.

Chapter Ten

Fletcher Boykin was a kid who grew up with me and Jimmy on 136th Street. His mother had actually ran with our moms for a while until she went down south and got religion. Miss Boykin was too busy preaching and ministering to the sinful souls at tent revivals to come back to Harlem and raise Fletcher, so just like a lot of us he lived with his grandmother and got raised the best he could.

Fletcher was a snotty-nosed kid with buckteeth and thick glasses. He followed Jimmy around like crazy, and all he ever talked about was how one day he was gonna make it rich and buy himself a Cadillac and a diamond ring.

I ignored Fletcher most of the time. He was always in our apartment trying to eat up our little bit of food, and he swore to my grandmother that one day I was gonna be his wifey and he was gonna take care of me like a queen. I was two years older than Fletcher and a whole foot taller. He was more of a nuisance than anything, but Jimmy loved him to death so I tolerated him for my brother's sake.

When I was in the eighth grade and Fletcher was in the sixth, something happened to him that neither me nor Jimmy ever truly figured out. There was a guy named Macaroni who lived in a building a few doors down from ours, but liked to hang out on the roof of our building. Macaroni was in his twenties and still lived with his mother and grandmother, who both dressed in all white and stood on the corner praying for winos and hoes who passed by. Macaroni was in and out of jail all the time, and Grandmother had warned me and Jimmy to stay away from him because he was crazy and didn't like little kids, so whenever we saw him lurking around our building we hurried up and booked up, running into the house.

One afternoon Jimmy and Fletcher were playing skelly in the hallway outside of our apartment. Grandmother was taking a nap, and I was laying on the pullout couch in the living room doing some math homework. Jimmy and Fletcher were loud talking each other and plucking caps right outside the door, and with all that hollering and carrying on I couldn't concentrate. I kept getting up and going to the door to yell at them, but they were both hardheaded as hell and didn't pay me much mind. I got mad and decided to make Jimmy's little ass come inside.

"It's your turn to clean the bathroom," I went to the door and reminded him. "And you better get it done before Grandmother wakes up." Now Jimmy was lazy and didn't care nothing about cleaning nobody's bathroom. Grandmother had already been cutting his ass left and right about showing out in school and forgetting to do his homework, but he wasn't scared of her the way I was so my threat didn't mean much to him. That is, until I said, "Besides. Grandmother got a letter about James Joseph today. I bet he can probably have visitors now, but she sure ain't gonna take you to see him if you don't start listening and doing like she says. She's probably so tired of telling you over and over to do stuff she hopes Bellevue will just gone and give you a bed right next to him."

Yeah, it was a low-down lie, but so what? Jimmy was still hyped about our father, who was just as crazy as they came. James Joseph hadn't even tied his own shoelaces since me and Jimmy were babies. Our father swore up and down he was Jesus in the flesh, and was forever talking cash mess out of his schizophrenic head, but Jimmy was blind to his shortcomings and still held out hope that one day he'd get better and Grandmother would take us to see him.

"I'll be right back, man," Jimmy told Fletcher, and ran to get the Ajax and the sponge to clean the bathroom. I hurried up and closed the door in Fletcher's face, just in case he had any ideas about coming inside and waiting until Jimmy was done.

I went back to my homework and forgot all about Jimmy in the bathroom and Fletcher out there by himself in the hallway. The sound of a woman's scream and running feet on the stairs sent me flying over to our peephole, and then running to look out the window.

"Jimmy!" I yelled as I leaned out the window and stared at the crowd of people running out of the building and others running toward my stoop. Jimmy squeezed in next to me and when we realized just what we were looking at all I could say was, "Oh, shit. Oh shit, oh shit, oh shit!"

"Oh, what?" Grandmother came up behind me. "I know you ain't grown enough to be cussing up in my house like you paying the damn rent."

I didn't even turn around to answer her. I couldn't. My eyes were fixed on the scene below. Macaroni was laying on the concrete just to the right of the stoop. He was on his back with his eyes open, and a puddle of blood was leaking from the back of his head.

Grandmother looked out the window on the other side of the chair and I heard her catch her breath. "Lord have mercy! That fool done finally fell his ass off that damn roof. He shoulda kept his crazy behind from up there in the first place. Now poor Mother Leland gone have to pray up some money to put his no-good ass in the ground."

But less than an hour later we were all back at the window again. This time it was the police car we were staring at. The morgue hadn't even come for Macaroni's body yet, although somebody had thrown a white sheet over him, and when Jimmy hollered for me and Grandmother to come look again, it was little Fletcher being led out in handcuffs that bucked our eyes this time.

We never did find out what happened to make Fletcher push Macaroni off that roof, but of course we made up all kinds of stories. Whatever it was that Macaroni had done to Fletcher when I made Jimmy leave him out in the hallway by himself, it was enough to make Fletcher kill him. And he 'fessed right up to it, too. Went right in his apartment and told his grandmother what he had done, and stayed there waiting while she prayed over him and called the police.

A few years went by before we saw Fletcher again. We'd heard he got sent to some boy's home upstate, but by the time I was a senior in high school Fletcher was back in Harlem again. By then his grandmother had died and some Puerto Ricans had moved into her old apartment, but Fletcher said he wasn't looking to stay there no way. He never did tell us where he lived, but Jimmy heard he was staying with somebody on the Lower East Side, even though he ran the streets of Harlem every day.

I had cut school and was hanging out with my girl Brittany down in Taft projects when I found out that Fletcher was scrambling for G.

"Whassup, Fletcher," I said as me and Brittany waited for the elevator. He was playing handball against the mailboxes on one wall, slamming killers like he was outside on a court.

"Flex," he said catching the ball and looking me up and down. "It's Flex now. How you doin, Juicy?"

"I'm good," I said, looking at him for signs of a killer. Fletcher's glasses were gone and his teeth were almost fitting in his mouth. He had gotten a little taller and put on a few pounds, but he still had that same grin and hopeful look in his eyes that he did when he was a kid.

"You looking good, too," he said, and I remembered the crush he had had on me all those years ago. "Know what?" he asked.

"What?"

"Remember when we was little and I used to like you?"

I nodded and laughed. "Yeah. You was a pain in the ass back in the day."

"Well, I still like you."

I shook my head and threw my hand in the air like I wasn't trying to hear it.

"Naw, naw," he said, grinning and bouncing his ball. "I know you G's woman now, and I respect that. I ain't stupid enough to step on my boss's dick. I'm just saying you was always real nice, Juicy. I still think you nice."

"You was a cool kid, Fletch—I mean Flex. We missed you when you left the building. I'm glad you're back in the city." I was hoping the elevator would hurry up and come so we could get this convo over with.

He nodded. "I missed y'all too. You and Jimmy was like the only real family I had." The elevator finally came and

Flex waved as I waited to get on. "Later, Juicy. Do your thing. But remember what I told your grandmother that time. I still mean that shit."

I waved at Flex and got on the elevator. When he was ten he'd told Grandmother that one day I was gonna be his. That one day he was gonna marry me and buy me mad gold jewelry and set me up in a big phat house with cooks and servants and the whole nine. It was a trip that all the things Flex had promised my grandmother he was gonna do for me were exactly the things that G was doing for me now.

Chapter Eleven

New York City was hot as hell. Sisters strutted the streets wearing shorts so tiny they showed the black of their asses, and I planned to be dressed just like them in a minute. Before long I'd be down in Brooklyn starring in a ghetto version of a wet T-shirt contest. I'd be hitting the streets with my titties busting out of a tank top and jumping in front of a Johnny pump to get sprayed with cold city water.

For now all I could do was hold back my excitement and count down the days. G was heading to the West Coast and he was taking Jimmy with him. They were going to his son Gino's graduation and would be gone for five whole days. I couldn't wait until they got on that plane. Me and Rita had all kinds of stuff planned. House parties in the BK, a Thug-a-Licious concert at the Garden, talent night at the Apollo, shopping till the stores closed down, you name it I was gonna do it, and do it all in five days.

G had asked me if I wanted to go and I almost screamed out hell no. Instead I ran him some line about how this would be a good time for Gino and Jimmy to get to know each other and how they didn't needed a girl hanging around stepping all over that. The truth was I wanted some down time, some time away from G and his damn Spot. I wanted to put on a pair of cut off shorts and let my hair hang down to my ass. I wanted to stroll up and down 125th Street, and maybe even Fordham Road, and eat slices of pizza with extra cheese and fried shrimp with hot sauce straight from a paper bag.

I also wanted to steal some time away from Jimmy, who was sho' nuff smelling his ass these days. Every time I turned around he was running his mouth about the jobs G had lined up for him and how much bank he was gonna be slinging. And he'd been right about Gino, too. He was coming back to Harlem with G, which was totally crazy if you asked me. Why would G spend all that money to send his son to college if he was gonna bring him back to Harlem and put him in charge of a bunch of crackheads and hoes? You didn't need no college degree to do that. The streets held class 24/7 and G was living proof of it.

That's why I knew I had to confront G. I didn't wanna risk him getting mad and putting me on lockdown while he was gone, so I decided to wait until he came back. But we were gonna talk, that much was for damn sure. Grandmother hadn't worked like a dog to raise us right just to have

Jimmy hustling up in no Spot. It was bad enough that I had
to put up with G's shit just to get my education, but have
Jimmy miss out completely on his? No. Just like Gino went
to college, Jimmy needed the chance to go too. G didn't love
his son no more than I loved my brother.

I rode with Pacho and Moonie to take G and Jimmy to La
Guardia airport in Queens. Inside the terminal I held on to
Jimmy's arm trying to cuddle with him like we used to do
when we were kids. He'd gotten so tall, so damned muscular it was almost like he wasn't my baby brother no more.
Dressed like one of them bad-ass thugged-out playas/
rappers/dealers who hung on the streets of Harlem, you
couldn't even tell he was the same kid who used to sleep next
to me on a pissy, bug-infested mattress.

I took his hand and made him hold mine tight. I could
tell he was embarrassed to have me hanging all over him, but
at least he kept grinning and squeezing my fingers so I could
feel his love. I clung to G a little bit too. Truth was, it was the
first time Jimmy would be out of New York City, and I was
scared the damn plane would crash and I'd find myself alone
without my soul or my source of income. I kept telling myself that nothing bad was gonna happen, that people had to
get where they were going and planes flew back and forth
safely every day.

Moonie said we couldn't go all the way with them to the
gate because of airline security, so we said our good-byes as
they got into a long line of people waiting to go through the

checkpoint. Despite my self-talk and all the stuff I was looking forward to doing for five days, I was still scared to see
them go. Jimmy looked happier than I'd ever seen him before. He was all up on G's dick, laughing and joking like he
climbed on a damn airplane and left me every day.

G came over and looked down at me. His clothes fit
him to a tee and even a fool could see how expensive they
were. I stared into his eyes. He was so damn fine. He hugged
me to his chest and his arms felt strong and warm around
my waist. Why couldn't he make me feel like this all the
time?

"Be good, Juicy," he said. "If you need anything, see
Moonie." He squeezed me tight. "You know you my girl."

I raised myself up on my toes and waited, begging him
from my heart. *Kiss me, G. Please. Put your mouth on mine
and let me feel your tongue inside of me. I'll be a good girl, G.
I'll make you feel so good. Just help me a little bit, G. Please kiss
me.* I was dying to feel his lips, let him taste mine. Whatever
issues I had with G, he was everything to me and Jimmy. He
put a roof over our heads when we didn't have nobody else
and even though he'd beat me, I knew he didn't really mean
it. Things could get better, I just knew they could. If we
could start with a kiss then maybe we could work our way to
a point where G wasn't turned off and disgusted by having
good sex and I wasn't afraid to show him how much I needed
it. But I was waiting in vain. G was old and set in his ways.
I was young and busting loose. He pressed two fingers to his

lips then touched my forehead. That was it. That was my good-bye kiss.

I sighed and stepped back. "You know you my man, G." I said it but in my heart I didn't mean it. I loved the things G did for me, loved what being his woman provided for me and my brother. But love him as my man? Uh-uh. I wasn't seventeen and cheddar-strung anymore. I was in college now. Meeting people and doing things. True, I'd gone from being the daughter of a crack-ho who slept on a pull-out bed in a rat-infested hole in the wall on 136th Street, to being chosen by the infamous Granite McKay and living so lovely I dripped mad jewelry and never had to play the same outfit twice, but just because I was raised poor didn't mean I was raised stupid. Yeah, poor sucked and rich was definitely the bomb, but a sister still had her bedroom needs, and the last time I checked a brick of hundred-dollar bills didn't do much to keep me lubricated at night.

I grabbed Moonie's arm and waved as they walked toward the security checkpoint. G never looked back, but Jimmy did. He looked just like a little boy again as he turned and waved, a gold hoop earring in his left ear and a pair of expensive headphones hanging around his neck. I wanted to run over to him and snatch him back, to tell him he couldn't go. But then he grinned, so excited. "You my heart, Juicy-Mo," he told me, just like he used to.

"And you, Jimmy-Jo," I said, loving him more than I ever had, "you my soul."

•   •   •

Five days was gonna seem like five minutes. Pacho and Moonie dropped me back at the apartment. "Make sure you call me before you make any moves," Moonie said. "If you need a ride over to the Spot, Pacho will pick you up. G said you supposed to stay close to the apartment and just chill until he gets back, so I'll give you a buzz a few times every day just to check. Okay?"

I nodded a few times and tried not to look like I was in a rush. As soon as they pulled off I ran upstairs to the apartment, changed into my hooch gear, and threw a bunch of stuff in a Coach bag and then called Rita. All the shit I packed was raggedy in comparison to the way I dressed when G was around. Yeah, I still had diamonds and designer labels hanging everywhere, but I was done with all those high heels and slinky-ass dresses G liked to see me in. For the next five days it was gonna be short-shorts, halters, jeans, and tank tops. And no damned makeup either. I wasn't putting nothing on my face except a little bit of lipstick and nothing hot was gonna touch my hair. It would get washed in the shower and brushed out with a little Pink Oil Moisturizer, then thrown back in a long curly-ass ponytail. That was about as much trouble as I was willing to go through since G wasn't gonna be around to make me get all dolled up for nothing.

G had told me to see Moonie if I needed anything, but that was the last thing I wanted to do. He didn't leave me no money and I'd been scared to ask for any because he would have gotten suspicious and probably ordered me to stay my ass inside the apartment. As it was, his boys had been ordered to keep their eyes on me, but they were gonna have to get up just a little bit earlier because I was outtie.

I watched from the window as Rita pulled up with her cousin Cat and gave the valet her keys. She was pushing her aunt's Range Rover, and hitting the FDR Drive and then sliding over the Brooklyn Bridge was our ultimate goal. But first we had some shopping to do. Thank God Rita had my back with the dollars. She and Cat took me to Delancey Street and showed me how they hustled the merchants down. Then we went to Chinatown and me and Rita looked at all those naked chickens and pigs hanging in the windows while Cat boosted stuff she planned to sell in Brooklyn later on.

I had been born and raised in New York, but I was taking stuff in like a tourist. I hardly ever got to travel to Brooklyn and I'd never stepped foot on Staten Island. My eyes were wide and excited and whenever I saw a sister my age who seemed like she was out doing her own thang I felt sad because that would never be me as long as I was trapped with G.

Rita had a friend who lived in Lambert projects in the Bronx, and we hung out there for a minute. We played handball in the park across the street, and then decided to take her cousin's two kids to the Bronx Zoo, which was another place I'd never been.

"Not even on a school trip?" Rita asked. I knew it was hard for her to understand that I'd been so sheltered, and I tried to explain that I'd gone directly from my grand-mother's house to G's house, with nothing at all in between. And with Jimmy acting all crazy half the time there was never money for school trips or stuff like that, so on those days I just stayed at home and helped Grandmother clean house.

There was something about the zoo that bothered me though. All those damn animals locked up and stuck behind bars. All they could do was look out at the people every sin-gle day and I recognized the look in a lot of their eyes. They were bored and pissed. Pissed and bored. I'd seen that look in my own eyes on many days.

The Bronx Zoo was really big, and Rita made sure we marched our asses from one end of it to the other. I had just followed her and the kids into the stink-ass monkey house when I thought I saw a familiar face. I didn't know how everybody else was standing that doo-doo smell, but it felt like it was getting into my mouth and skin and even in my hair.

I was trying to push my nose down into the low neck of my shirt when I saw him. He had on a white T-shirt and a beat-up-looking New York Yankees baseball cap, but it was him. A little girl was riding on his shoulders who looked to be about six. He was holding hands with a dark-skinned woman who had thick black locks down to her ass, and she had another little girl by the hand, this one slightly older.

Damn, I thought, messing around and breathing in that monkey air without even realizing it. Moonie looked just like a regular brother out chilling with his woman and his kids. He was such a small man that there was no sign of a killer in him, and the way he patted and stroked that sister and them kids almost made me jealous that he had a regular life outside of the Spot while that one building was just about my whole world.

His girl was slim but had a nice body, even if she did dress like an old woman. My shorts were ten times tighter than her jeans, even though we were about the same size, and compared to the Million Man March shirt she was playing, I felt real slutty with my titties hanging out of my tiny T-shirt that said SWEET POTATOES on the front.

I couldn't stop looking at them. Grandmother had sworn you could stare somebody into looking at you, and I guess that's exactly what I did. All of a sudden Moonie's head swung around and his eyes jumped dead on me. Scared that he'd bust me out to G, I tried to step behind a fat white man but I wasn't fast enough. For the briefest second we stared at each other and what I saw in his eyes looked a lot like disgust. When I blinked again he was walking away, pulling his woman quickly through the crowd. I followed him with my eyes as far as I could. Gone were the fine clothes and the jewelry and the playa-daddy image. The pants he wore looked like some white-boy Levi's and his sneaks were dirty and run over on the sides. It was like Moonie had completely shed his G-Spot persona for the day, and the sight of him with his family stayed with me for a good long while.

Five days went by in a big fat blur. I barely slept at all we were so busy running all over New York trying to see and do every damn thing we could. Rita liked showing me around. She had been on her own for so long that it was hard for her to believe that I had never gone to the Statue of Liberty or ridden the Staten Island ferry. She was real generous with me, too, offering to buy me outfits and sandals when we shopped, but I kept reminding her that I had more clothes than I knew what to do with and I promised she could come upstairs and raid my closet and pick out anything she wanted when she took me back home.

Day five snuck up on me when I wasn't looking. It was almost time to head back to the boring routine that was my life, and I had my lip poked out in resentment. It was my last night out, so I got loose. I put on my tightest booty-chokers and Rita took me to East New York to a house party where I slow-grinded for the very first time with some guy I didn't even know! I didn't wanna know him either, and when we pushed our way into the crowd and he asked me my name I just smiled and shook my ass. He was on the short side but he had a nice smile and that cologne he was wearing had cost over two hundred dollars a bottle. Best of all, he was a black man with a dick, and tonight that was my only requirement.

We started out dancing to a fast song, and even though I hadn't danced in so long that I probably looked crazy and off beat, the way dude was running his hands all over me told me he didn't care. He got that look on his face real quick. You know, the one where his tongue gets stuck between his teeth and he breathes real hard. Then the DJ changed the mix and threw on a slow jam, and as Maxwell's voice surrounded us I got bold and stepped straight into his body. He grabbed my ass and grinded, tearing me up, and I let him, too. Swaying to the music, I closed my eyes and let him rub his hard dick between my legs until my panties were soaked.

Two fast songs later we were still humping. "Let's go, Juicy!" Rita came up behind me and snatched me so hard I stumbled and he let me go. I backed away from him in a daze. I felt like he had dry-fucked me right there in the middle of that crowded living room, and I guess in a way he had.

Next stop was Cat's house in Bedford-Stuyvesant. Her people were throwing a fish fry and a card game and I sat watching from the sidelines because the only thing I knew how to play was pitty-pat, which was all Grandmother had allowed in her house, with her sanctified self. Even though she ran numbers on a daily, me and Jimmy couldn't even gamble with matchsticks at her table.

They had about five tables going. Rita and Cat were playing a game of Spades with two fine-ass guys, and the cutest one was Cat's older brother. His name was Frankie and he couldn't keep his eyes off of me. He kept looking at me over his cards and his partner kept getting mad as hell cause Frankie reneged twice from studying me instead of his hand.

Cat had a big-ass family. I wasn't used to so much action in such a small place! There were mad people coming and going, chicken and fish being fried, beer being drunk, and weed being smoked. It wasn't long before I needed a break. I stood up and stretched, then went into the small bedroom where Cat had told me to stash my Louis Vuitton, and stuck my head out the second-floor window.

It was after two but you couldn't tell it without a watch. Brooklyn never slept, and the stoop downstairs was packed and the streets were still rocking. I heard somebody come into the room behind me and I turned around so fast I banged into the window frame.

"Ouch," I said, rubbing my head. "You scared me."

He closed the door behind him and the only lights in the room came from the streetlight burning outside. "You ain't gotta be scared of me," Frankie said. "I'm harmless."

I laughed and leaned against the windowsill. "I heard that one before. That's what they all say. Right before they try to jump your bones."

"Don't lean back too far," he cautioned, "or getting your bones jumped won't be your problem. Breaking them will."

I don't know what got into me—okay, yeah I do. I was still stoked from the house party and Frankie looked better than sweet potato pie. Best of all, he was my age and his body was all that. It felt so damn different having a casual conversation with a guy like him, just a regular brother whose eyes told me everything I needed to hear. I turned around and leaned back out the window and when I heard him catch his breath I sure as hell knew why. Yeah, I had some nice titties, but it was the ass that got them every time. I had a phat ass on a fine frame, and the shorts I was rocking fit me just like panties.

He came up behind me and I bit my lip when I felt how close he was.

"Ain't nothing happening out there that's better than what we can make happen up in here."

My stuff was throbbing but I played it off without turning around. "How you trying to step to me? I don't know you like that. Shit. I already forgot what you said your name was."

He laughed behind me, then nudged me over and squeezed in next to me until he was looking out the window, too. "My name is Frankie. Cat's my little sister."

"I still don't know you."

"So? I don't know you either, but you don't see me complaining."

I cut my eyes at him, then laughed again. He was too cute.

"Pretty hair, pretty lips . . . I see why they call you Juicy. What's your real name?"

"That is my real name. Juicy."

Now he was laughing. "Yeah, okay. I must look like a

fuckin herb. Your name is probably Esmerelda or some shit like that."

"It's Juicy!" I shrieked, and elbowed him the best I could in that narrow space. The next thing I new his lips were all over mine, his tongue wiggling halfway down my throat.

"W-w-wait . . ."

I broke our kiss and pulled myself back until I was standing in the darkness. I wiped my mouth with the back of my hand, then dried it on my shorts. I had been dying to be kissed, but not like that. "What you do that for?"

He stood up beside me. "Because you wanted me to."

Yeah, I might have thought I wanted him to kiss me, but as wet as his mouth was and the way he had wiggled his tongue all over my tonsils had made me think twice.

"That was sloppy, Frankie. Don't no woman wanna be kissed like that."

He tried to play it off. "I ain't never had no complaints."

There were two twin beds in the room. A pile of clothes was on one, and the other one had a red spread over it. "C'mere," I grabbed his hand and pulled him toward the empty bed. "Swallow everything in your mouth except your tongue and your teeth," I commanded. "Now pay close attention. I'll be the teacher, you try hard not to be no fool."

I sat on Frankie's lap and took his ass to school, showing him how to kiss me just the way I was kissed in my fantasies. He was a real fast learner, too. It wasn't long before I felt heat rising from his groin and I was warming up, too. He slid me off of his lap and lay me back on the bed, pressing his body on top of mine.

Frankie kissed my lips and pulled my shirt up to stare at my naked titties. I let my hands flow through his curly hair, over his back, and down his ass. A door slammed and I heard a woman cursing somebody out on the stoop. I wondered if Frankie had locked the door behind him but I was too far gone to tell him to go check.

I felt his hands lowering the zipper on my shorts and I sucked hard on his bottom lip. He was inside my panties and I raised my hips off of the bed as he parted my pussy hairs and slid his fingers inside me. I shivered deliciously as he thrust into my wetness then used my juices to massage my clit. He whispered that I should spread my legs open and bend my knees, and I did. He moved his fingers deeply inside me and we settled into a pace: him plunging deep, then coming out to rub my clit and slide quickly back inside of me, and me holding on to his wrist and slamming my hips up to meet him as hard as I could. My stomach muscles clenched and I squeezed my legs closed around the hardness of his fingers. I was in heaven, it felt so good. I moved my ass in ways I had never moved it before, not even with my electric thruster. Frankie started moaning, too, and I looked down and saw his hand sliding in and out of my wet pussy. That shit looked so good I screamed into his chest as an orgasm tore through my body and completely blew my mind.

I wanted him to hold me for a minute while I caught my

breath, but Frankie wasn't having it. He wanted to get his too. He pushed his baggy jeans down, and pulled his dick through the pee hole in his drawers. I almost laughed when I saw what he was packing. It was the size of a magic marker, maybe even skinnier. He pushed my hand down on it and it felt wet and slimy.

"Hold up," I whispered, yanking my hand back and wiping it on the spread before pulling up my shorts. I fixed my shirt and closed my zipper.

"Whatchoo doing? Open your goddamn legs."

I pushed myself up on my elbows. "You got a rubber?"

"What?" He sucked his teeth and groaned, and I knew I was off the hook.

"You heard me. A rubber. Grown men who fuck usually carry rubbers."

"I just ran out. But I trust you. Your pussy is clean and I can tell you ain't got nothing. Besides, ain't you on the pill or something?"

I shook my head and sat all the way up on the bed. "Nope. I ain't on shit cause my man can't make no babies and he don't fuck out. You ain't running up in me raw."

He hesitated for a minute, then pushed his dick back in his pants. "You didn't mind raw when I was making your ass come."

I shrugged. A finger was one thing. A dick was something else. Besides, I wasn't attracted to him no more. I had gotten as much as I wanted from Frankie and now all I wanted him to do was leave me alone.

"Why'ont you go to the store or something? You got money, right? Go buy a pack of condoms if you want some pussy."

He got up off the bed and fixed his clothes. "Don't go nowhere." He pointed at me. "We gone finish this shit. I'ma give you some dick like you never had before, Miss Juicy. You just wait right here."

I looked at him and smiled. He must was gonna pick up a spare dick at the Spanish bodega because his finger was bigger than what he had in his pants. I watched from the window as he jumped down the stairs on the stoop and took off down the street looking for an open store.

Grabbing my purse from the closet I went back out to the kitchen and snatched a beer from Rita's hand. "I'm ready to go, Rita." I gave her a sad-ass look, then touched the low part of my stomach. "Cramps."

Ten minutes later I was riding in the Range Rover with the window down when I spotted Frankie coming out of a late-night corner store. "Later baby!" I screamed out the window, then me and Rita bust out laughing as he held his hands in the air like *Yo, what the fuck is up?*

G and Jimmy were due in the next afternoon, but I'd had a good last night out. We went to Rita's aunt's house and stayed up talking and listening to music most of the night. I wet Rita's hair and put it in some flat twists, and she put one big French braid down the back of my head, then we each took a pair of clean panties and tied them around our heads like scarves.

I laid down for the night with a smile on my face. Even though I had silk sheets and a ten-thousand-dollar bed waiting for me on Central Park West, I couldn't remember the last time I'd been so happy, and I got the best sleep of my life laying right there next to Rita on a pallet on her aunt's living room floor in one of the worst neighborhoods in Brooklyn.

Chapter Twelve

We got up the next morning hungry as hell and cooking up a storm. I made a pot of cheese grits that could have put Grandmother's to shame, and Rita fried beef bacon and made scrambled eggs and salmon cakes. We took our time eating and then cleaned her aunt's kitchen until it looked better than it had when we started. G, Jimmy, and Gino were due to fly in at 3:30, so I knew Pacho would be swinging by to pick me up at about 2:00 P.M.

It wasn't even 1:30 when we pulled up outside of the apartment building on Central Park West, but already Pacho was parked in the valet area and sitting in the limo. All I had to say was that we'd gone out for lunch, I told myself. Nobody told him to bring his ass over all early anyway. I waved at Pacho then turned away as Rita handed the valet boy her keys.

"You sure it's okay for me to come up?" she asked.

"Girl, please," I said striding toward the doorway. "You need to. Ain't nobody up in that big-ass apartment no way. Don't nobody never come up there except the maids. All that expensive shit and don't nobody ever get to see it."

We rode the elevator upstairs and Rita was tripping about the carpet, fresh flowers, and gold mirrors and crystal chandeliers that lined the hallway. True, it was a long way from the projects we'd just come from, but it wasn't nearly as much fun.

We stopped outside the door and I slung my purse over one shoulder and my Coach overnight bag over the other as I stuck the key in the lock. I knew what was up the moment I turned the knob and the door only opened half a foot, but at that point there wasn't a thing I could do.

"Where you been?"

G sounded like a pit bull as he slid the chain lock off the door and opened it all the way. He must not have seen Rita standing behind me the way he snatched me inside the apartment and flung me up against the wall.

My lie came pouring straight out. "G, this my friend Rita. She came by and picked me up earlier and we went out to breakfast. I had a taste for French toast and wasn't no bread in the house and you know I don't have no money."

He just looked at me for a minute, then he shook his head. "You're a big liar, Juicy. We came in on an early flight and ain't none of the doormen seen you come in or go out since the day I left. So where you been?"

G wasn't yelling but he might as well have been for all the rage that was in his eyes. I looked around and saw Jimmy sitting at the table with the finest man I'd ever seen. Jimmy looked disgusted and the other guy looked amazed. He had to be Gino, but since he wasn't a cop with a gun who could save my ass, I truly didn't give a fuck.

"For real, G!" I turned to Rita. "Right, Rita? Didn't you come get me and take me out for breakfast?"

I knew I looked pitiful, begging my girl to back up my lie, but I didn't care. My ass was on the line cause G didn't play. Rita nodded quickly. "Yeah that's right. I picked her up and we went to get something to eat. Dagg. We wasn't even gone that long."

G never even looked her way. Instead he snatched my Coach bag and turned it upside down, shaking everything out. All my dirty shit hit the floor. Thongs, belly shirts, push-up bras, cutoff shorts, even my toothbrush, deodorant, hairbrush, and the panties I'd used to tie down my hair the night before. There was nothing left to say, and even if there was, G wasn't trying to hear it.

"Why you lie so much, Juicy?" He grabbed the front of my shirt and tried to put me through the wall again.

"Hold up, goddamn it," Rita said, trying to squeeze between us. "Hold the motherfuckin phone. You ain't gotta be putting your damn hands all over her."

The next moment was a blur. It was almost like G hit Rita with me. He snatched me by the neck and slammed me dead into her, banging our heads together, trying to crack them like eggs. We collided so hard we both went down to the ground. I heard him cursing and beefing above us but my left ear was ringing and I was too dizzy to move.

"I don't know who the fuck you be, little mama," he warned, pointing down at Rita, "but if I ever set eyes on your ass again I guarantee your people'll be reading about you in the newspaper."

We stayed on the floor until G walked away, both of us too scared to move. Rita got up first, then helped pull me to my feet. Her eye was red and a bruise was rising on the side of her face. "You can come home with me," she whispered as I pushed her toward the door. It was all I could do to shake my head. Rita might not know any better, but I did. There was no betraying Granite McKay. And there was no escaping him either.

I found out why they'd come back early. On the spur of the moment G had decided to take his son to Hawaii as a graduation gift. Jimmy had wanted to leave straight from the West Coast, but G had insisted they come back to New York to get me. I felt like shit and Jimmy wasn't making me feel any better the way he was ragging on me.

"Why you always gotta mess everything up?" he asked, scowling at me like I was his damn child. I pressed an ice pack to the side of my head and tried to stop the room from spinning as Jimmy stormed around the kitchen opening and closing cabinets and drawers without taking anything out of them.

"I wasn't trying to mess nothing up." I sucked my teeth. "All I was trying to do was have some damn fun. Just like any other nineteen-year-old. Just like you do whenever you get ready to roll. I don't wanna go to nobody's Hawaii anyway."

"Well, you going. And you knew G's rules. You knew you was supposed to have your ass home while we was gone. How you think G felt when we got off that plane and didn't nobody know where you was? He was so mad he told Pacho to leave Moonie in Queens and let him find his own way home!"

"What Moonie got to do with me?"

"G left him in charge. He was supposed to have his people watching you, that's what. He failed G, so he had to pay for it. Shit, G should have left me running things. I'da made sure you kept your ass right here where you belonged."

Jimmy's words cut through my pain. Not only didn't I like the yang he was talking, he needed to get certain shit out of his head. Fast. "G didn't leave you in charge of nothing," I told him, "because you ain't getting involved in nothing. I already told you. You have to graduate next June, then come September you need to have your ass up in a college just like Gino had his ass up in one."

Jimmy leaned over me and spoke in a way I'd never heard before. In fact, a whole lot about him seemed to have changed after only five days alone with G. "Juicy-Mo. Get it

right. I'm not going to college, and that's word. I'm down
with G now. He made me a lieutenant and I got a job to do."

    This wasn't the time to argue with Jimmy. When shit set-
tled down I would talk to G. If he loved Jimmy so much
then he should want the same thing for him that he'd
wanted for Gino. An education. I pushed past my brother,
elbowing him roughly as I left the kitchen.

    "Get outta my damn face, Jimmy, before I fuck you up. I
might not be able to beat G, but I can damn sure beat you."

G said we were leaving in two days and would stay gone for
ten. I'd been real quiet all day cause my head was still banging like a drum. Jimmy had introduced me to Gino, then
spent almost an hour talking him up like he was some kind
of saint. It was Gino said this and Gino did that. It wasn't
long before I was sick of Gino-Gino-Bo-Bino and I didn't
even know him.

    But Gino was G's son, that much was for sure. Except for
the curly hair, which Gino must have gotten from his Puerto
Rican mother, they looked just alike. The same tall build,
solid shoulders, dark skin, and pretty teeth. But even as tight
as G kept his body Gino's youth outshined his father, and of
course he dressed hipper than G although his clothes were
just as expensive.

    For some reason G had put Gino in the guest room that
was connected to our bedroom, and I couldn't understand
why. The other room down the hall was much bigger and

had nicer stuff in it. A plasma screen television, a sitting area, it was laid. The room he put Gino in was the smallest in the apartment, and while it was still nice and had a good mattress on the bed, it wasn't where I would have put my son if he came to stay with me.

G acted like he'd forgotten about the scene with Rita. Forgotten about how he'd tried to bust our heads open like watermelons. Since it was Sunday, all areas in the G-Spot except the cut room were shut down. I usually cooked a big Sunday dinner for the three of us, but tonight G had decided to order in Chinese food and even rented a bunch of movies for us to watch. It seemed like he was trying to be nice to me around his son, who hadn't said more than a handful of words the whole day and spent most of his time talking on his cell phone or playing video games with Jimmy.

When I climbed out of the bathtub later on that night G was waiting for me. On any other Sunday night he'd jet over to the Spot before midnight so he could check on his powder, but tonight he was sitting up in the bed naked, the lamp shining from his nightstand, the white silk sheets tangled around his legs. I saw the way he was looking at me but I ignored him and did like I usually do. I rubbed myself all over with some scented lotion, then slipped into a pair of silk panties and a black lace teddy. I didn't bother to do anything to my hair because I knew G would insist I get it blown out and stiff curled first thing in the morning.

I got in the bed and closed my eyes and heard a click

when G turned off his lamp. I cursed inside when he reached for me and turned me over on my back. This was gonna be one dry fuck, and the only comfort was that I knew it wouldn't last long. It never did.

Pinch, pinch on the right titty. Squeeze, poke on the left. Sex with G was so stale and predictable I wished I could just put the pillow over my head and go to sleep while he did his thing.

I kept my eyes closed as he moved on top of me.

"Moan, Juicy."

For a second I was so stunned I couldn't speak. I just knew I heard him wrong.

"Moan," he said. "Make some damn noise up in here."

Moan? I didn't even know I was allowed to roll my hips during sex with G. A moan was likely to get my ass kicked. But I moaned. Moaned like a mother. I felt stupid as I did it, but considering the fact that he'd caught me hanging out for five days and all I got was clunked in the head with Rita, I moaned my ass off.

"Oh, yeah. Uh-uh-uh. Oooooh, baby."

"Louder," he said right in my ear as he rammed his dick up in my dry insides. "Much fuckin louder."

G had a wild hair up his ass and I didn't know how to take it. But I knew better than to disobey him in bed. I loved my asshole too much for that.

"OH GODDAMN, DADDY! EEEHH!! YOU MAK-ING ME FEEL SO GOOD!"

"Keep going, Juicy. Louder."

If G wanted me to wake up the dead then they asses better be prepared to get up.

"OHSHITDADDY!! YOUTEARINGTHISSTUFFUP-RIGHT! OHHHYESSSGIVEITTOMEBABYKEEPON-GIVINGITTOMEGOOD!!!!!!!"

Didn't no porn star have nothing on me, cause I performed like a pro for the whole two minutes G was fucking me. I don't know when I realized that my fake moaning had become real. That G's long dick was stroking me so nice I started purring like a cat, because for the last thirty seconds G had been giving it to me good. He slammed his dick up in me so hard and deep he touched my backbone and my whole body tried to go into shock. Damn! Negro should have been handling me like this all along! Now he was gonna have to bring it like this every single time! But thirty seconds still only lasted for thirty seconds. On his tenth stroke G almost cracked his spine getting his nut, and the moment he came he clamped his hand down over my mouth and smushed my face into the pillow. "Shut up, girl," he muttered, and pulled his limp wet dick out of me. "Just shut the fuck up."

So I did.

Chapter Thirteen

I got on that airplane mad as hell. Steam was rolling off me and I had enough fuel running through my blood to fly that bad boy all the way to Hawaii and back.

G had pulled some low-down shit.

I should have known he was scheming like a demon. He'd been too damn nice. Had let me off the hook too easily for staying out while he was gone. Now I knew why. I had just finished packing last night when I called Jimmy in my room to sit on my suitcase so I could zip it up.

"Your gear ready?" I asked him. "You got enough medication for the whole trip?"

He couldn't even look me in my face. "I ain't going."

"What?" I got up off my knees. "What you mean you ain't going?

Jimmy mumbled something under his breath and shrugged. "I ain't going."

I broke. "Uh-uh, Jimmy. Hell fuckin no. Ain't no way in hell I'm leaving you here for no ten days while I go way across the world to some damn island. How the fuck you sound, you ain't going?"

"How the fuck I said it, Juicy? I ain't going. You got any beef, see G."

And that's exactly what I did, too.

"G!" I bust into the bathroom while he was sitting on the toilet. "What's Jimmy talking about he ain't coming with us in the morning?"

That nigger pissed me off. He looked at me for a long moment, then spun the toilet tissue on the holder and bunched a wad of it up in his hand. I was tapping my foot and smelling his shit as I waited for him to answer. He took his time wiping his black ass, inspecting the tissue, then tossing it behind him into the bowl.

"Look," he said finally. "I'm taking my son on vacation. He graduated from college and he deserves it. But Jimmy gotta stay here. I got some work I need him to do."

Now my hand was on my hip. "G. You know Jimmy ain't right. He can't stay here for ten days all alone. That's my brother, and somebody has to watch him so I guess I'll be staying home, too."

"Kill all that noise, Juicy. You making my ass hurt. I'm putting Jimmy down on a little job. He'll be all right here. Pacho's gonna sleep up here at night and Moonie can watch him while we gone."

I just couldn't resist it. "Yeah, just like he watched me, huh?"

A vein jumped on the side of G's head. "You getting brand-new, Juicy. Brand-new. Don't push your luck, baby girl, cause my patience is getting thin."

I opened my mouth to talk some more shit, then closed it back. Damn. Motherfucker. This wasn't fair. I didn't feel good about going all the way to some damn Hawaii without Jimmy. This was some foul shit, and I made sure the look on my face told G just what I was thinking. Yeah, he could force me to go with him, but he couldn't make me have a good time. I wasn't gonna talk to his ass for ten whole days. Or to his stupid-ass son, neither. Dumb-ass niggah got a college degree just to come slanging and slumming up in Harlem. Fuck both of them.

I was so mad I slept mad. Our flight was leaving at eight A.M., and Pacho came to the door to take our bags down at five. I went into Jimmy's room and sat down on the bed next to him. "Jimmy." I shook his shoulder. "Wake up and tell me bye, Jimmy."

He rolled over on his back. "Bye, Juicy. Go have fun. Bring me back an island girl with some big titties, okay?"

I punched him on the arm. "Boy, you just too stupid. All them big titty bitches in the Spot and you need me to bring one way from Hawaii?" He had me laughing and I felt a little bit better about leaving him. "For real though. You gonna be straight while I'm gone?"

"Damn, girl. You act like I'm a baby or something. It ain't but ten days."

I nodded. "I know. But that's a long time." I stared into his eyes to see could I catch him in a lie. "What kinda job G gonna have you doing while we gone?"

"I don't know." He shrugged and looked toward the open door. "But I think I'ma be supervising some of the workers, or keeping books or something."

Yeah. I knew it was more than that, but without any proof there was only so much I could bitch. "Aiight, then. Be careful, Jimmy. There's some slimy motherfuckers out there."

He laughed. "I ain't worrying about nobody, Juicy. I'm down with G, and ain't a nigger out there stupid enough to violate that."

I kissed my brother on his cheek, then threw my arms around his neck. "Still. Be careful, Jimmy."

He hugged me back. "You too."

We were in the back of the limo about to pull off when Moonie rolled up.

"Hold up," G told Pacho. "Lemme handle something."

He pushed the button to roll up the car window, then got out and slammed the door. I was sitting across from Gino, and even though I felt bad about leaving Jimmy, I couldn't help notice how good Gino looked. He was listening to a

CD through his Walkman, and the look on his face told it all. He didn't want none of this shit either. He felt me studying him and looked over at me like I was a booger on somebody's fucking nose. "You got a problem?" I said.

"Yeah. You got one?"

I just crossed my legs and rolled my eyes. G finished handling his business and got back in the car. I looked out the window as we pulled away and locked eyes with Moonie. His face looked hard as hell, and before I could break my eyes away from him he nodded and turned away. I knew he was mad about me bringing G down on him and I prayed he wouldn't take it out on Jimmy.

Hawaii was far! It took us six hours to fly to California, and after a three-hour layover we still had another five and a half to go. It was my first time flying and I was scared as hell. Gino tried to be nice when he saw how nervous I was. He told me he'd flown from coast to coast more times than he could remember and gave me some line about how flying was much safer than driving. I didn't believe that mess for a minute, but I was glad he at least tried to make me feel better about being way up in the air without no parachute.

G didn't even try to comfort me. He practically ignored me during the whole flight. As usual, we had stepped out in style. We were in the first-class cabin where they kept calling us ma'am and sir and we were chilling in some phat leather seats that were so wide and soft they felt like a bed. Still, G kept shifting and moving around, complaining that he wasn't comfortable. He spent most of his time talking and kicking it with his son, and I was glad they were having a good time because it kept him from fucking with me.

Gino was on the end, G was in the middle, and I was in the window seat. I asked the stewardess for a blanket and wrapped myself up in it and kept praying the damn pilot knew what the hell he was doing. I had stopped at the airport bookstore and picked up a big bag of pistachio nuts and copy of *Skyscraper* by some chick called Zane, and I gobbled that book up in five hours flat. The story was so good I forgot all about being up in the air. All that fucking they had going on got my juices flowing and I waited until G and Gino shut up and fell asleep, and then I crossed my thighs and, fingering my nipples under the blanket, I got off right there in my seat and wasn't worrying about crashing to the ground at all.

I fell asleep during the last few hours of the second flight and the next thing I knew the stewardess was waking me up so I could raise my seat up and put on my seat belt. I pushed up the window shade and looked down at the bright lights. G said we were going to the island of Oahu, and this was the city of Honolulu. Except for the mountains that I could just barely see off in the distance, the bright lights kinda reminded me of New York, and even though we hadn't even started our vacation, thoughts of the city made me miss my baby brother.

As soon as we got off the plane and walked down to the

terminal there was a limo driver waiting. He was holding up a sign that read Purpose Driven, Inc., which was the name of one of G's front companies. I felt like I was in a foreign damn country or somewhere down in Chinatown. There was Japanese writing on all the signs and so many Oriental people it wasn't funny.

Honolulu didn't look nothing like New York from the ground. Yeah, the crowds were out there and the traffic was mad, but it was clean and smelled good and I rolled down the window in the limo and sucked up the saltwater smell all the way to the hotel.

G had booked two penthouse suites at the Kahala Mandarin Oriental Hotel, and if I thought our apartment was large, it didn't have shit on the Kahala. I knew all this had to be costing G some mad yardage, but I also knew he could afford it. Our suites had connecting doors and there was a king-sized bed, a dining area, and a separate spare bedroom in each one. By now I was used to quality stuff. G had exposed me to the best that money could buy and he didn't believe in skimping. After borrowing Gino's cell phone and leaving a message at the apartment for Jimmy so he'd know we'd landed safe, I checked everything in the room out thoroughly and decided it was up to standard.

We were all travel-tired and G was getting cranky. We ordered a bunch of food from room service, but by the time they brought it up G was shivering and sweating like he was running a fever.

"Let me run you a shower," I told him, trying to get back on his good side. If I was gonna be here for ten damn days I didn't want there to be no unnecessary tension. I started the shower for him, and while he was in there I took his silk pajama bottoms out his suitcase and laid them on the bed and put his slippers on the floor beside the tub.

Me and Gino both picked over our food until G got out the shower, and then Gino left to go to his room and I stripped out of my clothes and got into the shower myself. I was tired as hell, even though it was still early in Honolulu, because of the time difference. A few minutes later I was washed and oiled and had my hair tied down with my favorite silk scarf. I brushed my teeth and said a prayer for my baby brother, then climbed my ass in the bed next to G and crashed.

Chapter Fourteen

G had a boil. Right in the crack of his ass.

It was our first morning in Hawaii and I was ready to get out and see me some sights. Instead G had called me into the bathroom and showed me his split.

The hotel was even grander in the daylight, but there was no way I wanted to be cooped up in it. G had arranged a three-day private tour of the island for us and I was ready to hit it. The hotel clock had said 8:12 A.M. when Gino knocked on the door and asked if anybody wanted breakfast. G was still sleeping, after tossing and turning most of the night, so we went ahead and ordered some French toast, turkey sausage, and scrambled eggs and told them to bring it up to Gino's suite. The food came pretty fast so I slipped on a robe and went next door to eat so we wouldn't disturb G.

Gino was sitting on his bed dressed in a pair of Joe

Boxer pajama pants. He wasn't wearing a shirt and the hair on his chest was thick, black, and very curly.

"Hold up," he told me when I walked in. He snatched a shirt from a bag by the bed and put it on real quick, covering all those muscles he was packing. I really dug his complexion. It was milk chocolate like G's but more creamy. His hair was jet black and even his moustache was curly.

"Hawaii is pretty," I said, looking out the window. He had opened his curtains and the window and balcony covered one whole wall.

"Looks like it."

I didn't really know what to say to him. Even though he wasn't all that much older than me, we lived in worlds that were miles apart. I had no respect for him coming back to Harlem to roll with fleas, and the first time he ever laid eyes on me his father had had me up against a wall, busting my ass. Our first impressions had been ill.

The food smelled so good! I liked the way Gino uncovered my food and then pulled out my chair, then passed me a cloth napkin. I watched him on the sly as I shook the napkin out and laid it in my lap. He opened my Evian and poured it into a glass of ice, then asked me if I wanted him to say the grace.

Grace? Shit, I hadn't heard or said grace since Grandmother died. It was nice, though, to hear it again. I figured it was his mother or whoever had raised him that had taught him his home-training, because G damn sure didn't say no-body's grace!

I had poured coconut syrup over everything on my plate and me and Gino were chowing down and laughing at a Hawaiian cartoon when G bust through the connecting door and ordered me into our bathroom to look up his ass.

"What it look like, Juicy?" he asked, bending over with his black ass all up in my face. He'd been burning up with a fever all night and I could still smell it on him.

"Nasty," I said. "It looks real nasty, G. It's fat and has a pink head on it with some white stuff at the tip. Want me to try to squeeze it out?"

He jumped his ass back. "Girl, you crazy," he said letting his cheeks go and hobbling away. He could barely close his legs good enough to walk and I felt real sorry for him. Grandmother used to get them nasty-looking boils in her armpits all the time so I knew they hurt like hell.

"You need to put a hot washcloth on it, G. Draw it out with some Black Salve or some Boil Ease. Want me to call down to the desk and get you some Tylenol or something?"

He was running water in the tub. "No. Call down and tell them to bring me up a bottle of Courvousier and some ice." He climbed into the tub and eased himself down in the hot water. I'd never seen him look like this. Sweat ran down the sides of his face and his lips were dry and chapped.

"Don't you wanna eat some breakfast first?"

"No. I want some Yak."

Yak it was. I called room service and told them to bring my man a liquid breakfast. "So what about the tour today?"

G waved his hand. "Y'all go. I got some calls to make, then I'ma sit right here and soak my ass all day."

I eyed the tub. "We're getting picked up at nine, right? If I don't get a shower real quick I'll miss the ride."

"Damn, Juicy! Figure shit out, girl! Go across the way and take a goddamn shower! Gino ain't gonna bite you, and as much as I laid out for the tour them motherfuckers bet'not leave you neither!"

I got out his way. He was sick and mean and I knew it wouldn't be long before he was drunk, too. I'd only seen G get tight a couple of times, but I remember how ugly liquor made him.

Gino was already dressed when he opened the door for me.

"Your father is in the bathtub," I said, standing there holding all my shower shit. "Can I use your shower?"

He stepped aside to let me in, but didn't say anything. I went into his bathroom and closed the door. He was just like his daddy. A neat freak. I could tell he had just had a shower because the mirrors were still all fogged up from steam. His razor, toothbrush, and a diamond ring were sitting next to the sink, and the towel he had used was folded up on a little stand near the door.

My mind was going in ten different directions as I stood under that hot water. It was real hot and hard, just the way I liked it. I felt all funny inside but I didn't know why. Yeah, I was excited about seeing someplace new, and yeah, I felt sorry for G with that fat boil on his ass, but there was something else rumbling through me, too.

The Kahala was a top-quality hotel and the shower proved it. The water hit my skin like little fingers, massaging my muscles and my neck. I poured creamy shower gel all over my washcloth then stroked myself from head to toe, letting the suds glide over my skin as the scent filled the bathroom.

An image of Gino and that curly hair on his chest jumped into my mind, and I squeezed suds over my breasts then teased my nipples, pretending it was him who was touching me. Now my hands were everywhere. Down my stomach, between my legs, gripping my own ass, and then finally two fingers found my clit and slid deeply into my wet pussy.

I fingered myself deeply as the water beat down on me and the bubbles swirled over my body. My juices were so thick and hot I almost fainted as my hand moved faster and faster, stroking my clit and rubbing my slick insides, pretending my hand was Gino's dick. I had to clamp my hand over my mouth as I came, my whole body shaking, my ass pressed against the shower wall, and the feel of Gino's body playing with my mind.

I calmed down under the water and washed my hair, then soaped my skin again and let the hot water wash me clean. I wrapped a towel around my head and another one around my body before putting my robe back on. I made sure my shit was tight before opening the door, but when I went out there Gino wasn't even in the room. I felt a little disappointed as I slammed the door that connected our rooms and went to get dressed.

G was done with his soak and was laying in the bed with his knees up and a pillow underneath his ass. He didn't look nothing like the bad-ass King of Harlem who ruled niggers with just a glance. I turned my back and lotioned my body, then put on one of my new bikinis under my clothes, a pair of red denim Chanel shorts and a matching red and white cotton shirt. I had bought a pair of red Reebok flip-flops from 125th Street, so after rubbing some oil in my hair and pulling it back in a ponytail, I grabbed my shades and a beach towel and I was set.

"Bye, G," I said, leaning over to give him a hug.

"Uh-huh." He brushed his hand across my back twice then pushed me away. "Gone now."

"I hope you feel better."

"Yeah. Gone."

I closed the door and jetted.

As soon as I got a glimpse of Gino, G's whole asshole could have fallen out for all I cared. Gino was waiting for me downstairs at the desk. The hotel lobby was busy with people running back and forth in all directions. Tourist central.

Gino looked damn good. A baby blue Roc-A-Wear shirt and a pair of denim shorts that showed his muscular, slightly bowed legs. Fresh kicks, a diamond ring, smooth dark skin, and a Colgate smile. He was all that.

"Yo," he said, checking out my red shorts. "The driver is outside, so let's hustle."

A young Hawaiian guy who was almost as brown as me was waiting next to a white showroom-fresh Infinity SUV. His hair was straight and he had on a bright dolphin shirt and a pair of khaki shorts.

"Aloha!" He had a lei made of fresh flowers in his hands and I bent my head and let him slip it around my neck. Dude's name was Justin and he had been in Hawaii all his life. He told us he'd never even been to what he called the mainland and tried to talk us to death asking questions about New York. Finally he got behind the wheel and me and Gino settled into the back of the SUV as Justin took off driving toward Waikiki Beach, pointing out tourist sights to us the whole time. We saw houses that belonged to movie stars and professional basketball players, all the latest cars, and beaches along what had to be the bluest water in the world.

I wasn't a swimmer, and the only beaches I had ever been on were Coney Island and Jones, but even so I could tell how special the beach at Waikiki was. We had a lot of stuff to see so we didn't have time to stay and swim, but I did get out and take off my flip-flops and walk around and feel the sand between my toes. The beach was packed with bodies colored bronze by the sun. People were fishing and surfing and playing volleyball left and right, and little kids was running around kicking sand and splashing in the ocean. I went right down to the edge of the water and put my feet in and I was really surprised to see how warm it was.

Gino got out of the car, too, and I guess when he saw me start walking in one direction, he headed the opposite way. There was definitely a charge running back and forth between us. I wasn't gonna be the first to acknowledge it, but that didn't mean it wasn't there. I knew when a man was feeling me. I busted those sly looks at my ass and thighs when he thought I wasn't looking, because I was checking him out the same way. When I got back to the SUV I leaned against the bumper and tried to brush the sand off my feet while watching him walk back toward the car. He was even taller than G, I realized. Taller and finer.

"All this beautiful weather," I commented, fucking with him. "And you didn't even take off your shirt, let alone your sneaks," I said as he climbed back in the Infinity. "Don't be so uptight. Can't feel the Hawaiian sand through your shoes."

"Who said I'm uptight? Maybe I'm just principled. Not everybody believes in coming out their clothes just like that."

Boy had it twisted. He must have thought I was some stripper G had dragged in off the stage. I got in the back and put on my seat belt. "Seems to me you'd be down for that type of action, running back home to work at the Spot and all."

He stared at me. "Let's go ahead and get this straight real quick. I don't know you, and you don't know shit about me. Whatever your thing is with G, I'm sure it's either slimy or grimy—which is cool, 'cause it ain't none of my business. But I didn't come back to New York because I wanna be at the G-Spot, Juicy. Just because that's how you get down, don't put it on me."

Justin interrupted. "Next stop, the windward coast! In less than an hour we'll be nearing Chinaman's Hat, and after that it's taking pictures at the world's most beautiful lagoon!"

Both of us igged him so hard it wasn't funny.

"I'm not a stripper, Gino. I'm not a ho either. I don't work the stage or the rooms, so don't make no assumptions about how I get down."

He smirked at me like I was lying.

"For real. G takes care of me, that's true. But I don't get down like you think. I'm in college, for your information. I'm a fashion designer and I'm studying for a business degree."

"Well maybe you're smarter than you look then. G put me through school, too, and that's why I came back. Since he paid for my piece of paper he figures I owe him, and helping him open another Spot is how he wants to be repaid."

I frowned. "Another Spot? Get the fuck out of here."

"Yep." Gino nodded, looking out the window. "In Baltimore. He's already got Jersey locked in, even without a Spot. So now G wants to train a few loyals to slide down to Baltimore and expand his operation."

"Damn," I muttered. "Like father, like son."

"What you mean? I'm my own man. As soon as G opens in B-More, I'm out. It's back to the West Coast for me. I'm an architect, sugar. I'm about building my people up, not about having my sisters selling their ass to buy dope."

"So why are you even helping him then? When you lay down with dogs, you get up with fleas. If you're all about being positive, then why are you here?"

"Why the hell are you here, Juicy? G's my father, but what's your goddamn excuse? So what he kicks out the bank. He does that for all his hoes. Yeah, you're probably the first one he let go to college, but that doesn't mean you're smart. Smart would be getting out there and doing you for a living instead of letting a playa like G control you until he takes over your whole life."

I shook my head. "I'm my own woman, too," I lied, making shit up as I went along. "G doesn't own me. After I graduate, I'm outta here. I'm taking my little brother and going someplace where I can design a clothing line and Jimmy can get a decent job and maybe we can buy us a little house. I'm not down for the game either."

He looked at me real hard. "Okay, Juicy. You ain't gotta

prove nothing to me. I'm not here to make no waves. I'm just a temporary fixture. Give me six months, and I'm out."

For the next three days Gino and I toured the island together. G's boil wouldn't come to a head no matter how much he soaked in the tub, and I couldn't convince him to let me squeeze it either. It was red and pus-filled and still hurt him like hell. He stayed in bed ordering room service and running things in Harlem from his cell phone, while Gino and I worked Justin overtime by combing every inch of the island.

Being up under Gino had my pussy on fire. He was so damn smart and sexy I masturbated every chance I got, which was mostly at night in the shower. We hung out 24/7 doing things I'd never even imagined myself doing. Didn't even know I had the heart to do. We swam and snorkeled at eighty-leven beaches and I even surprised myself by climbing on the back of a Jet Ski and letting Gino take me so far out on the ocean I was scared we'd run out of gas.

"Go back!" I was screaming, dragging my feet in the blue water and punching his hard back with one hand while hanging on for my life with the other. I just knew the damn engine on the thing was gonna sputter and die, then send us tumbling into the ocean waves. But then I had a really scary thought. Jaws. Sharks like a mother. I jerked my feet out of that water and wrapped my legs around Gino's waist so tight we were like Siamese twins.

He called me a punk when I wouldn't go parasailing the next day, so you know I had to swallow my fear and take the challenge. Getting strapped into a harness positioned between his strong thighs felt like heaven, but once that wind lifted us almost up to the clouds I couldn't care less how fine he was—he didn't have no wings. By the time we came down and made it back to shore I was so airsick and seasick I had to go into a bathroom and throw up.

I couldn't believe I was having such a good time on a vacation I didn't even want to come on, especially since I hadn't been able to catch up with Jimmy. Gino had let me use his cell phone for the last two nights, but for some reason nobody picked up at the apartment. I'd broken down and called the Spot, and Cooter told me Jimmy had been in off and on, but spent most of his time upstairs supervising the workers in the cut room.

You should have seen how I was steaming as I hung up. I was mad as hell that Jimmy was working that close to drugs, and somebody was gonna have to explain that shit to me when I got back to Harlem.

Justin was taking us to a tourist spot called the Polynesian Cultural Center when I decided to call Jimmy again. We'd stopped at a roadside truck that had big shrimp painted on the sides, and Justin assured us that local gut trucks like these were the best-kept secrets on the island. Gino ordered fried shrimp and I ordered garlic prawns, and then sat down on an empty bench and Gino passed me his cell phone.

I dialed the Spot, but the line at the bar just rang, so I

clicked over and dialed another number. A female voice answered the phone in the cut room. "Jimmy there?" I demanded before she could get her "hello" out good.

"Nah. He left."

Too late, I recognized the voice. "Dicey?"

Click.

I pressed redial and the phone just rang and rang. But Dicey had answered that phone. Sure as hell, it had been her. I called the line at the bar again and this time Cooter picked up. I gave him a message for Jimmy saying he'd better call me at the hotel within twenty-four hours or his ass was gonna get kicked when I got back home.

I was so stressed when I hung up that I couldn't eat my prawns.

"Worried about your brother?" Gino asked.

I nodded. I was fronting like I was mad, but worried was a lot more like it.

"Don't be pressed. He'll be okay."

I shook my head and pushed my plate away. "I don't know . . . it just doesn't feel right to me. I don't know why he had to stay back anyway. He should have came with us from the door."

"G had other plans for him," Gino said. He opened a pack of hot sauce and squirted it all over his shrimp. "But if I was you, I'd watch that shit. Limit all that control y'all done gave him. Motherfuckers like G don't mean you no good."

I stared at him. This was the first time he'd said anything negative about his father and I wanted to hear more. "Why you say that?"

"Come on, Juicy. Why do you think?"

"G's been good to me. To Jimmy, too. I just have to convince him to keep Jimmy out of the Spot and let him go to college. Just like he did for you."

Gino laughed like crazy. "Oh, so you think G *let* my ass go to college? Let? 'Let' didn't have shit to do with it. I was going. One way or another, I was going." He wiped his mouth with a napkin. "Besides, he felt guilty behind the way he fucked up my life. If he didn't pay my way through school my grandmother woulda worked some Santeria roots on his ass that would make his dick fall off."

"Ain't like he's using it anyway," I mumbled.

"What was that?"

"Nothing," I said, shaking my head.

Gino laughed again. "Aiiight, now. Don't be putting the man's business all out in the street. I don't want to hear shit about what you do with him."

"There's not much to hear, so that shouldn't be a problem."

"Whatever, Juicy. Do you, sister. Just watch your back. You better watch Jimmy's back, too."

Now I was really worried. Gino sounded like he knew something I didn't know.

"Can I ask you something and have it stay between us?

You know, something you don't go running your mouth off to G with?"

His face got real serious and he put his hand on my arm. "Dig, I don't tell G shit. We don't roll that way. Anything me and you toss back and forth is strictly between us. Word."

Something in his eyes told me I could trust him. Besides, I needed some info and who better to put me down on G's true nature than his son. "Okay." I nodded. "I believe I can trust you, and even though you think I'm a chickenhead, you really can trust me, too. Tell me," I said, looking so deep into his eyes I could see his heart. "Tell me what happened to your mother."

Chapter Fifteen

Gino had some love in his heart for G, but judging by the things he told me, he had every right to hate him, too. Chills ran through me as I sat listening to him talk about the way G treated and controlled his mother. He had done her the exact same way he was doing me, only I didn't have a child to worry about protecting the way Gino's moms had. It always messed me up when I heard about foul stuff people did to their kids. It took me right back to that cold December night when a junkie ho tried to trade my life for hers.

"My mother was special," Gino said. "Not only was Salida the finest Puerto Rican chick in Harlem, she was smart, too. Her father died young and her mother was poor, so she thought she'd hit the jackpot when my father took her in, but G is a crafty nigger and when she stepped out of line he broke her down, mentally and physically."

I shivered and picked at my prawns even though the sun was roasting my back and neck. "I know what you mean. Whatever G wants, G gets."

"That's right. But what's worse, Juicy, is, G's truly cold. There's no margin of error with him when it comes to shit like loyalty and respecting his word. When you fuck up with him, you fuck up. It's all or nothing. He don't even know what it means to forgive."

I thought about all the people G had put down over the years, and a picture of that man's head hitting the Dungeon's door flashed through my mind. G ran his life the way he ran his business. Cut and dried. The game was his scripture and the gun was his bible.

Gino took a sip of my soda. "After my mother disappeared I heard all kinds of shit. I was only twelve, but her family put me down on everything that came through the streets. There were so many sightings of her you would have thought she was Tupac or Elvis. Her brothers and uncles looked for her for years. Even after it was obvious she had to be dead. I mean, if she could have come back home, she would have. Dig?"

"Didn't you ask G what happened to her?"

"Yeah. I did, and it was the only time I ever saw my father cry. He came to me one night and swore up and down he didn't know where she was. Fed me some shit about her running off with some dealer from Brooklyn. Said somebody told her he knew she was fucking around and dipping in the cut room, too, so she got scared and took off."

I had to ask. "Did you believe him?"

"C'mon, Juicy. I was a twelve-year-old kid, but I wasn't no fuckin sherm. I knew his ass was grimy. G hates women. In his game they're all either bitches or hoes, or training to be both. Whenever my mother tried to think for herself he would kick her ass to both ends of the house and back. Shoes, belts, brooms—even as young as seven I would hide in my closet just to keep from jumping in and killing his ass. But G was careful though. He could whip her ass all night long, but he never left a mark on her where me or anybody else could see it. That's why I got scared one morning when I woke up to go to school and her eye had been dotted and her nose was broke. I knew what time it was then. Once my father fucked up Salida's face, she could kiss it good-bye. I told you my mother was bad. She was G's Cadillac. His Jaguar and his Rolls-Royce. G is all about status and appearance, and the minute he stopped giving a fuck about what she looked like, she might as well have been dead."

Gino made G sound like a monster. I shivered again and was glad when Justin called us over to the car. I got in and turned my face toward the window as we drove. It shocked me when I felt Gino's fingers on my arm, and then he was holding my hand.

"Don't let me mess nothing up for you, Juicy. I'm sure you and G got a good thing going. All that stuff with my mother happened a long time ago. Every man can change. Even a man like G."

I couldn't say anything. There was still a big part of me

that was loyal to G, even though I knew it didn't make sense.
G might have been Gino's father, but he was my daddy.
How could I explain that it was G who made it possible for
me to take my first bath in truly hot water? That it was G
who bought me my first tube of lipstick, my first pair of
high-heeled shoes? That because of G me and Jimmy kept
the cold off in the winters and the rats and roaches away all
year round? Besides, G was one of the few links to my past.
Grandmother had trusted him and respected him; they were
practically family. What other sure thing did me and Jimmy
have?

Maybe because he had opened up so completely to me, or
maybe because I liked him and he was the first man to ever
really talk to me, but I found myself telling Gino all about
my mother and how the game she ran almost got me killed.
I had made it a rule not to talk about her, not even to Jimmy,
but for some reason I sat there and held Gino's hand and
shared that horrible part of my life with him. I told him how
it felt as I hid under the blankets while her bed rocked and
fuck sounds filled up the room And about the cold air coming from the kicked-in window. The *boom boom boom,* the
trick dead, Aunt Ree shot, and then my mother begging for
her pitiful-ass life. How her skanky ass was so fucking desperate to keep living and whoring she was willing to trade
her seven-year-old daughter so she could live to fuck and get
high another day.

I didn't tell him about Jimmy and the gun, though. I just

couldn't bring myself to speak on that. It had taken years for Jimmy to stop having nightmares, and to this day he was scared shitless of guns. Grandmother had been worried that Jimmy would grow up hating women because of my mother, and maybe she was right because that's how men like G were born.

Gino tried to lighten my mood. "Damn, there might really be eight million stories in this naked city, huh?"

I nodded. "Yep. And ours ain't but two."

"But we're rolling, Juicy. We survived those days and now they're over. The whole world is waiting out there. I got me a plan, sugar, and I hope like hell you've got one, too."

It took us another thirty minutes to get to the Polynesian Cultural Center, and by the time we pulled up in the parking lot me and Gino had put our pasts behind us and were back to acting the fool. He was telling me about his friends on the West Coast and all the crazy stuff he'd done in his college dorm, and it reminded me of all the extra things I'd been missing in my college experience by going to school in the city and having to be chauffeured straight home like a prisoner after classes every day.

We stopped to listen to a group of Hawaiian singers before going through the gate, and even though I was down for learning about other people, I wasn't really feeling Polynesia so I didn't expect to have a good time.

Boy was I wrong. Them Hawaiian sisters were shaking their asses and doing the hula all night long! We were riding on a little water raft watching them get loose on the shore, and everybody was clapping and screaming as the brown-skinned heffahs with the silky hair flung their hips around like fish out of water.

"I bet you can throw your stuff around like that," Gino leaned over and whispered and I almost fell out the boat. I knew we'd been vibing lately, but he hadn't said a sexy word since the moment I met him and now just because some hot island freaks were doing the Hawaiian hoochie-coochie he wanted to get brand-new.

"Put your money on this," I flirted with my hands on my hips, "and you'll win every time."

His eyes got all big and then he laughed. "Damn, girl. I bet you're one dangerous sumpthin-sumpthin when you wanna be."

"Damn straight," I said. "When I wanna be, and with who I wanna be."

Later that afternoon Justin took us to a resort where there were about five private lagoons. Gino had traveled some during his college years, but I had never seen anything so damn beautiful and peaceful in my life.

There were huge black rocks that formed a barrier between us and the open seas, so I knew there was no way Jaws could get me. We swam in the warm water, and even Justin took off his shirt and jumped in and helped me and Gino over to the rocks where we saw all kinds of colorful fish.

Still, I'm a Harlem girl, and I was paranoid as hell. The only place I like fish is either in a colorful tank or fried hard in cornmeal with ketchup and tartar sauce on my plate. Both Gino and Justin were laughing their asses off every time a fish swam near me and I tried to slap it away.

"Hold up," Gino said when we finally got out the water. I was walking ahead of him, climbing through the sand toward a huge grass umbrella where we'd stashed our towels.

I turned around. "What?"

"C'mere, girl." He motioned me toward him.

I gave him a look. "You meet me halfway."

He laughed and jogged a few steps until he caught up to me.

"You sure got that New York attitude, don't you?"

"Born with it. And what's wrong with that?"

I couldn't help but notice that his chest hair and the line of black fuzz that led down his stomach and into his shorts was slick with water and glistening under the sun.

"Nothing. I like it. Come here."

Gino grabbed my hand and we walked the rest of the way to the umbrella with him massaging my fingers. His hands felt so good and so strong. I knew if he could make my fingers feel like that he could probably put a serious hurting on the rest of my body.

I waited as Gino got some sunblock from Justin, then stood there as he rubbed it all over my back and my shoulders. The pole of the grass umbrella was thick and rough like the trunk of a tree, and I leaned against it and just enjoyed feeling a man's hands squeezing my muscles and smoothing cool cream all over my skin. He even put it on my lower back, my hips, and the back of my thighs.

It was only right that Gino should turn me around and do the front of me, too. By now my nipples were like missiles and even though my bikini bottoms were already wet, they were getting wetter.

"Gino," I heard myself saying as I leaned toward him, wanting to press my nipples against his hard chest.

He held me away from him and kept right on squeezing sunblock into his hands, then running them up and down my body. I squinched sand between my toes and closed my eyes, dying to feel more than just his hands on me.

"Let me do you," I whispered, opening my eyes and staring at his hard dick. It was so long and thick the head was flat against his belly and sticking out the waistband of his swimming trunks. "C'mon, boo. Let me do you."

But he wouldn't. Instead, he finally pulled me toward him, and when my body touched his I coulda sworn his skin was even hotter than the sun. There was no doubt we both wanted this, and I pressed myself against him feeling all that black dick poking into my stomach. And then we were kissing, tonguing each other down. Gino's style was perfect, too. Soft lips, sweet tongue, and not a whole lot of unnecessary spit.

Grandmother would have kicked my ass six ways to Sunday if she could see me getting felt up and kissing all out in

the open like that, but fuck if I cared who saw us. All I knew
was that both my body and my mind was digging the way
this man made me feel, and judging by the way he was nibbling my lips, sucking my tongue, and palming both cheeks
of my ass, he was digging me, too.

Chapter Sixteen

You know we had to do the do. There was just no way around it. The only thing we needed to figure out was when and where. I was game for going right to Gino's room and handling our business there, but he said no, the time wasn't right. We sat in the back of the car and he kissed me and sucked all over my neck and the tops of my titties all the way back to the Kahala Hotel. When we pulled up outside I hated that it was time to get out of the car. Hated that the ride and the thrills were over.

G was standing in the middle of the floor and looking evil when I walked into our room, and I was glad Gino had already let himself into his own room and closed the door.

"Hey," I said, dropping my wet towel on the floor.

"Back atcha."

I walked past him and pulled my shirt over my head

as I went into the bathroom to take a shower. "You feeling better?" I yelled to him, trying to act as normal as possible when all the while my pussy was still throbbing courtesy of his son, and I could still feel Gino's hands all over my body.

I didn't realize G had followed me to the bathroom, and I had just reached out to turn on the water when I heard him behind me.

"Yeah," G said, almost in my ear.

I checked the water temperature with my hand before turning around. I could feel G staring at me all funny, and when my eyes met my reflection in the mirror I thought I knew why.

Hickeys. Two big-ass hickeys. One next to my collarbone, one an inch or two down, right at the top of my breast.

I didn't realize Gino had been sucking hard enough to bring out a bruise, but then again my skin was light caramel and I welted up easily anyway.

You should have seen how fast I turned my back on G and pulled down my shorts and my bikini bottoms with one motion.

Not fast enough, though.

"What happened to you?" G's hand was on my shoulder, turning me around.

I followed his eyes down to the two red circles on my chest.

"Damn mosquitoes," I bitched. "This fuckin' place ain't

got a seasonal cycle so those damn things just eat and grow fat all year long."

"Ain't none bit me yet."

I shrugged. "You haven't really been out there, either. That nasty little creek at the Polynesian Cultural Center was a bitch," I lied. "Mosquito Central. You shoulda seen those people. Swatting at biting flies and mosquitoes so hard, one lady almost fell off the raft. I'm surprised two bites is all I got. Our tour guide had them all over his face."

I got in the shower and kept playing a role, singing under my breath like I didn't have a care in the world. G was twirling his ring and acting like he smelled a rat, and the last thing I wanted to do was come across as nervous or shady. So I tore up some old Mariah Carey jam that I didn't even like, but was the first thing that came to my head.

G played me close for the rest of the night. He made reservations for us to eat in the hotel restaurant, and made sure we knew he was joining us. I ached for Gino as I sat across from him, next to his father. They kept up a steady conversation, but I was real quiet, picking at my food and fuming inside at G for throwing shit in my game.

I wanted to be in bed tearing up some sheets with Gino! Not sitting next to his father squeezing my legs together and imagining how strong Gino would feel moving on top of me. But as usual, G was in control and his program was the one in effect.

Later that night I laid in bed next to G trying hard not to

cry. I was too young for this shit. There were a lot of things I'd never get to do as long as G owned my ass. I thought about Nae-Nae and her baby boy Maleek, and even though I wasn't ready to have no kids, it hurt me to think that maybe I'd never get to be a mother. If I kept messing around with G I would miss out on having a baby of my own altogether.

No matter how I tossed my situation around in my head, it kept coming back to the niggah snoring next to me. G was a buster to the max, throwing brick walls up around everything I wanted to do.

But then I thought about Gino over there in the next room, and my whole body got weak. Gino was the kind of man I shoulda been kicking it with. He was smart, he was educated, he was fine, and best of all he was about something. Something more than selling dope and pushing pussy, which is the only thing his father was good at.

I wanted me some of him.

Fucking G.

I couldn't help myself. My hands didn't even belong to me as they dove inside my panties and sank into my flesh. I arched my back as I stroked myself, feeling Gino's hands light the fire that burned between my legs. But I couldn't make myself come. No matter how I rubbed my clit and squeezed my own breasts, I just couldn't get me one, and the frustration of it all sent my anger at G boiling right over the edge.

I got out the bed and put on a robe, then walked barefoot out of the room. I didn't even look back as I headed for the front door. Fuck G. Stealing all my joy. I didn't care no more. Right now it was about making Juicy happy. Doing whatever it took to get my shit off, and that's exactly what I planned to do.

I used the house phone near the elevators to call Gino's room.

"Open your door," I told him when he answered. "I need to see you."

I hung up before he could tell me no and ran barefoot on the carpet back down to his door.

Gino was grinning when he let me in, and I put my finger to my lips warning him to be quiet. He barely made a sound as he closed the door, and as soon as it was shut he was all over me, pressing me against the wall, kissing me and feeling all over my ass.

"You was thinking about me too, huh?" he said between kisses.

"Couldn't even sleep," I moaned, opening my mouth for his tongue, then sucking on his bottom lip as we rubbed our groins together.

A drum was beating in my coochie and I didn't want to waste a whole lot of time getting that dick inside of me, but Gino had more control and he made me take it slow.

"Let's do it right," he whispered, laying me down on his king-sized bed. My robe and gown came off and my panties disappeared. Gino took his lips from mine and kissed each of my nipples, then sucked them into his mouth gently but tight, and just the sensation of his hands stroking my legs and his hot tongue on my sensitive knobs brought me to an orgasm.

But it was only a small one. The big one was still waiting to be released. I shuddered and tried to catch my breath as he entered me with two thick fingers. "Aaahhh," I moaned, holding his wrist and guiding it into my wetness. "Right there, baby." I worked my hips in deep circles as his fingers sloshed in and out of me. "Yeah, right there."

Gino was doing something to me with his fingers that I had never done to myself. First he used two, then three, as he slid into me and came back out to rub my wet clit, then pushed deeply back inside. I felt something deep inside my pussy awakening and it almost scared me, it felt so good. Gino's fingers were making a "c'mere" motion deep inside of me, and as I arched my back and spread my legs wider trying to stuff his whole arm up in me, something hot and delicious tore through my pussy and sent a gush of cum running out of me that wet the whole bed up!

"Agghhhhh!" I came screaming and kicking my legs and holding on to his arm with both hands, driving his hand deeper into me as I fucked up to meet him. "Ohmygoodness. Goddamnbabywhatyoudoingtome . . ."

Gino had found my g-spot.

Not only did I come harder than I ever had in my life, I'd ejaculated, too. The sheets were so wet under my ass that I was almost ashamed. But shame didn't last long because now that I'd come, Gino wanted to get him some.

He took a rubber from his wallet on the night table but I checked him when he tried to open the pack to put it on.

"No," I said, taking it from him and sliding it under the pillow. "Not yet."

And then I went to work.

I held his throbbing dick in my hands, amazed that it was so damn hard and thick. Yeah, you know I couldn't help comparing it to G's but as big and nice as G's dick was, his son had him beat in every way.

Slowly, I covered the head with my lips, then worked my mouth all the way down the shaft. I had never performed oral sex in my life, but it felt so good and natural to me that I guess I was born to do it.

I licked and sucked him with so much love that his dick was glistening wet and twice as hard as when I started. He was pushing my head down hard and fast, and I could feel his body tensing and shivering with each lick.

But Gino wasn't going out like that.

"Gimme the glove," he demanded and I slid it out from beneath the pillow and let him tear open the wrapper and roll it down over himself. Then he lay back and pulled me on top of him, holding me at the waist.

"Gone, girl," he said grinning up at me. "Get yours any way you want it."

I went to work! You know I did! It was my first time ever being on top!

I rode Gino like he was a bull, raising my ass up in the air, then slamming myself back down on his hard stick. I did this over and over, pausing to rock and whimper every so often, until I couldn't take it anymore and I came again.

I was limp and trying to catch my breath when Gino rolled me over onto my stomach. I felt him behind me, his dick touching the back of my thigh, and I froze.

"Uh-uh." I shook my head, balling myself up into a knot. "I don't play that back door shit!"

Gino looked confused. "Neither do I, baby. I would never hurt you like that. Don't you trust me?"

I gazed at him over my shoulder, the strength of his muscles jumping out at me. He could fuck me up if he wanted to. Do me just as bad as G liked to do me, but somehow I knew he wouldn't.

"Yeah," I answered, and lay down on my stomach. "I trust you."

Oh, man! I can't even describe how good it felt when Gino entered me from behind. For a moment I had a flashback about G and my asshole, but as soon as I felt Gino sliding up inside of my wet pussy I forgot all about G and concentrated on his son.

Over two hours passed before I snuck back into the room

I shared with G. I'd taken a quick shower before leaving Gino's room, so I knew I smelled okay, but my stuff was so nicely scuffed that I was scared my guilt would show.

G was still snoring as I climbed in the bed beside him, and I lay on the edge of the bed with a smile on my face and my hand between my legs, enjoying the ache that bounced through my body and laughed in my soul.

Chapter Seventeen

The next night I snuck into Gino's room again, and again he found my g-spot and sexed me so good I was slobbering when he finished. We went at it like rabbits, fucking in every position imaginable, doing all the things I had fantasized about but never actually experienced. I took him through almost every fantasy in the Juicy Journal, and Gino licked my pussy for hours and told me it was the sweetest he had ever tasted.

I was limping when I slipped back into my room before the sun came up. Limping and grinning like hell. But those two days of good dick must have given me brain damage because I stepped totally out of my mind when I decided to jump bad with G right after dinner on Thursday evening.

"Jimmy ain't no goddamn dope dealer!" I kicked open the connecting door to our rooms and stood over G. He was stretched out on the sofa in a pair of shorts and no shirt, and a black dress sock was on his left foot.

I had just gotten off the phone with Dicey. It was raining like crazy outside and G was taking a nap, so me and Gino had ordered a pay-per-view movie and were watching it in his room. Gino had dozed off right after the movie started, so when his cell phone rang I went ahead and answered it.

"I ain't supposed to be talking to you no more, Juicy," she said. "And after them motherfuckers bust up in my house like that I swore to God I was cutting you loose. But you know I love you and Jimmy both, so there ain't no way I can keep you in the dark about no shit like this."

"What, Dicey?" I almost screamed into the phone. "What??"

"Besides," she went on without answering me, "Gino's cell phone number came up on the caller ID in the cut room, so I'm taking that as a sign that pulling your coat is exactly what I'm supposed to be doing."

All I could think about was Jimmy. "Dicey, just tell me, goddamn it. Is Jimmy okay? Tell me, dammit!"

"Juicy, you know how hard your grandmother took it when Cara died. Shit, the way your mother was living, if she hadn't got shot she probably woulda sent your grandmother to an early grave."

"Dicey, please tell me." I was moaning.

"Your grandmother didn't cotton with no damn drugs,

and that's why when I was out there shooting duji I never came by to see her. Not once. I was too ashamed to let her see me that way, especially after Cara went down.

"But Jimmy. Jimmy ain't nothing but a pissy-tail baby, and it just ain't right that he's dabbling in shit like that. Juicy, I know G your man, but he got your brother running dope all over Harlem. I know you think he's just supervising or keeping books or some stupid shit like that, but ever since you left Jimmy been running with the connects and making road trips, too. Word on the streets is that he might be using, too. I just thought you ought to know."

And that wasn't all I needed to know as I stormed out of Gino's room and rolled up on G like I had a loaded gun to back me up.

"I need to know," I said to him, sweeping magazines off the marble coffee table and sitting down with my legs gapped open and grilling him eye to eye, "why my fuckin brother is up in your cut room handling duji and powder. Why out of all them motherfuckers out there dying to be down on your sour dick, you have to take the one thing that means something to me and dirty it up."

G didn't even look at me. "You been listening to the wrong people, Juicy. Don't let that smart-mouth bitch get your ass in a sling."

"This ain't about nobody but Jimmy. *My* motherfuckin brother."

"Did that yellow ho tell you she got caught dippin? That

she's the reason Jimmy got sent upstairs in the first place? I needed somebody I could trust to replace *her* thievin ass."

"Please." I waved my hand. "Dicey wouldn't even do no shit like that."

"So who you calling a liar, Juicy?"

I was steamed. "Whose motherfuckin face am I in?"

At first I thought some boiling water had been splashed in my face, and it took me a second to realize that G had capped me. I shook my head and blew blood out of my nose, scooting backward on the low table trying to get away from the two hammers that used to be his fists.

"Bitch!" he yelled, beating me like I'd stolen something. "Dirty, nasty, trick-ass bitch!"

I couldn't even scream. Blood was gushing down my throat, choking me, and my legs were so heavy my feet wouldn't move.

"Pwease, G!" I stretched out my arms to him and cried through my busted lip. "Pwease!" *Lord God,* I prayed as his fists crashed into my face, chest, arms, and head. *This nigger is trying to kill me.* I got as low as I could to the floor and balled up in a knot, my hands covering my head as he slammed his fists into me.

"Get your ass up! You bad enough to get in my face about the way I run my business, you bad enough to take what you got coming!"

It was just like getting beat with a baseball bat. Home runs were being swung at my back, head, and legs, left and right. I was tight though. Curled up so tight you could have bounced my ass. That just pissed G off even more.

G was in a beating frenzy and as I twisted and turned trying to get away, all I could do was pray that Gino wouldn't wake up and hear us and come try to save me. Both of us would end up dead. G grabbed my hair and pulled my head back, exposing my face and chest. His fist moved like a jackhammer, fucking me up with ease.

"I'll kill your fuckin ass!" G dragged me all over that room, wiping up the floor with me. My arms and back were on fire, but G also wanted my soft parts. He wanted some stomach. He swung his foot and kicked me in the ribs, then buried his heel in my gut so hard I threw up vomit that tasted like blood.

G beat me until he got tired; huffing and puffing and plain worn-out. By then I had crawled underneath the dining table, cringing and crying, my lips busted, my nose bleeding, my whole body in shock. I watched him from between the chair legs as he walked back over to the living room area and sat back down on the sofa, then pulled off his one sock and lay back on the couch in the same position he was in before I had come in and jumped bad in his face.

G fell back asleep, and I would have stayed under that table the whole night, scared to move, if he hadn't woke up about an hour later and threatened to turn that bitch over and drag me out from under it if I didn't come over to him.

"Go comb your hair, Juicy," he said real quiet-like. "And wash all that dried snot off your face. When you come back out here I want you in some red panties and a see-through top."

What this nigger got planned? I asked myself, because I sure as hell didn't know. But I did like he said. I hobbled into the bathroom and stood over the sink, all the while dying to fill that big old tub up with hot water and sink my aching bones down into it. I started crying again as soon as I looked in the mirror. G had fucked me up. My right eye was getting black and both my cheeks were red and swollen. I washed my face and put my hair back in a ponytail, then went into the bedroom and dug in my bag until I found some silky red drawers. I couldn't find a shirt that was see-through, but I had this sheer black throw that I'd bought to wear over a bikini, so I threw that on.

G made me stand there in front of him for about ten minutes. I was scared to move, and scared to speak. Finally he nodded and said, "Drag that table over to the wall."

I bent over and pulled that heavy-ass table across the room without opening my mouth.

"Now climb up there on it."

I climbed up on the table and stood there feeling stupid.

"Now dance."

"Dance?"

"Yeah. Dance. Pretend like you hear some music, and dance."

Slowly, I moved my feet from side to side, clapping my hands a bit and popping my fingers. G started shaking his head.

"Uh-uh, Juicy. You can do better than that." He stood up and came over to me, and even though I was standing on that coffee table he was still taller than me.

Something in G's eyes told me he wanted me to fuck up, even just a little bit, so he could kick my ass again. "Gone, girl. Dance like you one of them hoes at the Spot. Dance like you danced with that motherfuckin faggot in your class. Matter fact, Juicy, dance for Daddy until my dick gets hard."

So I danced. Sore and scared as I was, I danced my ass off, rubbing my hands over my titties, shaking my ass in his face, grinding my hips into the air. G didn't look the least bit turned on. In fact, it looked like he got madder and madder the more I moved, but each time I tried to slow down or stop, he would wave me on and tell me More ass, girl! Shake more ass!

The ultimate humiliation came when he called Gino's room and woke him up and told him to come over. I couldn't even look in Gino's face as G made him take a seat next to him and watch the Juicy-Mo Show.

I stood up on that table feeling worse than naked. I felt like a big ho, a cheap-ass slut, and a no-good bitch, which were all the things G was calling me as he pointed my good features out to his son, who had already explored them first-hand. "This one fine bitch, ain't she? Look at them titties," he said. "You ever see any that pretty before? Round as coconuts with them thick-ass nipples. And that ass. Lord have mercy. You could sit a cup on it that booty it's so damn round!"

I danced and I cried. G told me to take off my panties right there in front of Gino, and to slip two fingers into my pussy. I didn't want to, but what choice did I have? I knew he would've beat me half to death, and maybe Gino, too, if I didn't obey him, so I pulled those panties off and put my hand between my legs.

"Damn, G." Gino stood up and started walking away. "Chill, dawg. How you treating your lady? This your woman, man."

G just laughed at his back. "You damn right. This *my* woman."

Gino slammed the door behind him and I was left standing on that table with my thong in my hand. I knew the drill, so I wasn't surprised at all by what G told me to do. Minutes later I was on my knees, kneeling on that cold marble table with my ass up in the air. G had wrapped my panties around my head and rammed his dick up my ass. *"Pillow-biting bitch! Take this dick up your dookey chute, slut! Give Daddy some of that chocolate pudding!"* He rode me from behind and choked me with those panties until I thought I would pass out, but never once did I cry out or scream for help. Gino had already seen me violated worse than a dog, and there was no way I wanted him to see me being dicked down like this.

Later that night, I crawled into that tub and soaked myself in water so hot I should have got first-degree burns. G
had brutalized me in the past, but never had he showed me
out in public, and I realized that if G could let another man,
even his son, see my naked ass in his presence, then his feelings for me had taken a serious turn. There was no telling
what he had planned for me next, but between Jimmy working the cut room and selling drugs, and me sexing Gino on
the regular, either I was gonna take G out, or he was definitely gonna kill me.

I was so scared of my thoughts that I wanted to put
my head under the soapy bathwater and just stay like that
forever. As bad as G had hurt me, he was my comfort zone
and he took care of me and Jimmy. I'd never been on
my own before, and I was scared of us ending up on the
streets.

A few minutes later I heard G on the phone. He was
going back and forth about times and connecting flights, so
I knew he talking to someone at the airline.

I grabbed a washcloth and acted like I was soaping myself
when he bammed on the door and stuck his head inside.
"Get the fuck out, Juicy," he told me. "So I can wash my
dick. We leaving here tonight at nine, so pack your shit and
get ready to roll."

Our vacation was over.

·   ·   ·

The trip home from Hawaii took much longer than the one going there had taken. G wouldn't even look at me, let alone speak to me, and Gino got so mad when he saw the bruises on my face and the marks my panties had made around my neck, I thought he was gonna mess around and get us found out.

"Naw, Juicy," he said when G was at the counter settling our hotel bill. It was all I could do not to throw myself all over him, to hold his hands and press myself into his strong chest, but I knew better. "That punk motherfucker did my mother the same way."

"Sshhhh." I put my finger to my lip, knowing G was probably listening with one ear. "I'm all right," I whispered, hoping to calm his ass down even though he could see the welts on my face, arms, and legs, and my back felt like a horse had stomped me.

I could see the rage in Gino's eyes, and for the first time I felt bad about stepping between a father and his son. Yeah, G wasn't shit when it came to handling his business with a woman, but that didn't mean I had the right to bring drama between him and his son.

We were quiet all the way to the airport. G had called for a limo to pick us up at the hotel and we rode in that shit like we were going to a funeral. I tried not to look at Gino too often because every time I did, it looked like he was grilling G. He had already got funky and called himself messing with G's head when he climbed in the back of the whip.

"Damn, Juicy," he said, shaking his head. "Look like you fell off that table last night. If I didn't know no better I'd say those were fist prints on your face, but wouldn't no real man beat his woman like that, so it musta been that table that got a hold of you." Then he turned and stared at G, who stared right the fuck back at him.

It didn't matter how comfortable the seats were on the plane. I was so sore it was torture to stay on my ass in one spot all that time. Every few hours I had to get up and stretch my body, then walk to the rear bathroom and back before I could sit back down. I managed to hide my face with a pair of shades and a Donna Karan cap pulled down low over my forehead, but it still felt like everyone could see my red and purple welts and I thought they all knew that my ass had gotten kicked.

I was happy as hell when we landed in New York. City air had never smelled so good, but since I was still at the top of G's shit list, I could barely enjoy it. Pacho picked us up at the airport and I was disappointed to see that Jimmy wasn't with him.

"Where's my brother?" I asked him as he loaded our bags into the ride.

"At work," G answered for him, and the way he said it shut me right the hell up.

But shut up didn't mean backed up. Back at the apartment, G told me to unpack his stuff while him and Gino made a run down to the Spot. Gino gave me a look on his way out the door, but I didn't even ac-

knowledge it. G could beat my ass all day long, if he
wanted to. I was still gonna find a way to get Jimmy out
of that damn Spot, and even though she wasn't supposed to
talk to me no more, I knew just the person who could
help me.

Chapter Eighteen

As soon as G and Gino were gone I jumped in the shower, then got dressed real quick and caught the first train heading to Harlem. I stood outside looking up at Dicey's window and getting a crook in my neck for ten long minutes, but my girl didn't answer the bell and she didn't look out the nosey Susan either. Aggravated, I slammed my hand against the whole panel of bells, and finally somebody buzzed me in. I didn't even bother to hold my breath going up those pissy stairs. I hit them by threes and was on the second floor before my feet had touched the floor good.

The television was turned up loud and Dicey's door was sitting open, and for some reason something gripped me.

"Hey," I hollered toward the doorway, trying to sound cheery even though my mouth was dry. "Damn, Dice. You must think you down South or somewhere, chilling up in here with your door wide open."

She was sitting in her leopard-skin chair, and from where I was standing I could see both the TV and the back of her head. One of her hands was dangling over the armrest of the chair but she didn't even turn around to see who I was.

"Dicey," I said, walking into the apartment. I saw a pack of strawberry Twizzlers sitting on an end table and slid two out the pack. "Don't you know how to close your door? This is Harlem, baby! Your ass laying up here sleeping while niggers downstairs scheming on moving all your shit out on a U-Haul."

I was sticking the Twizzlers in my mouth when I smelled it. Blood. It had been a long time, but some things you just never forget.

"Dicey?"

I peered around that big old chair and my stomach lurched like a roller coaster. I dropped down to my knees and stuck my fist into my mouth to keep from screaming, biting down hard on my knuckles as the tears rushed from my eyes.

Blood was everywhere. Dripping from her mouth, covering her shirt, soaking into the carpet on the floor. "Dicey!" I whispered, terror damn near paralyzing me as I stretched my hands out toward her. All of a sudden I was right back in that pissy bed with cold air blowing through the room and the smell of gunpowder and shit choking me. No, not Dicey.

I wanted to shake her, to call 911, to grab something and

press it up to her neck and mouth to stop the bleeding, but a part of me also noted the glazed look in her eyes, the bruises all over her yellow face, and the way her left hand was clutched stiff and bloody against her chest.

"Oh my God," I moaned, hugging her limp body. I pulled her toward me, pressing her face into my stomach, crying and holding her cold stiff hand as I rocked her back and forth. I didn't give a damn about the blood that was soaking into my clothes, I just wanted my girlfriend back.

WHY? WHY? WHY? I cried. Dicey didn't have no enemies! Everybody loved her! She was cool with everybody and their grandmomma! My mind just couldn't comprehend it. The house didn't look robbed, and I just couldn't seen anybody having this much beef with Dicey.

All I could do was stand there crying and holding her and rocking her back and forth, and it took me a minute to realize that Dicey was clutching something in her hand. Something soft, and somehow still warm. I uncurled her fingers and stared, my eyes bugging almost out of my head when I realized just what it was she was holding.

It was her tongue.

I was way past scared. My life was on the line, and there was only one person I could turn to. I closed the door to Dicey's apartment and locked it. I was scared to be up in there with a dead body, but I was scared to leave, too. I needed to get across town, but my clothes and hands and even my shoes were covered in blood, and I knew I wouldn't get far on the streets looking like I'd just butchered somebody's whole family.

I was shaking and shivering, and had to force myself to walk into Dicey's bathroom, tears coming out my eyes the whole time. I wanted to block the reality of this situation from my mind as I turned on the water in the shower and stripped out of my clothes, but I wasn't that damn stupid. My girl was dead in the front room with her tongue cut the fuck out and this shit had G written all over it. He hadn't done it himself, of course. He was too smooth for that. But he'd ordered it done, and that was the same thing in my book.

I needed to think. Needed to come up with a plan, and I forced myself to forget the image of Dicey's dead eyes and the bloody stump of her tongue, and think about Jimmy and how I could scheme up a way to be free of G so that both of us could survive.

I let the hot water rinse my tears away as I scrubbed myself down and put my mind on survival mode. My hands were trembling as I soaped myself over and over, trying to get the smell of Dicey's blood out of my nose, and by the time I got out of that shower I knew just what I had to do.

I rummaged through Dicey's closet and dresser drawers until I found something that didn't swallow me. I pulled on a pair of flat leather Timberland mules I found near her bed and threw a belt around the waist of the size-sixteen sundress I'd found with the $180 price tag still on it. *Homeboy shopping network,* I thought, remembering all the crazy times I'd had with my friend. I knew damn well Dicey hadn't paid no yard and change for no damn dress. I wanted to start crying again, so I hurried up and grabbed a plastic shopping bag and stuffed my bloody clothes and shoes in it and left the apartment.

I stood in the doorway and gave one last glance at the sister who had proven she was totally down for me and Jimmy, and had died for us in the process.

Dicey was gone, but Jimmy was still alive. I had to focus my energy on him.

Thirty minutes later I was standing on Rita's stoop. I'd snuck on the train and cried all the way to my stop. I didn't care about how people were looking at me neither. There was nothing I could do to stop the tears from falling.

"Damn, Juicy," Rita said, opening the door to let me in. She was eating a sandwich but wrapped it in a napkin when she saw the look on my face. "What?" she asked, leading me in the back of the house to her bedroom. "That motherfucker hit you again? Huh? What?"

I shook my head miserably. "Dicey," I whimpered. "Dead."

Rita was on it.

"Oh, shit, no. G got her?"

I nodded. "It had to be him. Everybody else loved her."

"How she die?"

The vision of Dicey's slit throat and that lump of tongue in her hand sent me running into Rita's bathroom.

Rita came in behind me holding out a towel for my face, and when I was through she took me into her bedroom and made me lay down under the covers.

"It's my fault, Rita. It's my fuckin fault! If she hadn't tried to look out and put me down on what was going on with Jimmy, she would still be here. G blames her for hipping me to my brother, and that's why she's dead!"

"You gotta get the fuck away from him, Juicy. Everybody knows how coldblooded G's ass is. You gotta get away."

I nodded. Rita was right. Me and Jimmy had to go. But we weren't leaving empty-handed.

"Rita." I sat up in the bed and stared into her eyes. "I think I got a plan that might work out for both of us, if you willing to help me."

"Girl, if it means you say fuck that motherfucker before he puts you six feet under, I'm down. Just tell me what I gotta do."

"I need you to do what you do best, girlfriend. Do what you do best."

32-6-14-41.

Those numbers had been burned into my memory, and

later that night while G and Gino were still at the Spot, me and Rita went to the apartment and we took down that big-ass mirrored panel in my bedroom and hit G's safe. I was fully expecting to find a chunk of cash inside, but I also knew G had to have at least two shitloads of money stashed away in a bank. He always carried a lot of green on him, but it was chump change compared to the amount of yardage that rolled through the Spot and all of his other businesses around Harlem. G was a businessman above and beyond anything else. The majority of his money had to be earning interest in somebody's bank.

The plan was for Rita to read over every piece of paper that might be in that safe, and I would help her write down the names of G's banks and all of his account numbers. Then Rita could tap that ass through the computer lines. Get my name added to G's accounts so I could walk into those financial institutions, spank G, then walk out with almost all of his money. And then me and Gino and Jimmy could split. To where, I didn't know yet. But it would have to be far. Real far. Someplace where even G couldn't find us. Of course I planned to tear Rita off a lovely chunk of change for her help, but the majority of it would belong to me, Jimmy, and maybe Gino. With what G had to be pulling in, I'd be able to afford us all a new future.

Rita was pumped, too. "Don't worry, Juicy," she told me. "We gonna do that motherfucker just like he's been doing you."

At first I was worried that G mighta had some kind of

camera planted in the bedroom that was recording everything that went down, but then I tossed that shit outta my
mind. He was too paranoid to let somebody roll a tape in his
private room. They might find out that unless the great King
of Harlem was bumping him some booty, he was a two-
minute man who couldn't fuck his way from the bed over to
the bathroom.

32-6-14-41.

Rita and I went to work, and within a few minutes we
were staring inside of G's safe. "Oh shit," Rita said, but I
didn't know whether to laugh or to cry.

I counted out five thousand dollars in twenty-dollar bills.
That was it. Five thousand sorry-ass dollars, and no goddamn cents. There was also a black binder inside, and a few
pictures of the woman who I knew was Gino's mother. In
one of the pictures the woman was sitting on G's lap and
holding a baby. The baby was Gino, there was no doubt
about it, and even though they were all smiling at the camera I could tell the woman was faking it. Her eyes looked
scared as hell.

And that was it. There was nothing else inside the safe.
No stocks, no bonds, no securities, no gold bars, no secret
bank accounts, no Swiss bank accounts, nothing else. Nothing else except a key. In a small brown envelope. A tiny gold
key with the words RENO SUPREME engraved on it. RENO on
the top, and SUPREME directly underneath it.

The key didn't look familiar to me, so I left it there right

next to the cash. But I took the binder. Me and Rita were
gonna take that bad boy right down to Kinko's and make a
copy of every single page. Let G fuck with me or my brother.
I had the names and contact information for every single
one of his front men and his drug connects. I could put his
ass and all of theirs so far under the jail they'd need a back-
hoe to get them out.

"This is it?" Rita asked. She looked almost as disappointed as I felt.

I shrugged. "I guess so. Fuck! I thought there'd be more
money and bank statements and stuff. You know, account
numbers and records you could tap into."

Rita looked across the room. "What about the computer?"

I shook my head. G had that shit locked up tight. "You
gotta know the password just to turn it on. G is the only one
who knows it, so he's the only one who uses it."

"Did he ever tell you to stay away from it?"

"Girl, yeah. There's another computer in Jimmy's room
that G brought for us to use. He told me to stay my black ass
away from his because he changes the password every time
he signs on."

Rita's eyes looked all funny. "Is that right?" she said, already on her way over to the desk. "We gone see about that
shit."

Rita worked on G's computer for over two hours. I kept
running back and forth between the window and the front

door, scared Pacho or Ace or one of G's other flunkies was gonna come in and catch us. I was paranoid and spooked by every little sound I heard. When the phone rang it scared me so bad I caught an instant headache.

"Hey girl." Gino's easy voice met my ears through the line. "Shit is smooth over here, so we coming home early. We're on our way back. You want us to bring you anything?"

I felt happy that Gino was thinking about me, but I was even happier for the heads-up. I hurried up and told Rita to get her bony black Puerto Rican ass up and out of G's house.

"But I need more time," Rita complained when I insisted she had to stop. She'd been banging on the keyboard like a crazy woman, determined to crack G's code. "There's something on here, Juicy. I can feel it. The answers we need are right here on this fucking computer!"

I thought about Dicey and the way she'd looked the last time I'd seen her. "Nah, Rita," I said, pulling her up from the chair. "We gotta pick this shit up another time, my sister. Right now you gots to go."

By the time G turned his key in the lock Rita was long gone and I was laying on the couch with a cloth over my eyes like I had a headache. I peeked out and saw G walk right past without even looking at me, but Gino nodded and smiled and I smiled back.

I mighta looked all sweet and innocent, but deep inside I was scheming like a mother trying to figure out how to do like Dicey had said and get my own damn money. G had already proven he was crazy and didn't give a fuck about me or my brother. Now I needed to figure out how to get some of his ends, for me and for Jimmy, and if Rita could just get past that password on his computer, then nothing else in the world was gonna stand in my way.

Gino and I had already agreed not to even try to hook up in the apartment. We walked around each other barely speaking, trying hard not to give our true feelings away. We hardly had any time alone because G wanted Gino with him wherever he went. Gino was already getting mad props and respect from niggas on the street by virtue of being G's son, but G wanted him to learn everything about his operations so he could take over one day. Gino wasn't really down, but he went along with the program. Once or twice we managed to sneak in a few quick kisses when G went out alone, and we found ways to touch each other on the sly when we met in the kitchen or walked past each other in the halls, but there was never enough time for me to get some real dick, and with Gino sleeping on the other side of me and G's wall, he was getting frustrated too because of all that noise G had me making.

"Don't believe it," I told him. "Your father wants you to think he's getting mad pussy, but don't believe none of that shit cause I'm faking like a mother. That's the only reason he got you sleeping in that room anyway, so he can make sure you hear me hollering. But don't believe it, Gino, because G ain't got nothing on you."

Over the next few days I tried to lay low and play it cool at the Spot. They found Dicey's body on a Monday, and G had the nerve to say a prayer for her and donate some money to give to her sister for the funeral. He even told the day staff they could take off a few hours to go to her service, and while a lot of them went, I sure as hell didn't. The casket was gonna be closed, thank God, but the picture I still saw of Dicey in my mind was the last way I would always see her. It was a picture so foul that it made me cry every time I thought about it, but Dicey also made me stronger, too. That tongue in her hand reminded me to watch what I said around and about G to *everybody,* and that slit across her throat bore witness to just how far-reaching G's hands really were.

They buried Dicey out at Heavenly Works, but of course I didn't go to the cemetery. I still had flashbacks about falling into my mother's grave, and not even Dicey could make me go back there.

Two weeks later G and Gino took a trip down to B-More. They'd only been gone for two days when I saw Jimmy packing himself a bag.

"Where you going?" I questioned him. I'd been mad at him ever since we got back from Hawaii because he didn't believe me when I told him I thought G had got Dicey killed. I was so pissed off with his hardheaded self that it wasn't funny. Jimmy knew how much Dicey had done for us over the years, and he loved her as much as I did. Why he couldn't see that it was G who had her killed was beyond me.

He shrugged. "I'm heading upstate. Gotta make a run for G."

"What kind of run?"

He kept stuffing things in his bag. "A business run, Juicy. You know business. The shit men like me and G take care of so you can live in a house like this and walk around styling gear that cost more money than Grandmother ever saw in her whole life. Business. Where you think all this change comes from? A niggah gotta work for it."

"Not you," I said. "You ain't gotta work for G's business. Let him send some-fuckin-body else! Let him send—"

"Like who? Gino? You want him to send Gino out to handle this shit? Or you scared to let him be a man, too?"

I swallowed hard. "What are you talking about, Jimmy? Gino's already out. He's out in B-More with G right now. Why you trippin?"

"Ain't nobody stupid around here, Juicy. Blind neither. Both of y'all are wrong. You better get your shit together and stop worrying about mine. Get your shit together before G wakes up and smells the fuckin coffee."

"You know what?" I said, pointing at him. "G got your black ass brainwashed. You believe everything he tells you, don't you. Since when you started trusting him more than you trust me? Huh? Loving G more than you love me?"

Jimmy picked up his bag and pushed past me on his way out the door. "It ain't about loving him over you, Juicy. It's about staying in the game and staying alive. Watch yourself, big sister. Your shit is wide open."

"Fuck you!" I screamed, wondering if he was right and if G suspected something was going on between me and Gino. "Just fuck you, Jimmy!"

"I love you too, big sister," he said, and slammed out the door.

Chapter Nineteen

About a month later G called me into his office. By this time Jimmy was making regular trips both upstate and down to A.C., and he had even taken a few trips to B-More with Gino. I wasn't happy about none of it because I could see my brother sinking fast, getting deeper and deeper into the street life, but there wasn't much I could do to stop it. He had stopped taking his medication and I was looking for signs of that crazy bug to come out of him again. Rita was working on busting G's computer code as often as she could, and if I brought her around more frequently even the door-men were liable to get suspicious. So I chilled. I prayed for Jimmy and Gino, and kept my eyes and ears open.

"I need you to do something, Juicy," G said. He was sitting behind his desk, and that picture of Gino's mother was still there, turned facedown.

"Okay," I said, stepping inside. With him gone up

and down the road so much we had kinda settled back into our routine, and he hadn't even threatened me since we came back from Hawaii. "What you need, G?"

"I need you to take a drive. I got something I need picked up and brought back here, and the driver has to be clean in case they get stopped."

Shit sank in fast. G had made Pacho teach me how to drive over the summer, and now I knew why.

"But I don't have no license, G."

"That's all right. You ain't never been arrested before, and that's the main thing. Ain't too many niggahs in here without a record, and you the only woman I trust not to cross me cause every other bitch in here is dirty."

My heart hit my feet. What kind of shit was G talking about? He never even wanted me in his business before, and now he wanted me to make a pickup? That shit smelled foul from the jump, but I heard my voice come out of my mouth. "Okay, G. Okay."

"Don't tell nobody where you going, Juicy. Not even Jimmy."

"Okay."

For the rest of the day I walked around petro like a mother. I was scared G was sending me into a setup and I wanted to ask somebody to help me or to tell G to send somebody else to do his dirty shit, but I knew the next somebody he sent would be Jimmy, and I couldn't have that on my heart.

It was a Saturday night and the Spot was live. I made sure

my switchblade was in my purse, then I motioned to Gino to meet me in the coatroom, and while I kissed him and told him how much I loved him, I didn't tell him where I was going or what his father had asked me to do. The way I saw it, I was damned if I did and damned if I didn't, but if Gino found out about it and confronted G, we were all damned for sure.

"I miss you, baby." He held me in that coatroom and slid his tongue past my lips and I tried to suck it down my throat. As scared as I was, my pussy got wet. Damn, I wanted him. Wanted to feel his hard dick stroking me until I lost my mind and there was no room for G or his fuckin Spot in my head, but G wanted me on the road by midnight, so I had to be satisfied with a kiss.

"I miss you too," I told him, wishing I could stay right there in his arms forever.

Pluto brought the Z4 around to the front of the Spot at eleven-thirty. He was smiling all stupid when he opened the door and handed me the keys.

"Here you go, you stuck-up bitch. If you blow a tire or the engine falls out, walk your simple ass on back."

I went off. "You know what? I'm tired of you! If G knew half the shit you done tried with me, he'd fuck you up! Matter fact," I said, slamming the car door closed and heading back inside the Spot, "I'ma go let him know what kinda motherfucker Moonie got down on his staff. I'ma let G know just how bad you want a piece of his pussy!"

Pluto just smiled some more. "I don't know why all you

bitches think what you got between your legs is better than gold. I'd die for G, and he knows that. He ain't gonna hold your stupid ass up over me. Ain't you figured it out yet? Pussy comes and pussy goes. Loyal motherfuckers like me will be around forever."

Fuck Pluto. I was telling! I pushed through the Spot and ran back to G's office. I didn't see him, but I heard the water running in his private bathroom.

"G!" I yelled. "G, it's me, Juicy."

"Hold on. I'll be right out."

I stood at his desk mad as hell, drumming my fingers on the cherry wood. I glanced at that facedown picture frame again, and something made me pick it up and take another look. I almost hollered. The picture I'd expected to see of Gino's mother was gone. The girl smiling up at me was even more familiar. She had a Hawaiian lei around her neck and looked like she was on vacation.

She was me.

I dropped the picture and tried to play it off when G walked out the bathroom.

"What?" he said. "What you hollering about when you supposed to be getting on the road?"

"I-I-I just wanted to come tell you good-bye."

G came around the desk and patted my back twice. "Well, bye then. You got the directions, right?"

"Yeah," I said.

"Remember," he warned. "Do exactly like I told you and don't stop for nobody on them roads."

I nodded. "Okay."

G straightened his jacket, then put his hand on my back and led me out the door. "Later," he said, then closed the door in my face.

As I stood there shaking and trembling I understood my situation as clear as day. The only choice I had was to take my little ass back outside, jump in the whip, and get ready to roll.

The Z drove like a dream, but I still stayed at least five miles under the speed limit, hogging the right lane all the way. To say I was scared wouldn't come close to explaining it. I was shaking so bad that every now and then my foot would jerk on the gas pedal and the car would lurch forward, whipping my neck.

G had told me to drive up to the Bronx first and park on the corner of 167th and Jerome, killing my headlights but keeping the engine running once I stopped the car. He said for me to keep all the doors locked, and when I heard somebody tap three times on the tiny trunk I was supposed to pop the trunk release without turning around, and when I heard it slam shut again, I should drive off without looking back.

I followed his instructions to a tee. I wouldn't even let my eyes go near that rearview mirror as I sat there scared as hell. Fuck turning around. It just wasn't going to happen. Still, I almost hit the gas when I heard the three taps on the trunk, and I jabbed the trunk release so hard I broke one of my nails.

As soon as I heard the trunk slam closed I pulled off and headed toward the George Washington Bridge, just like G had said. Traffic was light this time of night, but I still stayed in the right lane and drove slightly under the speed limit.

I got to the New Jersey Turnpike and almost had a fit when the toll collector wouldn't take my money. G had E-ZPass for the Z, but he told me not to use it. He'd given me a ten-dollar bill to pay for the tolls and told me to go through the cash-only lane. And here this chick with thirty gold teeth and ten-inch nails was waving my money away and telling me to keep it moving.

"Why?" I shouted, about to panic. This wasn't going according to the plan. G had said not to use the damn E-ZPass. What part of that didn't this wench understand?

"Your E-ZPass already picked it up," she said, waving those damn nails at me.

"But this is cash only. I don't even have that E-ZPass thing on the windshield."

She had the nerve to suck on all that slum in her mouth. "Then maybe it's in the glove box or in the trunk or under your seat. All I know is I can't take your money, miss. E-ZPass already charged you."

I was steaming as I drove on, heading south toward exit 4. I was so scared my mouth was dry and I felt like I had to pee, even though I had gone to the bathroom not an hour earlier. My eyes were on autopilot as I drove, darting from mirror to mirror, checking for the police car I just knew was gonna pull me over and take my black ass straight to jail.

Who knew what kind of shit G had me walking into. It could have been a test. It could have been a setup, too, but for my brother's sake I had to see it through. I kept wondering, did somebody stick some dope or some money in the trunk when I made that stop in the Boogey-Down, or did they take something out? What was gonna happen when I got to the house in Jersey that G was sending me to? Damn! Plenty of stupid bitches were locked up in the joint for transporting dope for they man. G had put my picture face-down on his desk. Was he setting me up to take a bid, or would I just disappear like Salida did?

My head was buzzing as I followed G's directions off the turnpike and into a neighborhood that made Brooklyn look clean and Harlem look glamorous. This was Camden, New Jersey, the murder capital of the nation, and the hard-looking faces I passed on the streets made me check to make sure my doors were locked. Shit, I ain't fronting. I was scared. True, I came straight from the ghetto and was proud of it, but at least I knew the thugs who roamed my streets. These Camden people were strangers to me, and for all I knew I was carrying something they wanted in my trunk.

It took me about thirty minutes to find the street I was

looking for. I had messed around and took a wrong turn, and then couldn't make a left to double back until I found one of those stupid jug-handles that Jersey is famous for. I finally found the right street and as soon as I turned in to it I knew shit was flaky.

Most of the streetlights were out and there were niggahs everywhere like it was two in the afternoon instead of two in the morning. Lounging on the stoops, sitting on cars, shooting cee-low on the curb, and hanging off fire escapes. Every one of them turned to stare into the Z and check out the rims as I drove down looking for the right house number, and one or two of them had the balls to step up to my window and motion for me to stop, like I was stupid enough to do it and my damn head screwed off and on.

Even with my windows up I could hear the music blasting outside, the bass making my windshield vibrate. I got really scared when I drove in further and realized that the street was a dead end. That meant I would have to drive out again, right back past the same niggahs I had almost run over coming in.

The house I was looking for was at the bottom of the street, right at the dead end. G had told me just to do whatever the connect told me to, so I had no idea what to expect. I saw a buffed-up brother with a wild afro sitting on a crate with a whole crew of niggahs, and as soon as I stopped the car he jumped up and came over to me.

He had on jail clothes. A big-ass white T-shirt and some

baggy pants. A thick silver cross was hanging around his neck and I could see he was strapped.

He tapped twice on the window. "Roll it down," he ordered.

I hit the button just enough to drop the window about an inch.

"What?"

I had my finger next to the trunk release button, ready to pop that bad boy open and let him get his package of whatever was back there.

"Nothing," he said. "We changed the plan. You can go on back now."

"What?" I gave him a dirty look. I wasn't riding all the way back to Harlem with no hot package in my trunk. "Nah, G sent me—"

"I know who sent you. Now take your ass on back."

"But I got stuff—"

He slapped my window so hard I covered my face, expecting the glass to shatter. When it didn't, I put it up in a hurry, scared he'd somehow get his hand through that tiny crack and get to me.

"You got too much fuckin mouth! That's what the fuck you got. Now get your ass up outta here." He nodded up the street. "Before I get them niggers up there to strip this little toy car and then start on you."

I know damn well I left some tires on that pavement. I put the Z in reverse, then whipped around so fast I hit two garbage cans and almost hit a parked car, too. I came up out of that dead end so hasty them niggers at the top of the street weren't brave enough to run out at me this time. I didn't even stop at the corner, instead I took my chances with a glance, then turned right into traffic not knowing if I was going in the right direction or not.

I was mad enough to kick G's ass. Bad enough I drove all the way to Jersey in a drug dealer's car with no damn license. He had me riding around with who knows what in the trunk, swearing the cops were gonna stop me and take me to jail, and in a strange city where I didn't know nobody and the only thing I had for protection was my knife.

I was too scared to pull over and ask somebody on the streets how to get back to the turnpike, so I waited until I saw a gas station where an Indian man with a big turban on his head was pumping gas and asked him.

By the time I got back on the turnpike my foot was heavy and my mind was steady on driving north. But as scared as I was, curiosity was burning in me, too. I wanted to know. I wrestled with myself until I got to exit 8, then turned off at a gas station and parked on the side of the road. Looking around, I made sure nobody was anywhere near me, then punched the trunk release and jumped out of the car.

I stood there looking into the little ass trunk, getting mad as hell. It was empty. Wasn't shit in there. Either the connect in the Bronx had taken something out, or the one in Camden was supposed to put something in. Either way, I was going home. Back to Harlem, and if G ever asked me to make another drop we was gonna have a showdown right then and there. This kind of cloak-and-dagger shit wasn't happening for me no more, I didn't care what G said. Let him send Punanee or Honey Dew, or one of them other bitches who were always up in his face next time, 'cause it sure as hell wasn't going to be me.

Chapter Twenty

It was Ladies' Night at the G-Spot, but I had my period and the cramps were kicking me like a mother. All day long I moped around the apartment, holding my stomach, dragging my feet, and plain old looking pitiful as hell. G caught the hint and allowed me to stay home from the Spot for the night. He even told Jimmy to make me a cup of tea before they left so I could feel better.

Pacho came to pick them up, and as soon as the door closed I tore off my nightgown and put on a pair of shorts and a T-shirt. I ran into the kitchen and popped two Midols, then watched out the window until I saw Rita's SUV pull up out front.

Minutes later Rita's fingers were on G's keyboard, working their magic.

I'd had her come by every chance we could get. After that bogus drop G sent me on in Camden, I was more determined than ever to get my hands on some papers and get me and Jimmy out of Harlem. Rita kept a book of computer codes she'd already used on G's system, and today she was pulling some fresh ammo out of her bag of tricks.

"I don't know, Juicy," she said, her eyes staring at the screen in concentration. She looked in her book and started typing again. "G got this system locked down tight. Every damn trick I try has something protecting it. He's gotta have something to hide. Burying a password in all this—"

Rita almost jumped out the chair.

"Bingo, motherfucker!" she yelled. "We're in, Juicy. We're in!"

I was jumping up and down and screaming, too. Glad Rita had worked her magic and hoping we'd finally find out where G had stashed his bank.

An hour later Rita had picked G's computer clean, but not one damn bank account had come up. No account numbers, no stocks, no stash. Yeah, we'd busted into a hidden file and printed out the names of all of G's connects and the dirty-ass cops in Harlem and low-level government people who were in his pocket or who he'd had dealings with over the years, but that was almost the same information we had copied out of his binder and there wasn't even a mention of how G paid the rent on this phat apartment or how he financed his building leases or paid his taxes. I figured the Spot was just a front that he washed his money through. There was also a list of other businesses that he owned, some that I had known about and others that I didn't, but that knowledge didn't help me at all. I needed to find his money if I was gonna get Jimmy someplace safe, but my hope was dying as Rita read through the last of G's files.

"Damn, Juicy," Rita said shaking her head. "That motherfucker must have him another hiding place. The only thing left on here is a grave certificate registered to Orleatha Mae Stanfield."

Grandmother. I looked over Rita's shoulder, and sure enough there was a file from Woodlawn Cemetery with Grandmother's name on it and the section where she was buried.

"Print that out for me," I told Rita, but I didn't really know why. The only time I planned to visit a cemetery was when it was time for my own burial, and even then I wouldn't know anything about it.

As much as I hated to admit it, I was facing a brick wall. I didn't know where else to turn, and I was still broke. Gino had told me he was cutting out after six months, and in the back of my mind I wondered if he was still going, if he could just leave me like that.

He didn't owe me anything of course, and I couldn't roll with him even if I wanted to. I had Jimmy to think about, and unlike my mother I wasn't about to put a man above my own blood. I was back to feeling stuck and mad, and when Rita left I stashed the paper with Grandmother's gravesite on it in between the pages of the Juicy Journal, then put my nightgown back on and climbed into the bed to cry myself to sleep.

The following Tuesday was slow at the Spot. There was a playa's ball going on in Philly, and G and a lot of the old heads and other pimps had gone out there earlier in the day. I'd called my girl Brittany from school and we agreed to meet downtown on 42nd Street to go to the movies. I wanted to see *Barbershop 2,* and Brittany did, too.

Gino had slipped me some money and I wanted to treat Brittany since she was always so generous toward me and I was hardly ever able to give her anything in return except a couple of outfits and an occasional free night at the Spot.

We got to the theater early and I bought both of us some buttered popcorn and a box of Bon Bons. Brittany wanted some strawberry Twizzlers, but just the sight of them got me to thinking about Dicey and I convinced Brittany to get some Mike and Ikes instead, telling her the Twizzlers looked sticky and stale.

The theater was small and already crowded. The lights were still on and we sat toward the back where all the young rowdy people were. As usual, I felt free whenever I got the chance to hang out with my friends. Me and Brittany sat there throwing popcorn up in the air and trying to catch it in our mouths, laughing and spilling shit everywhere and not giving a damn.

At first I wasn't sure I was seeing right, but then Brittany nudged me and said, "Hey Juicy. Ain't that your friend? You know, the dude you grew up with who hangs out over in Taft?"

Sure enough, it was Flex with his little peanut head walking down the aisle and looking for a seat. But I was even more surprised to see who was with him. It was Cooter, walking right behind Flex and obviously there with him.

There must not have been any good seats down front, or maybe they couldn't find two side by side, because the next thing I knew they had turned around and were heading back up the aisle, directly toward us.

"Shit!" I said, dropping the box of Bon Bons I had just opened. I scooched down in my seat and bent down like I was trying to pick up those little balls of chocolate-covered ice cream off that nasty theater floor.

"Where are they?" I whispered up at Brittany.

"Sitting up there. Four rows up."

"Did they see me?"

She laughed. "Shit, how could they as fast as you fell out that chair!"

I eased myself back into my seat and took a deep breath. The lights were going down and the previews were beginning to roll, and I told myself to chill and get ready to enjoy the movie.

But something wasn't right about Flex and Cooter seeing a movie together. I didn't know they hung like that. I'd never even seen them two talking or even acting like the other one existed. As the movie played and we laughed and hooted, cracking up and falling out at the jokes taking place on screen, I couldn't help but keep one eye on Flex and Cooter.

I knew them niggahs was sho' nuff shady when they didn't laugh not one time. They weren't even watching the damn movie. Instead, they were leaning toward each other having some kind of deep conversation and I woulda paid a dollar to be a fly on the wall dipping on that dialogue.

The movie was so funny that eventually I forgot all about Flex and Cooter. But about halfway through the flick they both got up and walked up the aisle heading for the doors. I knew they couldn't see me in the darkness so I wasn't worried about being spotted, but I had damn sure spotted both of their asses scheming and I thought about them for a real long time.

Later that night I was dressed and pressed and my hair had been blow-dried and pulled back into flat twists. Me and Gino hadn't been together in almost two weeks, and I'd been aching for him like crazy. Masturbating next to G at night wasn't cutting it for me anymore. Not when I knew what was available to me just on the other side of the wall.

And Gino had it hard, too.

It looked like G went out of his way to slam the headboard against the wall when he was getting him a little bit.

Like he wanted Gino to know he was across the way ten inches deep in my stuff.

So both of us were horny as hell, but there never seemed to be a time where we could be together alone. Until late Tuesday night. Pacho had driven G to Philly earlier in the day, and Moonie was left to hold it down at the Spot. Flex was in the house again when he shoulda been out on the street, and I watched as he walked past the bar and headed toward the kitchen. A minute later Cooter headed that way, too, and again I wondered why the two of them seemed all of a sudden so thick.

But Flex and Cooter weren't my problem. Let Moonie check his barman and G handle his street thugs. While the big dog was away the cat was trying to get her some play. I was determined to get with Gino tonight, and I tipped my ass discreetly over to the phone on the bar and dialed his cell digits.

I climbed on a stool and crossed my legs as I watched Gino across the room fumbling at his waist to answer his phone.

"Yeah. Speak."

"My pussy is popping. I want some."

I watched as he turned his back on Jimmy and the rest of the brothers who were standing around.

"Hey. Whassup?"

"Meet me in room nine."

"Aaight." Click.

Yeah, I thought as I hung up the phone and watched him take his time strolling toward the back of the Spot. Gino was acting all low-profile in front of them niggahs, but I knew he was itching for me as bad as I was for him.

I made sure no one was watching, then snuck into room nine behind him. Gino sighed and pulled me close. I had on a sleeveless black slinky dress cut down low in the back, with no bra, and Gino pushed those straps off my arms and swirled his hot tongue wetly around my nipples. I wanted him to suck on them forever, but the hardness in his pants and the way he squeezed on me told me he was ready for something more.

We didn't even bother with the bed or a condom. Gino pulled my dress up around my waist and lifted me up, then leaning against the wall he pushed the crotch of my panties aside and entered me deeply. We got busy just like that. With my man lowering me up and down on his thick dick, my wetness soaking both of us.

Gino gave me a long, deep kiss when we were done.

"I love you, Juicy. You know that, right?"

I nodded. I knew. But what could I do? I was stuck with G for life.

Gino was in front of me leaving the room first. He had opened the door and stepped out with me right on his heels when I felt him reach back and try to push me back inside.

"Might as well come on out," I heard my brother say. "Y'all motherfuckers ain't foolin nobody."

Jimmy was standing right outside the door, with one foot propped up, leaning against the wall. I walked out of the room and he gave me a disgusted look, then went to grilling Gino like he wanted to fight.

"What's up, Jimmy?" I said, and then just like a guilty person I straightened my dress and pushed my hair back.

"Why'ont your man Gino here tell me what the fuck is up?"

I glanced at Gino, who had never taken his eyes off Jimmy.

They were staring each other down like dogs in the street and all of a sudden a tight feeling swelled in my chest.

"What the hell are you talking about, Jimmy?" I jumped defensive.

"Nah, Juicy." Gino waved me aside. "Let your brother speak. Niggah got something on his chest he wanna get out. Let him."

Jimmy laughed and shook his head. "Y'all motherfuckers are trifling and foul. As much as G done gave both of y'all, this is how you fuck over him."

"You accusing me of something, Jimmy?" Gino stepped toward my brother and I could see his body tense up. "You bringing a charge to the table on me?"

Jimmy stepped up to meet him. "Yeah, motherfucker. I'm accusing you of fucking my sister. Better yet, I'm accusing your monkey ass of fucking *over* my father."

"G ain't your goddamn father."

"Then he ain't yours either, you dirty motherfucker. Coming up in here violating his space like that." Jimmy turned on me. "And you. Scandalous ass! How could you do him like this? G gives you more than you ever deserved. If it wasn't for him you'd probably be strolling on 136th Street, or even worse, working this same back room with a whole crew of tricks."

"Watch yourself, Jimmy. Don't disrespect your sister like that—"

"Disrespect? What the fuck do you know about respect? If you was any other niggah I'd do G a favor and take you out. You better be glad it's my sister you fuckin or I'd take both of y'all out—"

Gino swung a left and it was on and cracking. Jimmy didn't have no wins, that was obvious from the jump, but I wasn't gonna let Gino hurt my baby brother neither. And I could tell he wasn't really trying to. He was mostly holding on to Jimmy and slinging his ass from one side of the wall to the other. Jimmy was big, but Gino was bigger, and no matter how much I cursed and tried to pull one off the other or get in between them, I couldn't break them up.

It was Flex and Cooter who came around the corner and managed to pull them apart.

"Yo, yo, yo!" Flex hollered. "Yo, Jimmy man. Chill, dawg. Chill!"

Cooter pulled Gino back, and Jimmy caught him with a right on the break.

The connection was so hard and solid everybody froze.

"Aaight, then." Gino shook Cooter off like a booger and knocked Flex down as he grabbed for Jimmy. "You my niggah, J, but your young ass needs to be taught a lesson."

I started hollering then. Gino punched Jimmy in the face three times, slamming him to the floor. He was standing over my brother ready to stomp him into the ground when he stopped and looked over at me.

"You better learn to show some respect, niggah," he said to Jimmy, then started walking down the hall.

Cooter ran behind Gino yelling, "What the fuck was that about? Huh? What was that about?"

It didn't sink in on me until later that Cooter had lost his stutter, and all I could do at the time was stand there as Flex helped my brother get up. Jimmy's nose was bleeding and anger still burned in his eyes. I rushed over and wiped away a drop of blood that fell on his lip.

"Damn, dawg," Flex said, leaning Jimmy against the wall. "What the fuck *was* that about?"

Jimmy pushed my hand away and stood shakily on his feet. He looked at me like I was somebody's criminal, then he turned toward Flex and said, "Ask Juicy."

Chapter Twenty-One

Jimmy didn't speak to me for three whole days. Even though I kept going to his room trying to talk to him, cooked his favorite foods, and tried real hard to reconnect with him, he just wasn't having it.

"Don't kiss his ass," Gino told me as I stood in the kitchen cutting up some potatoes to make Jimmy some fries. "He ain't no baby, Juicy. Jimmy is a man and you need to start treating him like one."

"But I disappointed him, Gino. He loves G, and it fucked him up when he caught us like that."

Gino shrugged. "Then he shouldn't have come looking for nothing he couldn't handle. Besides, everything is gonna come to a head one day anyway. If it wasn't Jimmy who checked us it woulda been somebody else."

I felt miserable inside. I didn't want to lose Gino, but I loved my brother, too.

"So are you saying we should stop then?"

Gino gave me a look like *Girl, are you crazy?* and then he snuck and kissed me on the neck. "Hell no. I don't ever wanna stop being with you, Juicy. Not for G or for Jimmy. You know I wasn't gonna hurt your brother. But I couldn't let him disrespect you like that neither."

I turned the flame down under the pan and dropped in a handful of fries, jumping back when the grease sizzled and popped out at me. "I know. But still, try to understand where he's coming from."

Jimmy eventually came around and started talking to me again. I knew he wouldn't stay mad at me forever, and I also knew that he would never betray me to G. But putting the burden of my secret on him wasn't fair to him either, and I would have done anything to turn back the clock to erase that disappointed look from my brother's eyes.

The summer was about to end and I was looking forward to going back to school. Yeah, my life still revolved around G and the Spot, but now I had Gino to fill all the holes and give me the love and the loving I had been missing.

It made me crazy trying to do everything on the sneak tip. I kept wishing that somehow G would just disappear and let me and Gino and Jimmy live happily ever after. But I wasn't a stupid young girl no more. I knew those fairy-tale thoughts were whack. And a part of me also knew that Gino had been right when he said things were gonna come to a head one day. But what I didn't know was how big that head would get and how far the fallout would reach. I guess that's why you should be careful what you pray for. Just in case you end up getting it.

By Thanksgiving Jimmy was in so deep with G I was scared I'd never get him out. I still hadn't figured out how to get out of my situation, with or without G's money, and I was scared that any day Gino was gonna announce that his six months were over and he was skying up.

He'd told me that G was only a few weeks away from closing a deal with some big-time connects in B-More, and that he'd already leased a building and started handpicking the crew he was gonna take down there with him to launch the opening of the G-Spot 2.

"Is he taking you?" I asked, hoping like hell the answer was no.

Gino shrugged. "I don't know if that's his plan, but it sure ain't mine. When I leave Harlem I'm heading back west, not south, so to answer your question, no."

Somehow that didn't make me feel any better. So what he wasn't going to Baltimore. He hadn't said shit about taking me with him out west neither. And even if he did, I could forget about making Jimmy go with me. He was on G's dick so hard he should have been gay. There was no way he was leaving that man. Jimmy would leave me first, and as close as we were, that was some knowledge that hurt me to my heart.

It was three days before Christmas when Jimmy came

home one night and told me he was making an overnight run to Atlantic City. G was at the Spot counting drugs in the cut room, and me and Gino were decorating the Christmas tree that G had brought home earlier in the day.

We'd never been big on Christmas growing up. It was easy to overlook it when there was never any money to buy presents. G always bought me and Jimmy expensive gifts for the holiday, but this would also be the first time we put up a tree in celebration of it, and the only reason he went out and got one was because Gino said he wanted one.

Like I said, G wasn't cheap. He believed in buying quality shit, and I was so happy when I saw the frosted glass ornaments and handmade balls and bells he had picked out for the tree. At first I was mad that he hadn't thought about letting me choose what to get, but as usual his taste was good and I knew I couldn't have picked anything prettier or classier myself.

I was standing back giving Gino directions on where to place the angel when Jimmy walked in.

"Hey. That tree is hot." He kissed me on the cheek and that's when I saw the overnight bag he was holding in his hand.

"Where you going?"

"South," he said.

"Baltimore?"

"Nah. Jersey. I'll be back sometime tomorrow."

This is what it had come to between Jimmy and me. I

couldn't even tell him what to do anymore, and I sure couldn't forbid him to do anything G had assigned him to do. I knew we hadn't lost our closeness, but Jimmy had moved beyond my reach and I didn't like it. If he had been stepping up to manhood in a different way then that would have been cool. But all this drug-running, money-washing shit he was involved in scared me.

And I knew that I had to take some of the blame for what was going on. I had convinced myself that being Granite McKay's woman was going to set me and my brother up lovely for life, when actually it had made us slaves to his operation. Jimmy wouldn't even be in this situation if I hadn't gotten with G and dragged him into G's world. In trying to take care of my brother I had actually ruined him, and while I didn't like to even think about it, in my heart I knew this was all my fault.

"Be careful, Jimmy," was all I could say.

He nodded. "I'm cool, Juicy. I'ma stop and check out Flex for a minute, then I'm out."

I almost dropped the glass ornament I was holding. "Flex? You hanging out with Flex now?"

"C'mon, Juicy. You know me and Flex go way back. What? You still wondering about that shit with Macaroni? Or since we live in the big house and Fletcher's still out in the fields he can't be my man no more?"

I shrugged. "That's not what I'm saying. I just thought . . . nothing, Jimmy."

He reached out and hugged me again. "Stop all that damn worrying all the time. Looking like Grandmother. Ain't nothing gonna happen to me. I'ma hit the Lower East Side and check out my dawg, then I'm headed south for the night."

When Jimmy didn't show up by the next night I started to get scared. I called his cell phone but the answering service picked up, and he hadn't called the house at all. I walked around the Spot with my chest hurting, I was so worried about him. Everybody else was dancing and fucking and drinking and eating and doing their normal thing, when my world felt like it was spinning out of control and I couldn't stop it.

I sat at the bar and for the first time I actually considered ordering a drink. My nerves were just that bad. Cooter came down wiping the counter and smiling at me, and for a minute I saw something flicker in his eyes, and then it was gone.

"Y-y-ou want something, J-j-j-uicy? Some s-s-soda? A bottle of w-w-water?"

He'd gotten his stutter back. I shook my head. "Nah. My stomach is too upset to put anything in it. Has Jimmy called?"

Cooter dropped his rag. "N-n-nah. I ain't h-h-heard from him."

He bent down and picked up his rag, and as soon as he walked away I snatched up the bar phone and called Gino.

"Gino," I said quickly. "Jimmy ain't back yet. I think something mighta happened to him."

"Why you think that?"

"Because he told me he was staying in Jersey overnight, and then coming right back home."

"I'm running the card room right now, but did you ask G what time Jimmy was due back?"

I sighed. "No. Not yet. I'll go ask him now."

"I don't know where the fuck your brother is," G said when I stopped him on his way toward his office. "He shoulda had his ass back here with my package by early this afternoon."

G was talking bad, but he sure didn't look concerned.

"Well, do you know if he at least made it down there safe? What if he got into an accident? Or maybe the cops got him? Ain't there somebody you can call in Jersey to see if they know where he is?"

G unlocked his office door and stepped inside. "If the cops had him he would have called. If he wrecked the car, the cops would have called. Jimmy's smelling his fuckin nuts, that's the problem. I thought I could trust him so I let him have a lot of area to move, and now the niggah's trying to test me."

I couldn't believe this shit he was talking.

"G! You know damn well that boy ain't testing you!

Jimmy *loves* you! He put you over *me,* and if it ever came down to it he would *die* for you. How could you even fix your mouth to accuse him of being shady?"

He turned around and stared at me. "Money will do that shit to you. It makes a whole lot of niggahs act shady." Then he left me standing there in the hall and closed the door in my face.

Now I was really scared, but I didn't know what to do. Who could I call in Jersey? Nobody. I didn't know the connect Jimmy was going to meet, and after what had happened to me in Camden, I didn't wanna know none of those Jersey niggers neither.

I thought about Flex and wondered if Jimmy had told him anything. Other than going over to his territory in Taft projects, I had no way of getting in touch with Flex either.

I went to the coatroom and got my cute little swing coat and put it on. Since all I ever did was run out of the apartment and jump into Pacho's warm ride, I never bothered with a hat or gloves unless it was way past cold and downright nasty outside. I knew I was gonna freeze like a mother, but I didn't care. G was talking shit that didn't make no sense, Gino was too busy to pay me any mind, and my brother was out there somewhere doing who knows what.

I cornered Moonie behind the bar and asked him for fifty dollars. He looked at me like I was crazy, but I think the tears coming out my eyes convinced him that I was desperate. I had never asked Moonie for anything before, and I gave less than a fuck about him running back and telling G, just as long as I had enough to get down to Taft Houses and talk to the man who had been the last person, as far as I knew, to see my baby brother.

Chapter Twenty-Two

There were hardly any cabs running at this time of night, especially in Harlem, but I managed to catch one that had a Black Pearl sign in the front window. It was cold as hell outside, and cute didn't mean shit as I sat in the back of that taxi shivering and blowing into my bare hands.

"How much do you charge to wait for me?" I asked the driver when we pulled up outside the projects.

"Depends on how long. I gotta make a living, you know."

Fuck you, I said under my breath. His ass would have charged me tourist rates anyway. Probably ten dollars for every two minutes, and I sure couldn't afford that.

I paid him and got out the cab in front of the housing office and walked deeper into the projects. Taft wasn't part of my stomping grounds and I didn't know too many people over here. I tipped down the walkways in my heels and flimsy coat trying to play it cool and confident like I lived in one of the buildings and wasn't down for no bullshit.

It was late but you know the freaks come out at night in New York, and corner runners were calling out to me from the doorways offering me crack and blow left and right. I knew my luck was bad when it started to snow. I was all for a white Christmas, but damn! Did it have to start right now? My A-line JuicyOriginal dress only let me move but so fast, and my coat sleeves were too wide to help keep my hands warm.

I was frozen by the time I made it to the building that Flex worked from. I wasn't even on the porch good when he pulled open the door and came outside.

"Girl, what you doing out here by yourself this time of night?"

"H-hey Flex," I said, shivering and going through the door as he stepped back and held it open. Inside the lobby wasn't much warmer than it was outside. About half of the windows were busted out, and the other half were boarded over.

"What you doing down here, Juicy? Looking all frozen. Don't you know it's too damn cold to try to look fine tonight?" There were about six men hanging out in the hall, lookouts whose job it was to make sure that 5-0 didn't rush in and catch nobody holding any product.

"Jimmy," I said, following Flex into the stairwell so we could talk in private. "I'm looking for Jimmy. He made a run for G yesterday and was supposed to be back this afternoon. He didn't show up yet, and I thought maybe he was down here with you."

Flex shook his head. "Nah. He ain't here. He did roll through yesterday, though, and I tried to get him to stay here with me, but that niggah loves him some G, so he stepped."

I leaned against the hand railing. "Why would you want him to stay with you? What's up with that?"

Flex reached out and took my hands. He had on some thick black gloves with fur sticking all out of them and he pulled them off his hands and put them on mine, warming me up. "Juicy. If anybody in the world should know what time it is with me, you and Jimmy should know. I told you a long time ago. I'ma be rich, girl. I'ma be holding all the stops one of these days, and I want you and Jimmy both to be down with me."

"Boy, you crazy—"

"Didn't I tell your grandmother I was gonna snatch you up and set you up for life? She believed me, so why the fuck don't you?"

"Flex!" I damn near shouted. "This ain't about you and me! This is about my brother, all right? This is about finding out where the fuck Jimmy is!"

He didn't say nothing for a minute. Then that little bucktooth niggah snatched his gloves off my hands and put them back on his. My fingers missed that warm fur. "You fine, Juicy, but you stupid. You and Jimmy both. A niggah wanna put y'all down, and y'all don't even know which line you should be standing on."

"Boy, what the hell are you talking about?"

Flex looked sad and mad. "Nothing, Juicy." He opened the door and pushed me back out of the stairwell. "Your brother ain't here, but if he shows up again I'll let him know you looking for him. Jimmy my niggah and I love him, but I can't make his eyes see what his mind can't believe is there."

I followed Flex back out into the night, and as crazy as he was he still had the decency to help me catch a cab going uptown.

"You coulda been Mrs. Boykin," Flex said, opening the cab's door for me. "Tell this cabby to go on about his business and stay here with me, and you still can."

I jumped into that cab so fast I broke the heel off my shoe. "Later, Fletcher," I said, waiting for him to close the door. "I'll check you later."

When I got back to the Spot Jimmy still hadn't showed up, even though I had been praying he'd be there when I walked inside, and I had already rehearsed how I was gonna curse his ass out for making me worry so much.

The next day was Christmas Eve, and he didn't show up

then either. I called his cell phone every thirty minutes and I almost wore a hole in the floor pacing, I was so scared of what might have happened to him.

I couldn't eat anything because my nerves were too bad, and my head was banging from grinding my teeth together all night. I was searching through the medicine cabinet for a Tylenol when G called for me to come out the bathroom.

I went into the living room where he was watching a movie with Gino.

"Yeah?"

G stood up. "I want you to take a ride with Gino. Jimmy still ain't showed up with my shit, and I want y'all to go to Atlantic City and check out a few places for me."

I glanced at Gino, who just looked at me and shrugged.

"G, I don't know nothing about Atlantic City. If I knew where to start looking for Jimmy down there I would have been down there already."

"I'ma tell y'all where to look, Juicy, damn! Gino's gonna be running things. Only reason you going is to make Jimmy come on back and face up to what he did like a man."

"Why do you keep saying that, G? You know Jimmy ain't done nothing wrong! He could be laying up hurt somewhere or even dead, and all you can think is that he might have crossed you?"

"Wise the fuck up, Juicy. Your brother broke out with my money. He didn't give a fuck about me, and he didn't give a fuck about you neither, or he would have took you with him."

I kept shaking my head. "G, you wrong. You know Jimmy wouldn't do nothing foul like that."

G ignored me. "Gone, Gino. Y'all get ready to go. Pacho is gonna take us all down to the Spot. The Benz is there, and it's already gassed up. You can get the keys from Moonie, then take it and hit all the places I told you about. Find Jimmy and bring him back up here to me. Don't hurt him, but make sure that niggah is back in Harlem before the night is over."

"I need to make a few stops," I told Gino as he pushed the fly Benz through Harlem. The weather was changing, getting real nasty. We'd left G at the Spot, and I told Gino to swing me back to the apartment on Central Park West so I could change out of the suede designer dress I was wearing and into something more comfortable for the ride to Atlantic City. It had started to snow again, real hard, and after I put on a pair of jeans and some warm Timbs, I made sure I grabbed a wool hat and some gloves, too.

But that's not all I grabbed.

My stomach was jumping from fear. I didn't trust G as far as I could smell his ass, and no matter how many times Gino told me everything was gonna be okay, I had a bad feeling about everything. About G, about taking this ride into Atlantic City, and especially about Jimmy.

If shit got crazy and I had to help my brother, I needed to be prepared. First I went into my bedroom and locked the door. I trusted Gino, but the less shit I had to explain, the better. I took down the mirrored panel off the wall again and opened G's safe. The same stuff was still in there as the last time. I took the brick of money and separated it in two stacks, sliding half of it into a MGM bag and leaving the other half in the safe.

I was about to slam the door closed when I caught a glimpse of the brown envelope, the one that held the small gold key. I shook the key out of the envelope then slipped it onto my key ring right next to the ones that opened the downstairs door and the front door of the apartment.

I threw the envelope back inside, not even bothering to put it back in the exact same spot like I had done before. G didn't go in his safe every day, but all he would have to see was half his money gone to know that somebody had been in there dipping, and of course the most likely suspect would be me.

Deep inside I had a feeling that I had just crossed the point of no return with Granite McKay. Nothing in my life was gonna be the same anymore, and as coldblooded as G was it scared me more to be ass-out and unable to take care of Jimmy than it did to steal G's money and risk him finding out. Yeah, if he knew I'd had the heart to go in his safe he would kill me, but just sitting around waiting for him to get rid of me was like suicide.

After closing the safe and putting the mirrored panel back, I grabbed a bag that I had used for my dance clothes, and then I opened my closet and found my school bag. I took the Juicy Journal, the copies I had made of G's black binder, and the folded sheet of paper that had my grandmother's gravesite information on it, and put them all in my dance bag and pulled the string closed. Feeling paranoid about G's money, I made sure the latch was closed on the MGM bag, but then at the last minute I opened it up again and stuck my key ring into the inside pocket, pausing just long enough for one last look at the picture of me, Jimmy, and Grandmother that was sealed in hard plastic and dangling from the ring.

And then I was set. Gino locked the front door as we left the apartment, and we went downstairs and got into the black Benz in silence.

"You okay?" he looked over at me and asked. Gino's voice was soft and he reached out and touched my cold cheek with one hand. "You hungry? You wanna get something to eat first?"

I shook my head. "Rita's," I said. "I need to stop at Rita's house."

He swung me by there and didn't even ask why I needed to see her at that time of night. Outside Rita's apartment, I stood on the stoop and banged until she opened the door.

"I gotta make a run, Rita," I said, passing her both of my bags. "Hold these someplace safe for me until I get back, okay?"

She took the bags without asking what was inside.

"What's up, Juicy?" she said, shivering. "Where you goin?"

I shook my head. "Looking for Jimmy. Gino is taking me so I'll be all right."

Minutes later me and Gino were on the road. As we drove down the highway I thought about the last time I had taken a ride for G. As scared as I was then, I was even more afraid now because I didn't know if I was gonna find my brother dead or alive at the end of the journey.

Still, it was cold outside so Gino had the heat blasting and the car was rocking me like a baby. Scared or not, I fell asleep about two exits after we got on the Garden State and when I woke up again I saw the bright lights of Atlantic City in front of us.

"You aaight? Feeling better?" Gino asked when he saw that I was up.

Hell no, I wanted to say. But instead I just shook my head and kept looking ahead so he couldn't spot the tears trying to fall out my eyes.

G had given Gino a list of three places he wanted him to go to. The first place was a first-floor room in a small hotel off the main strip, and the second place was an Italian seafood restaurant that was so crowded I just knew the whole damn Mafia was up in there.

Jimmy wasn't at either place, but people at both spots claimed they'd seen him a few days earlier when he came to make his pickup. I just couldn't believe that my brother would sky up with G's cheddar, but according to everybody we talked to, he damn sure had G's dollars on him when he disappeared.

The snow was really coming down now, much harder in New Jersey than it had been in New York. Gino had the windshield wipers going at the max, and we could only drive about twenty-five miles an hour because the roads were so bad. Traffic was backed way up and it took us a whole hour to get to the third stop, even though it was less than twenty miles from the Italian restaurant. G had told Gino to check at this lady's house who was the last person Jimmy was supposed to see before heading back home. She lived in an apartment complex that was small, and since the snow plows hadn't even cleared the main roads I was scared we'd drive into the complex, get stuck, and not be able to drive back out.

It was late and I was gonna stay in the car while Gino got out to knock, but then I got scared of being left alone and jumped out and ran through the icy snow and up the stairs behind him.

"No, baby," the little old woman said when she answered the door and Gino asked if Jimmy was there. I was surprised to hear the door unlock just seconds after we hit the porch, and thought maybe she should try looking out her peephole before she opened the door for strange people standing on her porch. "He was by here a couple of days ago, but I ain't seen him since."

She reminded me so much of my grandmother. Not because she looked like her—Grandmother had been real light and thick with big hips and a slamming shape for an older woman, and this woman was tall and skinny and almost bald—but it was something in her voice that was sweet and comfortable. I felt like I could go into her house and lay my head in her lap forever.

"Did he seem all right when he was here?" I asked her, stepping from behind Gino. "Jimmy is my brother and I'm worried about him because he should have been home two days ago and nobody's seen him."

She shook her head. "No, he seemed fine, with his sweet little self. That boy sure is mannerable! He been raised right. You kin tell!"

She stood out on the porch in the cold, waving as me and Gino pulled away through the snow. "She sure was nice," I said waving back until I couldn't see her no more. "She oughta be careful about opening up her door at night like that, but at least she was nice though."

Gino gave me a crazy look. "Juicy, you can't be that damn blind. That old lady is the connect! One of the biggest rollers in New Jersey. You must didn't see that Glock sticking out under her housecoat, huh?"

"Boy, quit it!" I said, laughing and punching his arm. "Grandma wasn't strapped!"

Gino nodded. "Oh yes she was. And so was all them niggahs hiding behind curtains and checking us from the windows."

All I could do was shake my head. She seemed so sweet and grandmotherly I figured one of her kids was working for G. I woulda never guessed that Grandma was the drug queen, but then again, if Jimmy had come down here to do a pickup from her, what else could she have been?

Gino didn't know what to do next and neither did I.

"I'ma call G," he said, pulling over on the side of the road. The embankment was piled high with snow that passing cars had managed to clear as they cut a trail through the road. "Maybe Jimmy made it back by now."

My stomach sank as I listened to Gino's conversation with his father. The way he was talking I could tell that Jimmy wasn't back, and G was mad as hell.

"It's snowing pretty bad down here, G. The roads are so bad and cars are moving so slow it'll take us five or six hours to get back to Harlem. By the time we roll up it'll be day-light."

Gino paused, listening. "Where? You sure? Aaight. Yeah. Nah, I'm cool with it. Aaight, later."

"What?" I said as he turned toward me.

"Check this out. Jimmy's not there. G thinks he dipped on his money and then cut out. Somebody said they heard he was hiding in Brooklyn. G is sending Moonie down there to look for him, but he said we should stay at the Taj Mahal for the night and then try to make it back to Harlem in the morning."

I have to admit it. As scared as I was for my brother, the

thought of staying all night in a phat hotel with Gino helped me feel a little better.

"You know we gotta get two rooms," I said, grinning.

Gino grinned back. "Yeah, but we only have to sleep in one."

Chapter Twenty-Three

The Taj Mahal was one of G's favorite hotels. I'd come with him once or twice when he got the urge to do some big-time gambling with the high rollers of New Jersey. G would hit the casinos and stay at the tables for hours, leaving me on my own to get into whatever I wanted. He'd tear me off a huge chunk of cash and I would shop my ass off. For me and for Jimmy, and every now and then I'd even pick out something nice for G, too.

Walking into the lobby with Gino felt funny though. Good, but funny. G had connects at the Taj and he'd told Gino to charge our rooms to his account, and as much as his operation had infiltrated New Jersey, the management knew he was good for the money.

We decided not to go all out and get suites. Two regular rooms with king-sized beds would do. But even a regular room at the Taj Mahal was the shit, and I looked forward to loving my man down in a nice soft bed that came with the most expensive sheets and blankets.

Gino was given room 202 and I had room 204. Both were lanai suites.

"We don't need suites," Gino explained. "Double rooms will be cool."

The young white guy at the desk shook his head. "These are the rooms set aside for Granite McKay. The computer won't let me change them, and even if it did, with the weather being so horrible we're booked solid."

We took the elevator up to the second floor. The halls had mirrors and cherry wood everywhere. "Yours or mine?" I said as we stood outside our rooms.

Gino laughed. "Always yours," he said, sliding the card key into room 204. "Always yours."

The suite was sweet. There was a fluffy white 100 percent down comforter on the bed, and the thread count on the sheets had to be somewhere near a thousand. The bathroom was marble and onyx, and the view was like a postcard.

I plopped down on the thick mattress and laid back staring at the ceiling. Gino sat down next to me and squeezed my thigh, then slid his hand between my legs and rubbed on my stuff.

"You wanna take a shower before I get me some, or you want me to hit it just like it is?"

I pushed his hand away, squealing. "Quit, nasty! Why you so damn nasty, huh? Why you so damn nas—"

Gino covered my mouth with his lips, his tongue swirling around so gently inside my mouth that it made me dizzy. He climbed on top of me and started moving his hips, the thickness of his dick pressing into my stomach. I grabbed his ass with both hands and matched his pace, my pussy on fire as I aimed his dick where I needed it to be. We lay there grinding into each other for a long time. By the time Gino stood up and pulled me to my feet my panties were soaked and my lips felt swollen from his kisses.

"C'mon," he said, leading me toward the bathroom.

We couldn't even get into the shower good we were kissing and touching so much. This was the first time we were able to really be together without sneaking, and it felt so damn hot. Gino rubbed soap all over me from my neck down to my feet, and even washed between my legs and seemed to like doing it.

My hands were all over him the entire time. The sight of suds dripping from his dark skin turned me on, and I squeezed his hard arms and played with the hair on his chest as he slid two fingers into me and made me come standing up.

There were two plush white bathrobes hanging behind the door with the initials TM over the breast pockets. Gino dried me off like I was a baby, then rubbed some expensive hotel lotion on my arms, ass, and legs before helping me into the robe.

We came out of the bathroom together, laughing and

looking forward to what we were gonna do once we got between those sheets. As soon as Gino sat down I dropped to
my knees and opened his robe and held his thick dick in
both hands, then went to work licking and sucking it like it
was made from sugar.

Gino was moaning out loud and I was moaning right
along with him, slurping that thang to death, my head bob-
bing up and down faster and faster as he fucked up at me
and held me by my hair.

A moment later Gino pushed me away and stood up.
"Take that shit off," he told me, nodding at the robe and
panting as he closed his fist around his wet dick and held it
tight.

What I felt next was indescribable. Gino took his time
working on me. He sucked my toes and put hickeys on both
cheeks of my ass. His tongue moved down and licked behind both of my knees. My titties were past swollen as he
turned me over and licked at them, nibbling on my nipples
as they stood straight up in the air. For the first time in my
life I was being done totally right. Sexed and loved at the
same time. Hickeys on my arms, my ass, and my stomach.
Gino licked my pussy for an hour straight, stabbing it with
his tongue and gently sucking on my clit. I must have come
about five times before he finally let his go, and when he fell
on top of me I squeezed my pussy muscles trying to milk
every single drop of cum from his nuts.

We slept together all tangled up in the sheets. During the

night I felt Gino pull the comforter over me and kiss my cheek, but I was too dick-whipped to respond.

The next morning I woke up first, and as soon as I stretched my body I felt a pleasing ache from the delicious sex Gino had put on me. I turned over toward him smiling, but suddenly thoughts of Jimmy came rushing back to me and my smile became a frown. Yeah, I'd been getting my stuff stroked all night, but what had been happening to my brother?

Gino rolled over and ran his big hand roughly over my hair.

"You alive?"

Despite myself, I smiled. "Just barely. You wasn't even trying to beat this stuff up, was you? No, you tried to kill it!"

He laughed. "Hurt me. . . . Hurt me. . . ."

I sat up and my full breasts jiggled. Gino reached over and cupped one in his hand, his fingers lazily trailing over my erect nipples. My stuff thumped and became slippery, and I quickly slid back down in the bed letting Gino pull me into his arms. We spent the next hour trying to stock up on the loving we had missed living under G's roof.

After ordering breakfast we showered and put back on our clothes from the day before. Housekeeping brought us some toothbrushes and we joked each other about who needed to use them the most.

When it was time to leave my stomach started humming again. Stress was kicking me in the ass, and for a minute I wanted to do something crazy. I didn't wanna go back to Harlem, back to G and all of his damned drama. Especially if G found out I'd been in his safe. I was ready to fix my mouth to tell Gino to drive west instead of north when we got back out on the road. He was all the time talking about California and how he was going back there to start his architectural firm. At this point I was game to go with him. He could start his business while I finished college, and maybe then we could raise us some cute curly-haired babies with smooth chocolate skin.

All of this yang was floating through my head, but none of it came out of my mouth. How could it? Gino mighta been down to jet and leave his father, but there was no way in hell I was leaving my brother. No. Fuck the dumb shit. I was going back to Harlem to wait for Jimmy, and I promised myself that if my baby brother hadn't shown up within twenty-four hours after we arrived, I'd be calling the feds on G.

The weather was still nasty on the drive back home but at least the snow plows had been out clearing the roads overnight. Gino drove slow on the Garden State Parkway anyway, taking his time as we listened to a few CDs by Beyoncé, 50 Cent, and Outkast.

All too soon we were going through the Lincoln Tunnel, up toward Port Authority, and the end of our trip was only minutes away. What me and Gino had shared was way past special, but now it was time for us to get back to reality.

It was just after two when we pulled up in front of the G-Spot, and almost as soon as Gino stepped out the Benz, Moonie bust out the door with Pluto and Ace right behind him. They bum rushed through the snow toward us with killer looks on their faces.

I saw a bat gripped in Ace's hand. "W-w-what the fuck?"

Pluto and Ace tried to grab hold of Gino, who broke loose and started throwing blows. It was two against one, but Gino was holding shit down like a superstar, fucking both of them fat niggahs up.

But then Pluto caught him with a good punch. Gino was spinning around from drilling Ace when Pluto put all his ass behind the blow and connected with Gino's temple. Gino went down and I screamed. Moonie was trying to hold me back, but I was a Harlem girl who'd eaten beans out the can, and if my man was thumping in the street then I was damn sure gonna jump in and help him.

I swung my Timbs and kicked Moonie in the balls and then jumped on Ace's back. He was swinging his bat at Gino's head when I bit down into that fucker's back like it was a piece of lobster dipped in butter. That grimy nigger tasted just like salt pork.

"Get this bitch!" Ace yelled, and Moonie grabbed me from behind putting me in a sleep-hold.

"Get the fuck offa me!" I tried to scream, but he was choking me so hard all that came out was a wheeze.

"Chill, Juicy," I heard Moonie whispering in my ear as Pluto and Ace beat the shit out of Gino. "Quit fighting it, girl. G set y'all motherfuckers up. Jimmy's safe on the Lower East Side with Cooter, but G knows all about you and Gino, girl, and one of y'all is gonna have to die."

Chapter Twenty-Four

They dragged us both down to the Dungeon, kicking and fighting the whole way.

Moonie tossed me onto a nasty mattress, while Pluto, Ace, and two other big niggas pinned Gino down on the ground. The Dungeon looked just like it sounded. Dingy and dark. We were in a small, bare room and the mattress I was laying against was the only furniture in sight.

G came down the stairs and I started shaking like a mother. As usual he looked pressed out in expensive everything, and even his cologne smelled like money.

Jimmy is safe, I reassured myself. Moonie said Jimmy was safe, and that was all that mattered.

G stood there staring at his son. He didn't even bother to look at me, which was cool because I was scared of what I'd see in his eyes.

"Gino, Gino, Gino. You always were your mother's son."

Gino cursed at Pluto and tried to ram his shoulder in his gut.

"Know why I didn't give you my name? You ever wonder about that? How you came to be Gino instead of Granite II?"

"Do I look like I give a fuck?"

G laughed. "I knew you wasn't shit the minute you jumped out of that bitch's ass! I knew you wasn't gonna be man enough, hard enough to handle my name. Damn." G shook his head. "You almost inherited an empire. A ready-made cash cow that I built with my own two hands, and you let a stink piece of pussy get you bent."

G moved closer to Gino, who was straining to break free of all the rough hands that held him back. I saw his muscles jumping through his shirt and all I could do was hold my breath and pray.

"Salida the slut," G continued. "You just like that dirty bitch. I should have been a better magician though. Instead of wasting my paper on that white-boy college I shoulda made your punk ass disappear right along with hers."

Wasn't no holding Gino back. He broke free of all them niggas and jumped on G, knocking him backward and down to the ground. For a moment, they were scrapping, the young against the old, the father against the son. And then Gino was muscled down again, niggas five deep dove on top of him and pinned him once more, then pulled out their guns and started denting his head.

G got up, wiping his lip. Both of them were strong and built, but Gino had drawn first blood, and I was proud of my man for that.

"Take him back to the apartment and guard him for the next two days," G said. "Don't give this niggah a bite of my food or a drop of my water neither. If he gotta piss, let him do it in his pants. Let him shit in them, too. I want four of y'all on him. Twenty-four/seven. Fuck him up good if he gives you any flack. Forty-eight hours from now I want you to take this motherfucker down to Kennedy and put his ass on the first thing smoking out west."

Ace looked up from the fighting heap and asked, "What if he don't wanna go? What if this nigga won't get on the plane?"

G didn't even hesitate as they dragged his only son fighting and bleeding up the basement steps.

"Then kill him."

G was gonna kill me, too. I could see it in his eyes.

He told everybody to get the fuck upstairs and they jetted with a quickness. As soon as they were gone G went crazy, slapping me, punching me, and bending my arms back until my shoulder bones popped. That motherfucker kicked my ass. Plain and simple, that's what he did.

All the time he was beating me G was also cursing me out. My whole body was in pain, but I could still feel G's pain, too. I had humiliated him. Violated him in the worst kind of way. Everybody knew how particular he was over his pussy, and my fucking Gino had just put the word out on the wire that the great Granite McKay couldn't hold it down in the sheets.

At first I screamed and begged him not to hit me, but I soon realized that G didn't even hear me and I would do better trying to duck and roll and use my energy to run from one side of the small room to the other.

Sweat was coming off both of us in that hot-assed basement, but G looked like he was enjoying his workout. After a while I started screaming again. How much longer did he think I could take this? My stomach, my back, my ribs . . . I just knew he had ruptured something in me and I would die from internal bleeding.

I was scooting backward on the floor screaming and trying to dodge his kicking feet when G crouched, then jumped straight up into the air. And then life started moving in slow motion. It took forever for G to land, but when he did he came down hard on both feet. Surely this shit was happening to some other chick, I thought as the bottom of G's two-thousand-dollar shoes descended on me, but when I felt all that hard leather come crashing down into my face, I damn sure knew it was me.

I came awake sputtering, hot liquid splashing in my face.

G was pissing on me.

All over my face and right into my half-opened mouth. When I opened my eyes and closed my lips, his pee stung my eyes and ran down into my ears. I couldn't have been knocked out long, probably only a few seconds, but staring up at that big niggah holding his dick and aiming his flow down at me, I wished like hell I could go back unconscious.

"This is all you worth, you rotten-ass bitch!" G stood over me until he squeezed out his last drop, and then he tucked his dick away and zipped up his pants.

I thought he was gonna start beating me again, but we both turned around when the door opened upstairs and somebody came running down.

It was Moonie. He gave me a pity look when he saw me laying on the floor, my face and hair soaked in G's piss, but then his mask came down and he turned to stone again as G laughed and dapped him out.

"Private party tonight," G said as I whimpered on the floor. "The best pussy in the house is up for sale and I want all my niggahs to get some." He rotated his onyx ring on his finger and then nodded toward me. "Have Kadijah put her nasty ass in some water, then make sure she's out there when the girls go onstage."

They left me down in that stanking little basement for almost twelve hours, and by the time they came back I was dying to get upstairs and breathe some real air. My whole body was throbbing, but I didn't protest when Ace and Pluto grabbed my arms and dragged me up the steps. Upstairs, the show was getting heated up. I limped down the halls of the Spot being manhandled by Ace and Pluto, embarrassed as hell, my eyes on the floor. Mouths were opening and closing left and right, and I could hear the steady buzz . . . *G done fucked Juicy up, and now he's putting her ass out to work the rooms!*

As we turned a corner, Monique stepped out in front of me styling and profiling. Every inch of her shit was tight and she had this big-ass smile on her face like she'd just been crowned queen of the Spot. I was ashamed to be caught out there looking all dirty and fucked up and smelling like piss, but I stared at her like my hair was did and my clothes were fly.

She looked me up and down. "Damn, Juicy. Your shit is way raggedy! All this time you been perpetrating like you all that, when you really just another low-profile ho. So you don't fuck behind nobody, huh? Well, before it's all over you'll be fuckin behind me and every other ho up in this Spot."

"Fuck you, you three-titty bitch!"

Monique just laughed and shook her long silky weave. "Just *who* you'll be fuckin is anybody's guess, and while your stank pussy is getting scuffed and plunged, G's gonna be suckin all three of these titties!"

I doubted that cause G didn't suck no titties, but I didn't bother to tell her. I was too embarrassed at being seen hemmed up like a criminal. Most of the staff looked at me like, Be strong, Juicy. This ain't nothing but a thing. But for the most part all I saw was pity. Pity and fear, like they, too, were scared of what G had planned for me.

Deep down I was shitting bricks, but I told myself that as long as Moonie was right and Jimmy was safe, that was all that mattered. I had to force myself not to think about Gino cause that could break me all the way down. Seeing him beaten and pistol-whipped like that had hurt me to my heart, and the look in his eyes when they dragged him up those basement steps was gonna haunt me until the day I died. I prayed they would have mercy on him for being G's blood, but I also remembered G's cousin from all those years ago, the one who G had fucked up so bad he still limped around Harlem begging for change with his one-eyeball self.

They took me into the massage room and told Ursula to get out so Kadijah could get me ready. An hour later I'd taken a shower and washed my hair, and Kadijah had taken me into the dressing room and put a bunch of makeup on my face and body to cover the bruises, and then tossed me an outfit that screamed hoochie mama/club stripper/ two-dollar ho.

It looked like every nigger in Harlem was in the house that night. G made me get onstage and fuck the poles and do a slow funky striptease, too. I didn't even try to play with him by acting out. I moved my ass like a natural ho and did all the freaky shit I'd seen Monique, Punanee, and Honey Dew do night after night after night.

I guess I was good, too. Money was flying up on the stage,

and every time I turned around and let them see my ass, brothers clapped and hooted and dug in their pockets for some more. I cried inside the whole time and tried to block out all the noise. I pretended I was dancing for Gino, that it was him urging me to lick my titties, ride that pole, and spread open my ass cheeks. Picturing Gino's long black dick was the only way I got through the segment, and by the time it was over I felt lower than ever before in life.

But G wasn't done with me yet. When I got off the stage, he put my ass up on the block. Monique was happy to swish her ass over and be the bitch to bring me the bone.

"Juicy girl, them motherfuckers LOVE you! You gonna have the cleaning crew working overtime washing sheets tonight!"

"What?"

Pluto and Greco were each clocking one side of me as I stumbled back into the dressing room. I was G's prisoner and everybody knew it.

"You didn't know? Girl, your fine ass got twelve chips already and a crew of cash niggas lined up waiting for you! I think it was that ass thing you did that got 'em all hot. Whatever it was, thank you, girlfriend, cause you giving all the other hoes a break up in here tonight!"

I was in a daze. As many times as I had been in those fuck rooms gossiping and helping change cummed-up sheets, I'd never thought I'd have to one day stoop down to sexing strangers and flat-backing to save my life.

"Here." Monique slipped me something she took out of a tiny piece of foil. "After about ten of them dirty-dick, stank-breath niggahs, you'll need this to help get you through the next ten."

Ironically, Pluto threw me in fuck-room number nine, then stepped inside and closed the door. "You on the clock now, bitch, and I'm customer number one. I want mine first, before all them other niggahs stank that punanee up."

"You ain't fucking me, Pluto," I told him. "Your fat ass ain't hardly fucking me."

He slammed me back on the bed, then sat his buffalo ass on my chest.

"No shit, stupid. I don't wanna fuck you no way. But you *are* gonna suck my dick."

The funk coming off his ass was incredible. Here the niggah had on three g's worth of gear, and his drawers and ass smelled like two weeks ago. Pluto put his fat knee in my chest and pulled out his dick, and I almost threw up at the sight of it. It was fat and uncircumcised and had a glob of slimy juice dripping from the head.

"If you put that shit anywhere near my mouth, I'ma—"

Pluto knocked the shit out of me. "Suck it, bitch," he yelled as I tried to clear my head and catch my breath. "You gonna *suck it!*"

That dick was halfway down my throat before I knew it. I gagged and fought as he pumped in and out of my mouth like it was his own personal pussy. Tears were blinding me, but I heard that fat niggah laughing on top of me as he slammed his dick in my mouth up to the balls. "Yeah, bitch. Suck it! Suck it!"

I forced myself to wait until he pulled back, and the moment he went in for another slam, I bit down on that shit so hard it made my jaw ache.

The next thing I knew Pluto was screaming, fists were flying, and my mouth was filling up with blood. A bunch of somebodys bust into the room and pulled Pluto off of me, and I could hear Monique laughing in the doorway. G came in and looked down at me with ice in his eyes.

"Pluto paid for that pussy, bitch. Next customer that comes up in here better get his money's worth." But even G couldn't make me suck no dick. When those niggahs saw Pluto with blood all over his pants, none of them were bad enough to stick their dicks in my face.

The first five tricks were the worst. Some of them I'd known and had dissed for years because they had tried to get with me even though they knew I was G's. Others were straight-up strangers who were all about getting some cold sex. Only a few of them bothered with a rubber since I was considered prime fresh meat. G stayed right there in the room with me, too, and even told me what to do. "Grab his ass, Juicy. Don't just lay there! These niggahs done paid good money for that pussy! Fuck back at 'em!"

Five turned into ten, and then into even more. By then my nipples were chewed raw, I was bleeding between my legs and scraped so sore that all I could do was lay there and moan. G looked down on me with a strange look in his eyes, and I thought about all the nights I had lain in bed next to this man while he slept. I prayed he would remember how much he used to like me and say fuck his reputation and have a little mercy on me.

"All right, now," G said as the next customer came through the door. "Y'all bout wearing this pussy out now. Quit sending them niggahs in here one by one. Let's get us a train rolling, keep this pussy hot. One niggah jump out, the next one jump in. Let's move it, fellahs. Time is money."

I turned my head toward the wall, but I didn't cry. I couldn't. I didn't have no more tears left. But what I did have was a little purple pill Monique had slipped me. *See there, Dicey,* I thought. *Maybe that three-titty bitch ain't so bad after all.* I opened my mouth and threw that pill down my grateful throat.

Chapter Twenty-Five

I had survived the first night and was back in the Dungeon. It was dark and foul, and to top it off the toilet didn't flush. I jumped at every little noise, and I made myself sing out loud, scared that there were some big-ass New York City rats living in the walls and just hungry for a piece of me.

For the next two days G was his usual generous self. He brought all of his young lieutenants through—the hard-core niggas who worked the projects and served as lookouts and the ones who manned the corners of each avenue passing his product—and let all of them sample my stuff for free.

"Yeah! Yeah! Yeah!" They screamed into my neck, gripping my hips and trying to knock a hole in my back. "You thought you was too good for a nigga! Huh? Huh?"

At night G had Ace and Pluto take me upstairs and

get me ready for the stage, and when the show was over I worked the back rooms until closing time.

By the third night I had a fever, and one of the customers refused to fuck me. He told G I was talking out of my head and looked half-dead, so G gave him his money back and told him to pick another ho.

Flex came through on the morning of that third day, during the daytime when he coulda got him some for free. He stepped up to the mattress and stared down at me laying on that dirty sheet.

"Damn, girl. You used to be a Porsche. Now you just a regular putt-putt."

I tried to give him the finger, but I was too weak. Besides, I was laying on one hand and the other one was chained to the pole.

"Fuck you, Flex," I whispered, my throat raw.

"Nah, baby. That's okay. Your pussy stanks, and plus, you been run through."

"Where's Jimmy? You seen Jimmy?"

Flex got quiet for a minute. "Yeah. I seen that niggah. G set both of y'all up, Juicy-Mo. He sent Jimmy to the A.C. and then had some niggahs jack him for his yards."

"You knew about it, you motherfucker!"

"Uh-uh." Flex shook his head. "Not when you came down to Taft I didn't. I tried to talk Jimmy out of making that run to A.C. but he wouldn't listen. See, G arranged the whole thing, and Jimmy was scared to come back without his money, so I let him chill at the crib with me and Cooter on the Lower East Side."

"Where is he now, Flex?" I whispered. "Where the fuck is my brother?"

He shrugged. "You got me. I been looking for him my-self. Word got around that G had you and Gino, and the next thing I knew Jimmy rolled. I thought he was heading up here, but I ain't seen him in two days."

I started crying again. I couldn't help it. Loud, heavy tears.

"This is fucked up, Juicy," Flex said. "I feel for you, girl, but you put your money on the wrong nigger. Shit is about to change big time. I told you one day I'd be runnin thangs in Harlem. You shoulda had some faith in me. You and Jimmy both. G is getting old. That motherfucker ain't got much longer on the throne. But since we go way back, I tell you what. Make it through this, and I'll hook you up with a job. You can be my main bitch when I take over the Spot. Me and Cooter gonna rename it Flex-n-Effect."

Cooter? I thought. Flex was bugging. He was worse off than me and I was beat and fucked and chained to a bed. I closed my eyes and willed myself to doze off before the next pair of balls were dangling over me. Fletcher Boykin could take his job and stick it up his ass. If I lived through this, I was definitely gonna be my own boss.

·   ·   ·

The door slammed at the top of the stairs, and I opened my eyes and tried to sit up. My mind was so confused I had lost track of time and couldn't tell if it was morning or night. Heavy footsteps boomed down and I looked up to see Pluto standing over me, looking like he wanted to beat my ass again. He grabbed me and unlocked the chain, then started dragging me toward the stairs by my ponytail and the back of my shirt, but I was already so bruised and banged up I couldn't even feel any additional pain. I could tell he was still mad about the way I bit up his dick, and he slung my ass from wall to wall as we came out of the Dungeon and headed toward the main room.

Right before we turned the corner Pluto gripped the back of my neck and spit dead in my face. "You about to get yours now, you scab-ass bitch. Before the night is over you gone be a dick-suckin pro." I wiped his funky spit out of my eyes and told him to kiss my ass.

"That's why we capped that mothefuckin Gino, tramp. Cause he was too busy kissing your ass to handle his business. You shoulda seen how that bitch bled."

Gino was dead.

I moaned and my whole body went cold. To keep from screaming, I bit down into my lip and fought to clamp my mouth closed.

Pluto snatched me in a headlock and I stumbled beside him as we climbed the stairs to the stage. It was dark in front of the Spot, except for a few low lights over the bar. My eyes adjusted and I could see there were people sitting and waiting in the darkness, and I smelled weed and cigarette smoke and heard shot glasses clinking together.

"Right there," I heard somebody say, and my stomach clenched. It was G, and just the sound of his voice almost made me pee on myself.

Pluto threw me on the floor, and the funk of thirty different dicks rose from my body. *Just make me dance*, I prayed. *Please don't beat me no more. Just make me get up and shake my ass, lick my own titties, hold my pussy open, and let these freaks stare at my uterus. Just don't beat me no more.*

Suddenly somebody turned on the spotlight overhead, and I saw that I wasn't up on that stage by myself. Some guy was sitting in a chair, slumped over with a hoody pulled over his face like he was asleep. I couldn't see any of his features, and his clothes looked just like every other playa who rolled at the Spot. He was wearing a fresh pair of Timbs, some Sean Johns, and the rest of his gear was Roc-A-Wear.

"Stand up, Juicy."

I looked out into the audience and saw G sitting there twirling that goddamn ring. Moonie, Ace, and Cooter were also there, along with a few regulars. Slowly, I pulled myself up to my feet, shaking so bad and in so much pain that I almost fell back down. Somebody pointed the spotlight right in my face, and I put my hand up to shield my eyes, squinting as I waited for his next command.

"You like sucking dick, right, Juicy?"

I swallowed hard, fear stealing my breath.

"N-o-o, G," I whispered. "That's why I bit Pluto. D-d-dick sucking is nasty. I don't like to suck no dick."

A glass came flying toward me, barely missing my face. It shattered against the back wall and I almost peed again.

"Lying ho. Next time it'll be a whole bottle and I won't miss." He started talking again, his words real slow and evil. "So now you think that shit is nasty, huh? Turn around, Juicy."

I was scared to turn my back on G, but I had no choice. I turned around slowly, bracing myself for the shot that would blow the back of my head all over the stage. Instead, the big screen was lowered and the projector started rolling. G was showing a movie, and I was playing in the starring role.

I started crying when the camera picked up a shot of me and Gino chilling in that phat-ass hotel room in Atlantic City, courtesy of G. It showed us coming out the bathroom wearing fluffy white robes after showering together, and then taking turns rubbing our naked bodies down with designer lotion from the Taj Mahal. Gino looked so good to me, so real and unhurt, that it was painful to imagine him all beaten up like he was the last time I'd seen him, and it almost killed me that I'd never see him again.

But then the camera rolled on and I was on my knees, smiling and taking all ten inches of Gino's big black dick in my mouth, licking it like it was candy, stroking it with both hands, sucking it so hard my cheeks collapsed.

My shit was done for. To G, this was the ultimate betrayal

and disrespect, and I turned back around, ready to face whatever I had coming. Yeah, G had set us up, but I already knew that. His revenge was to humiliate me and keep me fearing for my life. Well, I didn't give a fuck no more. G couldn't do no more to me than had already been done. Let him kill me, I didn't care. He dictated the game and called all the shots, but I wasn't my mother and I wouldn't beg or try to trade somebody else's life for mine.

I stood there waiting, and for the first time in a long time, I wasn't scared at all. I was ready for G and ready to die. The lights were on me so bright I could barely see G, but I knew he was twirling that ring with a killer look on his face.

"So you *do* like sucking dick, huh Juicy?"

I glanced over at Pluto. He was holding his shit through his pants.

"I guess."

"Naw, bitch. Don't look like you was guessing just now to me. Say that shit out loud. Don't be shy. Say you like sucking dick, cause that's exactly what you was doing."

I went ahead and said it. What did it matter? "Yes, G. I like sucking dick."

"Good," he said. "Cause you gonna suck some dick tonight. Pluto, wake that niggah up."

Pluto came up on stage and snatched the hoody off the brother in the chair. He turned a whole bottle of vodka over and poured it dead in the guy's face. Ace and G started laughing as the guy sputtered and coughed while coming awake, and as I strained to see around Pluto's big wide ass I almost passed out when I peeped who was struggling and choking in that chair.

It was Jimmy.

My brother looked more dead than alive. His face was all fucked up and blood was caked up everywhere. He had a dented gash deep in his forehead and his jaw swung back and forth like it was broken.

"Jimmy . . . ," I moaned, dropping to my knees in front of him. He had come back for me. "Oh, God . . . Jimmy-Jo . . . what did they do to you?"

His eyes were so puffy he could hardly open them. He reached out to touch me and I saw that his fingers were swollen and broken and pointing every which way. "You . . . my heart . . . Juicy."

I couldn't stop crying. "And you my soul."

I turned to G. "What'd you do to him, G?" I screamed. "I thought you loved him like your own! How could you do him this way?"

"Bitch, you thought I loved Gino, too, but that didn't stop you from sucking his dick!"

"Get a doctor for him, G. Please. Do what you wanna do to me, but Jimmy is hurt for real. At least get him a doctor."

"Everything Jimmy's gonna get is right here."

I put my head down on my brother's lap and cried some

more. His insides were so busted up that he was bleeding from the mouth and blood sprayed out his nose every time he exhaled.

G said, "You in just the right spot, Juicy. Now, since you like sucking dick so much, pull out that niggah's shit and get to sucking!"

I looked up. "W-w-what?"

G's voice was cold as ice. "You heard me. Suck . . . his . . . MOTHERFUCKIN DICK!" And then he added softly, "Or watch the motherfucker die."

A chill ran through my body and I fumbled for Jimmy's belt. I'd suck his dick. I'd lick his ass, I'd swallow his balls, just as long as G let him live.

Jimmy fought me as I tried to get to him, cursing and protesting. "Juicy . . . no . . . stop, Juicy. No . . ."

Ace and his niggahs was laughing like crazy as I slapped at Jimmy's hands, crying louder as he winced in pain from my blows. I didn't give a fuck. I was gonna suck his dick until the skin fell off. I'd do anything to please G and to keep my brother alive.

I managed to undo the top button on Jimmy's pants and he finally quit fighting me and let me get his zipper down, but as soon as I reached down into his underwear he brought his knee up and caught me in the chest, and if I hadn't grabbed hold of the chair I would have fallen over backward.

Jimmy looked down at me with love and tears in his eyes

and I knew the only reason my brother was here was because of me. We stared at each other for a split second and I tried to make him see without words why we had to work together, why we had to do whatever it took to keep him alive. But he shook his head no.

"I love you, Juicy-Mo," my baby brother whispered with blood on his lips, and as I opened my mouth to tell him the same thing, he stood up and reached into his pants and then I saw a quick flash of silver and heard two thunderous booms.

The first shot got G right where he stood, and the second shot, the one that Jimmy turned on himself, sent blood and brains and shattered pieces of bone raining down all over my head as my soul broke free of his body and floated up to heaven.

Chapter Twenty-Six

As soon as the shooting stopped Moonie grabbed me and led me back down to the Dungeon. I'd screamed until my throat was raw, hysterical at the sight of my brother's faceless body and his brain matter clinging to my skin. Jimmy's body had landed on top of me, slamming me down to the ground and protecting me from the rounds that sank into his dead flesh as Pluto opened fire. It was a miracle, but I didn't have a hole in me, except for the one bleeding from my heart.

Pluto had actually screamed when G went down, and if it wasn't for Moonie he would have shot me on the spot. *Click! Click ! Click!* Pluto kept on pulling his trigger even after all the bullets were gone, and if he'da had any rounds left my ass would be dead. Moonie and Cooter rolled Jimmy off of me, and I caught a quick glimpse of G laying against a table with half of his chest blown away.

"This is some fucked-up shit, Juicy." Moonie took me in the tiny bathroom and tried to use his shirt to wipe the blood out my eyes. "Shit's about to get hot cause too many niggas got emotional and fucked up!"

Moonie pulled my bloody T-shirt over my head and helped me take off my filthy panties. My period had come down earlier that morning, and I'd made a pad out of the last of the toilet tissue I'd found in the nasty little bathroom.

There wasn't even a rag to wash up with, so Moonie turned on the rusted tap and wet my bloody T-shirt down, then used it to wash my face and chest, and get what gore he could out of my hair. I stood there naked and crying in grief, that last look in Jimmy's eyes haunting me down to my bones.

I didn't even know Pluto and Ace had come downstairs until they were standing in front of me. Pluto was still crying, and the way Ace was looking at me made me glad that Moonie was standing between us.

"You gonna do her, Moonie?" Pluto asked, slinging snot. "Or you want me to? Either way, this ho gotta go."

Moonie looked at him and shrugged. "Don't matter who do her. But Pacho is still in Brooklyn and we ain't getting three bodies in the trunk of no Benz." He grabbed my arm and dragged me over to the mattress on the floor, and flung me down on that nasty, cum-stained sheet. I was shaking as Moonie slipped the chain around my wrist and then looped it around the pole again and locked it. "We'll come back for her ass later. This time we'll make sure the bitch treats you right. And then we'll do her."

I tried to turn over in my sleep, but I was still chained to the pipe on the filthy mattress. I didn't know how long much time had passed, but ants had been chowing down on me, and I'd scratched my leg down to the white meat while I was asleep. I'd been dreaming about Grandmother, and grief was all over me. I'd seen her as clear as day, wearing the same dress we'd buried her in, her smiling face still caked up with mortician makeup. "Look out for yourself, Juicy," she had whispered to me. "Jimmy-Jo is right here with me and Cara, and that hardheaded boy is doing just fine."

The realization that they were all gone hit me hard. I was left in this world all by myself, alone without nobody to love me or look out for me. I willed myself not to cry again, and instead I started praying, wishing Moonie hadn't stepped in front of Pluto when he pulled out that gun and hoping that the next time Pluto pointed it at me he'd have enough heart to take me out fast.

At the top of the stairs, the door opened again, but I didn't even bother to open my eyes. Why should I? I'd lost my soul in the G-Spot, and there was nothing left to live for anymore. I heard Pluto coming down, this time real slow, like he thought I was scared and he wanted to punk me some more. I could feel him standing there looking down at me, but if he thought I was gonna open my eyes and beg to suck his dick in exchange for my life, his ass was dead wrong. I wasn't Cara. I didn't even want to live.

I waited his ass out as the minutes went by. I pushed those dead images of G and Jimmy to the far corners of my mind, and instead thought about my brother being whole and happy, and my man, Gino, loving me with everything in his heart. Pluto could go ahead and shoot now, I thought to myself, and I was just about to open my mouth and tell him so when he spoke first.

"Juicy, we fin'ta find somewhere to stash them bodies, so I'ma give you the chance that somebody shoulda gave my little sister."

My eyes flew open and I found Cooter looking down at me.

"What?" I said softly, confused as hell.

"Dig this," Cooter said, and he sure as fuck wasn't stuttering. "You lucky, Juicy, cause ain't no such thing as an ex-bitch with G. You don't just walk away after fuckin with a niggah like him. You end up in a graveyard. G fucked my whole family up when he killed Charlene. Broke my mama's heart and she ain't been right since. So I'ma do for you what I wish somebody woulda been man enough to do for Charlene. I'ma accidentally forget to lock that door when we leave up outta here, but if you still around when me and the crew get back . . . I sure hate it for ya."

"W-w-where's Moonie?"

"Moonie? He's outtie. My man kept his family in a one-bedroom on Tiebout while G tricked his money away over on Central Park West. Don't worry about Moonie. He done stashed away enough yardage to live larger than ten Gs, and ain't a dime of it traceable back to this Spot." Cooter tossed me a fat envelope. "He left this for you, though. It should help you start over again."

I bit down on my lip as Cooter turned a key in the chain's lock, and the next thing I knew my arm was free and I was staring at his back as he walked up the stairs.

It coulda been a trap, but I trusted Moonie and somehow I believed Cooter, and two seconds after that door slammed I was on my feet. Weak and sore, I searched around trying to find something to put on, but the only thing in the room besides my bloody shirt and drawers was the sheet on the bed and one dirty tube sock.

I wrapped that sheet around me the best I could, then grabbed the envelope and crept up the stairs and listened at the door. Even the air at the top of the stairs was foul, and I forced myself to chill and wait, instead of busting through the door and running.

I figured if I counted to one thousand real slow, chances were they'd be long gone. When I got up to 999 I turned the knob on the Dungeon's door and crouched down low. Moving through the doorway and into the darkness, I hugged the wall and led myself through the warehouse by touch.

Moments later I pushed out the front door of the G-Spot, wrapped in a dirty white sheet and squeezing a sock between my legs. Running barefoot through the ice and snow, I staggered to the curb, flagged down a bootleg taxi, and collapsed inside.

Chapter Twenty-Seven

I fell into Rita's arms as soon as she opened the door. I was numb and could barely answer her as she yelled in Spanish and her sisters ran and got me a blanket and a housecoat.

"Oh my God, Juicy," Rita switched to English as she pulled me into the bathroom. Even though I'd made it out of the Spot alive, most of me was already dead. I was like a baby as Rita put me in the shower and washed the blood off of me with soap and warm water. All I could think about was Grandmother and Jimmy. Gino and Dicey. I cried my heart out and Rita just let me. She didn't even ask me what had happened. She just did her best to help me the only way she knew how. She had to climb in the shower with me in order to shampoo my hair, and for the life of me I couldn't lift a finger to help her. I was just that through.

"Jimmy's dead," I told her after she had dried me off

and given me a tampon, a housecoat, and some warm socks to put on. "G and Gino, too."

Rita cried along with me then. She'd gotten soaked trying to get me cleaned up, and now she sat next to me wearing a green duster and holding me in her arms as I told her how G had set us all up, how Jimmy found out G was gonna kill me and had come back to help me. I cried as I told Rita how guilty I felt because me and my bullshit had cost my baby brother his life.

"Jimmy came back because he loved you, Juicy. Don't let that grimy motherfuckin G steal what you and your brother had. G is the one who was guilty. Jimmy was straight-up loyal to him, but G still set him up too, right? Just like you wouldn't have left Jimmy out there hanging, your brother couldn't leave you out there like that neither. Come on," she said, pulling me to my feet, "you need to lay down, Juicy. Get some rest, chica. Later, we'll figure out what to do."

I followed Rita into her bedroom dragging my feet.

"I got that package for you," she said, and reached into a closet and handed me my dance bag and the MGM bag that contained half of the money that had been in G's safe.

I dropped the bags on the dresser next to the envelope I'd gotten from Cooter and just stood there.

Rita had just pulled down her blankets and was ordering me to get in the bed when I eyed the telephone on her night-stand. I knew it was crazy, but my emotions were wrecked and I needed to hear his voice one more time, even if it was only on his voice mail. "Okay, Rita," I told her. "I'll lay down for a while. But first let me make a call."

I dialed his cell phone digits and screamed out loud when the phone was answered on the second ring.

"Speak."

"Gino!" I started babbling and crying all over again. I couldn't believe it. Gino was alive. I was expecting his machine to pick up, but my man was alive and somehow I wasn't by myself anymore.

"Juicy, Juicy, Juicy, Juicy . . ."

All he could do was say my name. Over and over again.

I heard all kinds of noise in the background and it sounded like somebody was making an announcement over a loudspeaker.

"Baby, you okay?" he shouted. "Juicy, where are you? I've been calling the Spot. Are you okay?"

"Yeah," I sniffled. "I'm . . . okay. They said you were dead. I'm at Rita's house. In Harlem. Where are you?"

"At the airport, baby. I just landed at JFK. I caught a flight back as soon as I could. Hold tight, baby. I'm coming to get you."

I reminded him of Rita's address but I was scared to hang up. Scared the whole thing would have been a dream if I disconnected the call.

"I'm on my way, baby. Just let me rent me a ride, and I'll be there in a minute."

I forced myself to hang up the phone. Rita was squeezing my hand and we both started crying again. "He's alive, Rita," I said, still trying to convince myself. "He's really okay."

"Yes," she nodded, and wiped her nose. "It's all right now, Juice. Everything's all right now."

I waited like a crazy person. Pacing back and forth around Rita's living room table. Wearing a path in the floor between the twelve steps from her kitchen to her bedroom, and then the four from her bedroom to her bathroom. I darted to the window every time a car went by, although common sense told me it was gonna take a minute before Gino could rent a car and get here through traffic.

I was doing my best to hold on until my man arrived, knowing how bad grief was gonna come down on both of us when he heard about G and Jimmy. I didn't have it in me to tell him about them over the phone. That was something I thought he should experience with me right by his side.

What seemed like ten hours was actually closer to two. Gino pulled up in a rented Sean Jean edition Explorer and I forgot about how cold it was outside. I was busting out the front door, duster and all, before he could step on the sidewalk good.

Gino almost broke down when he saw me. "Juicy." his whole body shook and he cupped my face in his hands, careful not to touch my thousands of bruises. "Damn, baby. Oh, Juicy."

Gino had a black eye and a long slash down the side of his

face that had about thirty stitches holding it together. His left arm was in a sling and a cut had scabbed over on his top lip.

In the privacy of Rita's bedroom, me and my man cried together as I told him about Jimmy and G. Gino cried even harder when he heard how Jimmy had sacrificed himself for me, and he said he was sorry he wasn't there to protect both of us.

My man was a rock for me as he held me in his arms and we drew strength from each other. I saw the deep pain in his eyes as he traced the bruises all over my body. I knew I looked bad, and it hurt him to see how G and his friends had beaten and abused me.

Even though I knew Gino loved me, I didn't want to tell him how I had worked the rooms at the Spot. I couldn't tell him how his father had pissed all over me and brought in mad niggahs to use my body like a piece of meat.

I was hurting so badly for my brother that I didn't want to relive all of that pain and humiliation and Gino was cool with that. He said he'd never press me to tell him anything and that I didn't have to talk about it ever again in life if I didn't want to.

We fell asleep in Rita's bed holding on to each other as tightly as we could. I kept waking up during the night, startled and crying, and checking to make sure Gino was still there.

"I'm right here, Juicy," he whispered in my ear. "I'm right here and I ain't going nowhere."

. . .

We hid out at Rita's for two days until it was safe to slide downtown. Shit was hot on the streets of Harlem with G gone. The police, his connects, everybody was out of control. Rita told us G's whole crew was being shook down and locked up left and right. She said Flex was in the hospital on critical after getting popped by some kid trying to take over the projects, and Moonie's apartment had got raided but the cops were too late. The house was empty and nobody had seen Moonie in days.

Gino had mad family in the Bushwick section of Brooklyn. A bunch of loud-ass close-knit Puerto Ricans who loved their Gino to death. They took us in and treated us right and gave us time and space to get our heads together and heal, which was exactly what we needed.

Three weeks had passed since I'd run naked out of the G-Spot, and the backlash from G's murder was still vibrating through New York City. With all the arrests and street hits we were reading about in the *Post* and the *Daily News,* Gino and I both agreed that it was time to put this crazy city behind us. We had kept the Explorer even though renting it for so long had gotten expensive. I wanted to pay for it out of the twenty-five hundred I'd stolen from G's safe, but Gino said he had some decent change and that I should hold on to what I was carrying. We were planning to turn it in at the airport later on today, right before we hopped on a flight out west.

Gino drove slowly as we headed toward Woodlawn Cemetery on 233rd Street in the Bronx, and I held on to his thigh real tight the whole time, dreading what I was going to do, but knowing it had to be done.

I hadn't stepped foot inside a cemetery since the day I almost fell into my mother's grave, but with Jimmy gone and no closure to be found, I was determined to visit the spot where my grandmother was buried and tell her good-bye before I left New York for good. Maybe I would feel better just being near her final resting place since I didn't have a clue to where Jimmy's bones were buried.

The Boogie-Down was hopping when we came off the Cross Bronx Expressway and headed for the Bronx River Parkway, and when we got to the cemetery the tall black metal gates were open and we drove right in. I looked down at the slip of paper in my hand, and read Gino the name of the section that Grandmother was buried in.

There were crazy rows of tombstones in here. Woodlawn was seriously overcrowded. I couldn't help reading the dates on the bigger tombstones as Gino drove slowly down the narrow road, following the signs to the section I'd given him.

We drove past what looked like a small city of the dead and buried, and into an area that was full of mausoleums. These dead folks musta had some money, I thought. There were no in-the-ground graves over here at all. Just those little concrete houses built for people who could afford not to go six feet under.

"This is the area," Gino said, and I nodded as I rechecked the paper in my hand. He was right. We were in the right section, but I wasn't sure if it was where I wanted to be. G had taken care of Grandmother's funeral and burial. Since I was too scared to walk close to a ditch, let alone stand over somebody's open grave, G had paid for a private burial service for Grandmother.

I remembered it like it was yesterday because right after her funeral he had put me and Jimmy in a limo and sent us straight back to the apartment on Central Park West. I'd already written down what I wanted to have engraved on her headstone, and G had promised me that everything had been taken care of.

But a mausoleum?

This couldn't be right. Where in the hell was my grandmother's grave?

All of the little concrete houses had a number on the outside, and I told Gino to stop near the one that matched the gravesite number Rita had gotten from G's computer files.

"I don't know . . . ," I said as we got out the Explorer. "This don't look right. Ain't even no headstones over here. G had my grandmother put in the ground."

Gino took my hand and pushed open the door with his shoulder. He didn't look scared at all, and I was suddenly so happy that this big strong man was still by my side. "C'mon," he said. "This gotta be her. Who else could be in there?"

We went inside, and suddenly I wasn't scared no more.
There was a smooth wall with the name Orleatha Mae Stanfield carved in script in the center, and a long brass hinge ran
sideways almost halfway down the wall.

"Grandmother," I whispered, and held on to Gino, and
then I started crying just like a baby. Being here, this close to
the woman who had loved me and raised me was just too
much. So much shit had happened in my life, and most of it
I didn't think I deserved. And now, except for Gino, I was all
by myself in the world. No grandmother, no brother, and
not even a junkie for a mother. I was totally assed out, and it
hurt me to my heart. I stared at my grandmother's name on
the slab and more tears than I knew I had left just fell from
my eyes.

"It's okay, baby," Gino kept saying over and over. "You
gonna be all right, Juicy. Everything is gonna be all right."

There was a bunch of dried-up flowers on a small table
against the back wall, and a metal chair right beside it. As
bad as G had done Jimmy, I couldn't believe he had still been
coming here visiting with my grandmother, but the flowers
proved it. Nobody else could have left them there. Gino
held me as I collapsed into the chair, and when I put my
head on my knees and hollered, he stayed right by my side,
rubbing my back and rocking me the whole time.

I don't know how long I stayed there with my head down
in my lap. Lost in my grief. I hurt so bad inside I wanted
to die. Not even all those ass-whippings and beatings I had

taken, all those men who had run up in me and used me like animals, none of that shit came close to causing the kind of pain that losing Jimmy and Grandmother did.

Gino let me cry it out. He just stood quietly letting me know he was there if I needed him. At some point I was done. Just empty. But I still didn't have the strength to move.

"C'mon, baby," Gino said, putting his hand on my arm and taking my hand. We had a flight to catch and needed to get moving. I was lifting my head, just about to let him lead me to my feet, when I saw it. It was round and gold, and even from where I sat I could make out the words RENO SUPREME, one below the other, engraved in the metal.

I snatched my hand away from Gino and stuck it into the side pocket of my MGM bag. My keys clinked like crazy when I pulled them out in the stillness of the crypt, and I dropped them twice before I was steady enough to grab hold of the right one.

"Shit!" I yelled, my eyes already comparing the size of the key to the size of the lock on my grandmother's crypt. "Oh, shit, Gino." I passed the key ring to him, holding out the one I'd taken from G's safe. "This is the key to Grandmother's grave!"

For a moment Gino looked at me all crazy, then his whole face changed and I could tell we were thinking the same thing.

"That low-down motherfucker," he said, shaking his head.

"We can walk back out of here right now, Juicy. You don't have to open that lock, but I don't put shit past G's grimy ass. This looks just like something he would do."

Gino offered to open the crypt up for me, but I knew this was something I needed to do for myself. Yeah, I was scared shitless about what I might find when I turned that key and slid open that gigantic concrete drawer, but there was no way I could just walk away without knowing. How could I? I'd lost too much for that. My soul had died so that I could live, and I owed it to him to find whatever it was that G had tried so hard to hide from us.

I slid the key into the lock and it fit just like . . . well, like a key.

Taking a deep breath, I closed my eyes and braced myself. For what, I did not know. *Don't be so damn scary, Juicy,* I yeasted myself up. Grandmother would be in a coffin. Wasn't like they just threw bodies into these things just like that. There was no way I'd slide this bad boy open and be treated to no bunch of decaying bones.

Gino was reading my mind.

"Even if it's her, Juicy, you won't see nothing. First they put them in a coffin, and then they put the coffin in a metal box."

Slowly, I turned the key. It moved real easy, like it was either oiled or a new lock. Feeling along the ridge handle underneath the lock, I pulled once and nothing happened. Grandmother was heavy. Twice, and still the shit didn't budge. Gino stepped up like he wanted to help, but I shook my head and put some ass behind my pull, and the entire drawer slid open.

My heart almost stopped, and by the way Gino's body shook, I knew his did, too.

We stared down into the darkness of that drawer with our mouths wide open.

But it wasn't Grandmother's moldy body that had me and Gino sprung.

It was every dime of G's money.

And at the end . . .

Gino and I missed our flight, and neither one of us was mad about it.

Plus, they don't let you transport the kind of cash we were holding in your suitcases anyway, so flying out west was out of the question.

There had been rows and rows of bank in Grandmother's crypt, each one stacked at least three bricks high and I don't know how many across. All I saw were 50s and 100s. All of it banded and sealed in clear plastic.

My hands were shaking so bad Gino had to help me lock that bad boy back up, and then we jetted to a cheap motel off of White Plains Road and came up with our plan.

We bought four duffel bags from the Army-Navy store, then found one of the car dealerships that were known for taking cash under the table in exchange for a brand-new ride. Back at the cemetery it took us over an hour to clear out the crypt and stack the money inside of the duffel bags, and as soon as we closed the trunk we hauled ass getting out of there.

Cash talked real loud with the dealer we went to, and I had picked out a gray 2004 Volvo. Nice ride, lots of features, but not flashy enough to scream "drug money" and get us pulled over for driving while black. Gino was chilling behind the wheel, taking us out west, and I sat back in the leather seat and tried to stop my head from spinning.

Finding G's money didn't bring my family back and it didn't solve all of my problems neither. I had no idea where Grandmother was actually buried, and the location of Jimmy's body would always be unknown to me, but I comforted myself with the thought that I had done something for the living even if I couldn't do anything for the dead.

We had hit Harlem one last time before watching the bright lights of New York City fade in our rearview mirror, and I felt good about what I'd done. Gino had taken me to Rita's house where I gave my girl enough cash for her to not only buy herself a slamming house and pay her tuition in full, but enough to put both of her sisters through college and treat herself to all the Naughty Girls toys she wanted. I'd tore Brittany off a hunk of change, too, dropping it off at her crib in a big red box and making her promise not to open it until after I left. I had a feeling Cecil and his little detail shop were gonna be like last week's dirty drawers once my girl saw how lovely I'd left her rolling.

And now, Gino had checked us into a Hilton Hotel in Ohio off I-70, heading west. We could have stayed at a posh luxury hotel like we used to when we were traveling with G, but neither of us needed all the bells and whistles or the reminders of that kind of high-rolling lifestyle. Besides, we wanted to keep a low profile. Money had a way of drawing trouble to you like flies to shit, and we were way past all that. We were starting over from scratch, just me and Gino, and even though we had mad money to burn we both wanted to put it to better use.

"California . . . I can't wait until we get there," I said, whispering into Gino's chest. He held me close as we stood in the middle of the hotel room. It was nice and clean, but it sure wasn't the Taj Mahal. "You can build your business any way you like it, boo. As a matter of fact, the way we'll be clocking we can do just about anything we want."

Gino kissed me and nodded. "But, what do *you* wanna do, Juicy? We both know what I want, but let's talk about something that you really want."

I thought for a quick minute.

"I want . . . ," I said, moving even closer to him and squeezing him around the waist. During the three weeks we'd been in Brooklyn we hadn't had sex once. Gino had known how bad I was hurting, and all he had done was hold me and kiss me and be there for me every single moment.

". . . I wanna do something that I like to do. I wanna push my JuicyOriginals from my own dress shop. *And* . . . I wanna have me some babies, Gino."

"Babies?"

His lips were on mine again, so soft and wet I started getting dizzy.

"Yep. Babies."

He was teasing his tongue along the softness of my lips and my coochie started coming alive.

"Well, come on then," my man whispered, leading me toward the bed, pressing his hard dick against me and sliding two fingers down into my panties. "Come on, Miss Juicy Juice. Let's go get started."

About the Author

NOIRE is an author from the streets of New York whose hip-hop erotic stories pulsate with urban flavor. Visit the author's website at www.asknoire.com.

About the Type

This book was set in Garamond, a typeface originally designed by the Parisian typecutter Claude Garamond (1480–1561). This version of Garamond was modeled on a 1592 specimen sheet from the Egenolff-Berner foundry, which was produced from types assumed to have been brought to Frankfurt by the punchcutter Jacques Sabon.

Claude Garamond's distinguished romans and italics first appeared in *Opera Ciceronis* in 1543–44. The Garamond types are clear, open, and elegant.